Men tried to erase ... ... history.
Yet she remains,
The Poetess,
Ψαπφ

PSAPPHA

A NOVEL OF SAPPHO

By

Peggy Ullman Bell

Published by
Upstart Press

Peggy Ullman Bell

Published by: UpStart Press, 305 West 45th Street, Suite #3-I, New York, NY 10036. For further information, please contact: UpstartPub@aol.com

This book is a work of fiction. Names, characters, places and incidents are either products of the author's imagination or are used fictitiously. Any resemblence to actual events or locales or persons, living or dead, is entirely coincidental.

The cover illustration is a detail from "Sappho and Alcaeus" by Sir Lawrence Alma-Tadema reproduced with permission from ArtToday.com The layout of the cover was effected by Scott Fowler.

ISBN: 0-9701274-9-9

Printed in the U.S.A.

Psappha

**Dedicated
to**

Daughters

and

Generations

of

Daughters

Thanks

~~~~~~~

Psappha

To all of those who encouraged my attempt to add to the body of literature that surrounds this truly remarkable woman, thank you.

To librarians everywhere, without whom an historical novelist could not function.

To Bliss Carmen, Canada's poet laureate, whose work with the fragments provided inspiration for this book. (Sappho: One Hundred Lyrics, Boston, 1903)

To Henry Thornton Wharton, for the research and motivation behind Carmen's insightful interpretations. (Sappho: Memoir, Text, Selected Renderings and A Literal Translation 1885; 2nd. ed. 1887)

To Algernon Charles Swinburne, whose use of the extant lines provided the impetus that got me started. (Poems and Ballads, London, 1866)

To Paul Roche and his publisher, for granting permission to include his poem "Please", which fit my plot so perfectly, I did not have the heart to paraphrase.
(The Love Poems of Sappho, Prometheus Books, 1999)

To these and to the many and various others who have translated and interpreted the bits of Psappha's nine books that remain available to us, thank you for keeping her voice alive.

Thank you, also, to Paul Harris, whose vision and faith placed this volume in your hands.

Peggy Ullman Bell

"There was a time when you were not a slave, remember that. You walked alone, full of laughter, you bathed bare-bellied. You say you have lost all recollection of it, remember.... You say there are no words to describe this time, you say it does not exist...remember. Make an effort to remember. Or, failing that, invent."

Les Guerilleres, Monique Wittig; Beacon Press, Boston 1985 (c 1969 Les Editions de Minuit [English translation c 1971 Peter Owen, Viking Press Inc.])

Psappha

Excerpt from The Life of Greece by Will Durant
Simon & Schuster, N.Y., 1939.

Above the Ionian Dodecapolis lay the twelve cities of mainland Aeolia, settled by Aeolians and Achaeans from northern Greece soon after the fall of Troy opened Asia Plinor to Greek immigration. Most of these cities were small, and played a modest role in history; but the Aeolian isle of Lesbos rivaled the Ionian centers in wealth, refinement and literary genius....

"Sappho was a marvelous woman," said Strabo, "for in all the time of which we have record I do not know of any woman who could rival her even in a slight degree in the matter of poetry." As the ancients meant Homer when they said The Poet, so all the Greek world knew whom men signified when they spoke of The Poetess.

Psappha, as she called herself in her soft Aeolian dialect, was born at Eresus, on Lesbos, ...Pittacus, fearing her maturing pen, banished her...she married a rich merchant of Andros; some years later she writes, "I have a little daughter, like a golden flower..."

After five years of exile she returned to Lesbos and became a leader of the island's society and intellect ... Eager for an active life, she opened a school for young women, to whom she taught poetry, music, and dancing; it was the first 'finishing school' in history....

Her verse was collected into nine books, of some twelve-hundred(sic) lines, six-hundred survive, seldom continuous. In the year 1073, of our era, the poetry of Sappho and Alcaeus was publicly burned by ecclesiastical authorities in Constantinople and Rome (sic).

Then, in 1897, Grenfell and Hunt discovered ... coffins of paper-mache, in whose making certain scraps of old books had been used; and on some of these scraps were some poems of Sappho....

In truth, we do not know when she died or how; we know only that she left a vivid memory of passionate poetry, and grace.

Peggy Ullman Bell

~~ 1 ~~

The half-forgotten storm tossed Psappha naked from her berth. Wrapped in a blanket, she rushed on deck. Rain and salt spray stung her eyes. The wind whipped the blanket against her legs. A wave broke over her head and took the blanket with it. She slipped on the wet deck and her stomach clenched. Just as she was certain Poseidon had claimed her, someone grabbed her ankle.

"Here," the captain shouted. "Put this on," he said, thrusting a soggy wad of cloth into her hand.

Psappha struggled to turn the length of dripping fabric into a serviceable kiton while the wind tried to rip it from her hands.

"Go back inside," the captain told her. "I don't have time to look after you. We're taking on water. I have to man the pump!"

"I can work the pump!" Psappha screamed above the thunder.

"Nonsense, milady, the pump's bigger than you. If you won't go inside, I'm tethering you to the mast."

"What about you and the others?" she asked as he secured the knots at her waist.

"We're used to it," he boomed.

No one could get used to this, she thought as she followed him as far as her tether would allow. The sway of the lumbering vessel wrenched her from side to side. Rain stung her body and blurred her sight. Waves scoured the deck, curling around her ankles like fingers trying to pull her from the ship.

Twenty oarsmen took up the yeoman's beat. A keening chant rose, more terrorizing to Psappha than the thunderbolts that split the sky. Psappha countered their lament with a prayer.

Oh, Lady without Peer, Mother of all gods, she prayed. Protect me on this journey and let me hurry safely home to thy blessed temple.

Thinking of the temple, a sob stuck in her throat. She blocked fear with memories of walking among sacred olive trees, composing songs as young leaves shimmered in the sunlight. "Like a thousand needles sewing up the sky," she whispered past cracked lips. Tears

Psappha

flooded her eyes. They burned. She should not have insulted the Tyrant, although her words were true.

'Truth is the most dangerous of weapons,' her betrothed told her before they boarded separate ships. 'We will return,' he had said.

Yes, Psappha decided, grateful for the taut rope that held her to the mast. I will live again in Mytilene, she vowed, someday, when they applaud my verses in palaces and every street beggar knows my songs.

A gigantic wave rushed toward the foundering ship. Psappha shrieked in terror and got a mouthful of salty water. The mast cracked and fell. Poseidon snatched Psappha from the pitching deck and hurled her and the mast far out to sea.

"Poseidon!" she screamed. "I can't die now. No one will remember my name!"

~~~~~

Psappha drowsed between sheets of dry linen and imagined herself at home in Mytilene. The bunk on which she lay rocked with the gentle roll of waves beneath the hull. Memory swamped her euphoria. She thought of the squat ship upon which she began her hated exile, but the soft linen told her she was no longer there. Terror and grief rushed at her in expanding waves.

Her eyes clenched against reality, Psappha pounded the bunk with raw, cracked fists and rage at offending gods. "Capricious charlatans. Why weren't you watching what you were doing?"

Her fingers rasped across sun-scorched flesh as she searched for broken bones. Realizing she was naked, her hands flew from her body, dislodging her covering. She grabbed at it and felt other hands tuck it around her. She blinked and thought she saw Pittakos, Tyrant of Lesbos, standing over her – sending her into exile all over again.

Psappha rolled toward the bulkhead, her eyes awash with terror. Where was she? Peeking cautiously through wet lashes, she saw polished teak walls instead of an unfinished bulkhead. Through the open porthole, she glimpsed the shadow of towering mast and vast sails. The ship must be huge, she thought.

Someone spoke. Psappha rolled toward the sound ready to rise and flee. Her wide eyes met a smoky, indigo gaze. Ebony hair framed the man's sun-bronzed face. He had a straight hook–tipped nose and a thick, black beard. An arrow tail of crimped black hair splashed over his chest and shafted downward out of sight beneath a simple kilt.

When he spoke again, his words hovered just beyond her understanding.

9

"Who are you?" she asked. "Were there other survivors?"

He shrugged.

"Answer me, damn you!"

He smiled.

Father Poseidon to whom have you delivered me? She raged in silent exasperation. What vengeful brother is this?

"I am Psappha of Lesbos," she said, pointing to herself. "You will answer me at once."

The dark man grinned and left.

She watched him go. His upper body was a small miracle of muscles but his legs were slender and bowed. An oarsman, she decided and she dismissed him from her mind.

Listening to the garbled conversations beyond her door, she gradually realized they spoke an odd and varied dialect of Hellenic Greek. Though different from her own Aeolian, she knew the language.

Nevertheless, when she used flawless Hellenic to ask the scruffy old seaman who brought her supper about survivors, he gave her a bewildered shrug. Tears of frustration scorched her salt scoured eyes. She fought to believe the kindly old captain was safe somewhere. "Lord Dionysus," she prayed, pouring a small libation from her dinner wine. "Don't fall asleep over your cups and allow a dear worshiper to get away."

~~~~~

They must have put poppy juice in the wine, Psappha thought when she awakened. Her limbs felt heavy, her head seemed light. It hurt to move. Nevertheless, she knew the longer she stayed still the stiffer she would get. It took several nauseating tries, but she managed to stand.

The massive mahogany furnishings provided support as she searched the cabin for some form of clothing. Finding nothing better, she settled for a sheet, which she knotted at one shoulder, using a bit of rope to hold it around her waist, and off the polished deck.

"Who are you?" she asked the russet-haired youth who bustled into her cabin without knocking. She thought him somewhat older than her own sixteen years, although his face was hairless as a babe. The emerald tunic that pretended to cover his lean body matched intelligent green eyes.

"My name is Lycos," he said in dulcet tones that should have soothed her.

"Were there other survivors?" she asked hopefully.

10

Psappha

He arched copper brows.

"Survivors?"

"Yes, survivors, you simpering fool," she almost shouted from frustration. "From my ship. Was anyone else saved?"

"There was no ship, milady, only you and a log and a lot of seaweed. Kerkolos spotted you from the lookout, slid down the starboard shroud, and fished you out of the sea with a cargo net. You should have seen him. He hauled you aboard all by himself, broken mast and all." The boy's voice was soft and merry.

His grin infuriated her. "I don't see anything funny about the loss of an entire ship and everyone aboard."

"Not everyone," he corrected. "You're here. Maybe others are somewhere else."

"Almost everyone, then."

"I'm sorry."

Psappha was in no mood to accept his smile. "What are you grinning at, you rude boy?"

"I'm still picturing Kerkolos plucking you from the water like a sturgeon."

"Who is Kerkolos?"

Lycos gaped and gulped. "Kerkolos of Andros," he said, his bright eyes wide with astonishment. "The captain. Didn't he tell you?"

"I haven't seen him."

"Of course you have. He sent me here."

Psappha felt blood rush to her face. I thought he was an oarsman, she remembered, mortified by her unpardonable lack of manners. "Why didn't he identify himself? If I had known it was he who rescued me, I could have thanked him."

"That's probably why he didn't tell you."

"Are you the one who undressed me?" She had to know. She could not bear it if it had been the other one.

"Nothing to undress," he quipped. "Old Poseidon stripped you clean."

Psappha wanted to cry. She visualized a leering crew. No wonder the dark captain had smiled so much.

"Don't worry," Lycos said, as if privy to her thoughts. "The African whisked you out of the net and into Kerkolos' cabin so fast nobody saw much."

"The African?" Psappha frowned, picturing some heathen oarsman daring to touch her naked flesh.

11

"She wouldn't let anyone get a good look at you," Lycos said.

"She? There's another woman aboard?"

"Not just another woman," he said, beaming. "A queen."

Psappha frowned. "Don't lie to me, boy. Pharaoh would not allow his wife to sail on another man's ship."

"Oh, the African is no man's wife," he said, chuckling at the thought. "The African is a warrior."

A warrior, Psappha thought, a savage. Yet, judging by the glow of respect in the young man's eyes, he either liked savages, which was unlikely, given the delicacy of his appearance, or the African was something else, something far more interesting.

"I would meet this African," she said.

"Oh, she'll come by. If she chooses."

~~~~~

The African strode through the cabin doorway the next afternoon, and Psappha decided she had never understood the definition of a queen until then. Taller than most men, with cinnamon skin as richly hued and as lovely as the polished teak walls, the woman filled the cabin with her presence.

Psappha succumbed to an unexpected shyness. Suddenly sixteen did not seem so worldly after all. "If it pleases you, I would like to know your name," she said, her voice tremulous and inexplicably timid.

"I am called, Gongyla."

"I am Psappha." Awed by the magnificence of the woman before her, she left the aristocratic 'of Lesbos' off her introduction.

Gongyla's deep chuckle warmed her like sudden sunlight amid a blustery day.

"How came you here, oh Queen?" Psappha asked, wanting to hear the vibrant voice again.

Gongyla's elegant face saddened. "There was a war, little dove. My people fought bravely and I, myself, killed many enemies with my bow, but victory gained us nothing. My people were hungry. If not for Lord Kerkolos, my people would have sold themselves to the slavers. I could not let them be sent to the market beyond Tyre."

Psappha shuddered. She had heard of the market beyond Tyre. Rumor had it that no one returned from there: the men went to the mines, to die slowly; the women to brothels to live, though their souls were soon dead.

Psappha

"Tell me of your country, oh Queen," she said, hoping to coax a smile.

"My land is far," Gongyla said, her head high on her long, arched neck. "A green land, past a white land, beyond the land of the Carthaginians; near the birthplace of the river Niger." There was love mixed with the pride in her resonant voice. "My people are as free as eagles in flight," she said, her tone rich with feeling. "The women are strong and fleet of foot and the men as gentle and watchful as the great cats with whom we share the hunt. There are birds in my country with plumage brighter than Egyptian brocade. And small animals like creeping children that fill the air with endless chatter like gynakeoni."

"Gynakeoni?" Psappha asked, her brow furrowed.

"You will see," Gongyla said, smiling softly.

Psappha answered the smile by touching Gongyla's long, tapered hand. "What of your gods? Are they gentle like the little animals or fierce like you?"

"We worship no gods, Ivory one. We worship only Cybele, whom you call Queen of Heaven."

"You know The Lady!" Psappha exclaimed joyfully.

"What lady?"

"Not lady, Oh Queen, The Lady, Cybele, Isis, Asharah, Astarte, The Lady of a Thousand Names, The Lady by whatever name. My mother was her priestess."

"I, too, am a priestess. A priestess of Cybele," Gongyla said. "And what of you? How came you here?"

Psappha shuddered, ashamed before such majesty. "I'm an exile," she whispered, head down.

"Oh?" the queen murmured, and her eyes narrowed. Psappha pictured the great cats so recently mentioned. She tried to imagine Gongyla striding through a jungle on the heels of a panther, no, not on its heels, beside it, almost a cat herself – dark, silent and dangerous in the undergrowth.

"I spoke truth when I should have stayed quiet," Psappha said. "I challenged a gutter-rat who became a king . . ." Her voice cracked, and her mind reeled with visions she would rather forget.

"Don't think of it if it hurts you," Gongyla said in a voice that whispered through Psappha's veins, like a spark in the woods flashes through the underbrush.

"It's hard not to think about it," she said. "We poked a snake and lost our home, my birth-betrothed and I. I should've known I was pushing Pittakos too far. He wanted men to die for his beliefs, but he accepted no responsibility for their pain. 'Bloodshed solves nothing,' I told him. 'What you propose is nothing but your greed pitted against another's.'

"He dared to say he did not expect me to understand, me being so young and being female and all! Nevertheless, he expected the people to understand. I demanded that he ask them, thinking that would end his death–creating schemes.

"I did not expect my betrothed to take up my cause and make matters worse.

"'Come, my fine man of the people,' Alkaios said. 'Shall we put the question before your public? Shall we ask the populace if the husband of a porna is their choice of leaders? Let's hear it for Old Crack-toes,' he toasted. 'Hear, hear for the people's champion.'

"I can still hear goblets crashing to the floor. I retreated then, my courage destroyed by mass confusion. Why couldn't I have just kept quiet?"

"Perhaps because it was not in you," Gongyla suggested, the hint of a smile lifting the corners of her lush mouth.

Psappha glumly agreed. "I intend to be a professional poet like Alkaios, and being quiet isn't part of that. Poets are the chroniclers of history, the keepers of truth. But, sometimes it is expensive to be honest when the world seeks platitudes and lies."

"Don't worry," Gongyla said. "I've heard Kerkolos has a fine gynakeon."

~~~~~

"What in The Lady's thousand names is a gyna whatever?" Psappha asked Lycos the next time she saw him.

"Guynah-KHEE-ahn," he pronounced for her, seeming amazed by her question.

"A gynakeon is the secluded and well-guarded women's quarter of all fine homes," he explained.

"I grew up in a fine home in the world's finest city," Psappha said, indignant at the thought of guards. "And I enjoyed total freedom in all of both, not just in a quarter of a single house."

Lycos gawked. "Are there really places where decent women wander as freely as boys?"

"In Mytilene, boys don't wander anywhere," she lied. "They mind their manners and speak when spoken to."

Psappha

Lycos surveyed her face then burst into laughter. Psappha was still laughing herself when Kerkolos appeared in the doorway.

Remembering that he had seen her naked, Psappha blushed as Kerkolos' dark eyes swept over them.

"It appears you approve of my choice of servants," he said.

"A fine choice," Psappha agreed, with all the dignity she could muster. "But not a servant, Master Kerkolos. A friend."

"So, you know my name," he said, his full lips widening into a smile. "What else has this scamp told you?"

"Not much." She winked at Lycos, whose eyes were bright with longing. "He was attempting to explain why a proper lady should confine herself to a prison within her own home."

"Gynakia," Lycos injected nervously.

"Gynakia are hardly prisons," Kerkolos scoffed. "Most women enjoy their privacy, although some of the gynakeoni's customs may seem strange to those from backward cultures."

"Backward!" Psappha bolted to her feet. "Lesbos is not backward! Lesbos had an advanced culture when Athens was still a suburb of Mycenae. How dare you call us backward? Lesbian women live free while you can't trust yours in the company of men. Or is it that you fear they'll run away?"

"So," he said with an infuriating chuckle, "the little fish can fight. Save your fury, small fry. When I've decided what to do with you, I'll let you know. Meanwhile, I'll leave you children to your games."

"Isn't he wonderful?" Lycos bubbled the moment Kerkolos was gone.

"Wonderful? He's a monster. He's pompous. He's . . ."

"A sphincter," Lycos supplied, and Psappha's embarrassed anger was lost to laughter.

When their giggles subsided, she picked at the sailcloth robe she had fashioned for herself. "Do you think you could find me something better to wear?"

Lycos scampered out like an eager puppy and was back before she had time to miss him. For reasons she did not bother defining, she felt as comfortable with him as she would have felt with a female attendant. She did not hesitate when he signaled her to strip.

Lycos stared but said nothing.

"What ails you, boy? Surely you've served women before?"

"Of course, milady. But you look different from the ladies of the gynakia."

"Am I ugly?"

"Oh, no, milady, you're beautiful, but you're --"

"I'm what, you fumble–tongued whelp."

"You're hairy."

"I'm what?"

"You're hairy, milady."

"What're you talking about? Are the women you've seen so disfavored they've no badge of womanhood to break the monotony of flesh?" She could not imagine being without The Lady's sacred symbol. Still, if the African . . .?

"How do they do it?" she asked as she climbed onto his massage table and stretched out on her stomach.

"Do what, milady?"

"Remove the hair, of course. How do they do it?"

"With creams." She saw his satisfied smirk from the corner of her eye, but she chose to ignore it.

"Do you have such things?"

"I have them," he said, blushing. "Would you like me to use them?" he asked, rubbing the tension from her shoulders.

"You're sure it wouldn't hurt?"

"Yes. I'm sure. I could do it while you sleep. Roll over."

Psappha did as instructed. The touch of his hands on areas of her skin that usually started her dreaming felt friendly, sisterly, and not at all erotic.

"Shall I fetch the creams, milady?"

"M-m-m-m

Psappha awoke to an astounding transformation. Lycos had changed everything. Stark teak walls bore filmy lavender draperies. Soft, sheer violet curtained the bunk in which she lay. A silk, down-filled comforter had replaced the rough blanket that chafed her tortured skin. Wriggling contentedly beneath it, she let her hands explore her body. Her skin tingled with life. It startled her to find The Lady's most precious temple naked of adornment. Yet, it felt strangely sensuous. She smiled.

"It pleases milady?" Lycos perched on a stool nearby, delight and mischief competing on his lightly freckled face.

Psappha blushed. "Yes, Little Fox, I think it pleases me."

At his silent suggestion, she gathered the coverlet around her and went to the newly acquired chaise. He dragged his stool to her side and reached for her hand. She yanked it away and tucked it beneath

Psappha

her. He fished her other hand from beneath the coverlet and held it firmly, his eyes daring her to pull free. When she did not, he began filing her cracked and broken nails with deft strokes of the pumice.

"I must look horrible," she worried.

With a self-satisfied grin, Lycos reached beneath the couch then held a hand mirror before a face she barely recognized. "I don't wear paint!" Psappha protested, trying to wipe it off.

Lycos grabbed both her hands in one of his, being careful to avoid the injured wrists. "Look again," he said. "Lycos knows." He gave her a stern look as he again raised the mirror, moving it back and forth when she tried to look away.

Unable to avoid him, Psappha gave in. Her eyes, their lash lines darkened with kohl, stared defiantly at her from the flawless glass. He had painted her face so skillfully she was not sure exactly what he had done. Not bad, she decided. Even with her nose crinkled, the overall effect was gratifying. He had woven russet ribbons into her hair to create a high coronet of braids.

As she relaxed the aspect changed. Her pupils shone like huge amethysts, set in mother of pearl. Her full, red lips invited kisses. She puckered at herself and chuckled. "All right, Little Fox, you can let me have my hands now."

He jerked away and dropped to his knees beside her.

"Forgive me, milady, please. I didn't mean to hurt you. Please don't tell Master Kerkolos. I won't do it again."

He looked as frightened as a fox in an unguarded chicken house. Psappha laughed until her eyes filled with tears.

"What would your master do if I told him?" she asked when she caught her breath.

Lycos shrugged and shook his head. "Not a thing, milady. I'm too small for his anger."

"Well, Little Fox, since you are no bigger than I am, and will not conduct yourself as a proper slave –- "

"I'm not a slave, Psappha. I can serve you well enough, but I am free born."

Then, don't you think it's time you stopped miladying me?"

~~~~~

Lycos became Psappha's constant companion. They walked on the open deck together every sunny day. At first, her worn and beaten condition made her dizzy and she spent most of her time sitting in the shade of her cabin, watching the African's daily routine.

The priestess stood poised on the top right yardarm, wearing only in a narrow swath of amber cloth around her loins. Her oiled body glistened in the sunlight like polished cinnamon. When she dove, Psappha's breath released slowly, her chest deflating almost painfully.

Gongyla knifed the water like a glittering black swan, wings folded; neck arched to meet the foam. A glory worthy of The Lady Cybele and a distant throne, Psappha thought as Gyla paced the ship with strong sure strokes. Her fear of strange shores and guarded houses seemed manageable, whenever the African was nearby.

~~~~~

Eventually, Psappha grew strong enough to walk with the motion of the deck. She no longer needed Lycos' hand at her elbow but he seemed to like having it there, so she let it stay.

One hot afternoon, they stopped to watch Kerkolos command his crew with crisp shouts from the tiller. "He looks like Hades staring across Styx in hope of fresh victims," Psappha claimed, irritated because the captain had only spoken to her twice in all the time she had been aboard his ship. "Who does he think he is? When HE decides what to do with me. The nerve of the man!"

Lycos giggled.

"What are you laughing at?"

"You. You're falling for him," Lycos sputtered.

"Don't be absurd. I have to worry about him. He owns my destiny. When do we reach Andros?"

"We're not going to Andros," Lycos said. "We're going to Syracuse. In fact, we should have sighted it two days ago, but the wind's been slack. That's why we don't usually sail these waters in mid summer. Look!" he shouted.

Psappha's gaze darted to where the African had sliced through the nearest wave. "Where? Where?"

"There," Lycos pointed beyond Gongyla. "That bit of white on the horizon. Can you see it?"

Psappha nodded stiffly, her body reluctant to release its tension. "What is it? Another ship?"

"No. It's Sicily."

The crew rushed to the prow, straining toward the horizon. Psappha marveled that the ship did not nose under. Only she noticed when the African pulled herself aboard. She, too, watched the speck grow larger, then turn brown, green and gray, and slowly disappear in the gathering darkness.

Psappha

"How long?" Psappha asked as the men returned to their posts.

"Dawn," said Lycos. "We'll dock soon after first light."

Psappha shivered. The air had turned chill the moment Helios dropped from sight, but that was not what troubled her. While Lycos went to light the braziers in the cabin, she worried about her reception in Syracuse. Kerkolos had ignored her. Would that change when he had her among his women? She shivered again as Lycos returned to fetch her. The only light she could see was the bow lantern and a faint glow extending an inch or two outside her cabin door. A sliver of moon peeked from behind a low cloud.

The cabin warmed quickly, but Psappha still felt cold. She trembled as she removed her clothes and loosed her hair. She did not feel her usual proud glow when it cascaded down her back. "What awaits me in this place?" She whispered into the near darkness. "How will I survive? What sinister plan does the dark merchant have in mind for me? Am I to disappear into a gynakeon, never to be heard from again?"

Her mind protested the thought of becoming unknown. She was speculating grimly on her future when someone called her from beyond the cabin door. Recognizing the voice, she cringed.

"Psappha," Kerkolos called again.

Psappha threw on a robe and opened the door.

Kerkolos gave no indication of wanting to enter. Instead, he shifted slightly on his bandy legs, took her into his massive arms and kissed her. Then, before she could decide whether to respond or not, he released her and left.

"What manner of man is this?" She grumbled at the walls as she closed the door. "How dare he march in here and kiss me as if I expected it?" With a startled gasp, she touched her fingers to her lips. "I did expect it," she whispered. "I wanted him to stay. Am I that afraid?"

Peggy Ullman Bell

2

Breakfast was late and, when Lycos brought it, he apologized for it being only cold barley-cakes and honey. Psappha took a nervous bite of a honey-dripping cake before gathering her possessions into a small wooden box. There were the few garments Lycos had sewn for her, an onyx-backed boar-bristle brush on loan from Kerkolos and a pair of carved ivory combs she had not seen before.

Lycos shook his head when she held them out to him. "No," he said. "They were never mine. I removed my cosmetics while you slept."

Wondering who had made a gift of the delicate combs, Psappha tucked the box beneath her arm and took a last look around the cabin. It looked as it had when first she saw it, stark and masculine. No trace of her remained.

"Oh, Lady, guard me in this new place," she prayed.

Lycos smiled and opened the cabin door.

A sedan chair, heavily draped in magenta velvet, blocked their way. Psappha sniffed in distaste. Use of precious purple dye for such a mundane task seemed to her the grossest ostentation.

"All the comforts of the captain's home," Lycos said with a suspicious chuckle.

"His gynakeon you mean."

"His gynakeon is full, Psappha, and is presided over by his mother. She sent these for you," he said, gesturing toward the chair and its handsome bearers.

Psappha entered the deeply cushioned chair, wondering what Kerkolos' mother would think of having two more women dumped on her unexpectedly. In a way, Psappha was grateful to her for providing the chair. Behind its curtains, she could imagine that the familiar harbor smells were those of her beloved Mytilene. Tears filled her eyes when she remembered they were not.

The chair rocked upward. Psappha peeped between the drapes, and saw sights that bore no resemblance to her beloved Mytilene. Instead of cerulean twin harbors, a single greenish bay stretched to and beyond an immense bridge.

20

Psappha

From the moving chair, she saw white buildings, most of them larger than the citadel on old Mytilene, glaring at her with a thousand black eyes. She followed the terraces upward with her eyes until the canopy on the chair cut them from view.

The chair tilted forward as the bearers started down the gangway. More people crowded the docks than she had ever seen.

"Oh, Beloved Lady, guard your frightened daughter in this vast metropolis. Protect me, Oh Mother of Tenderness. I am so far from home."

She saw Kerkolos coming toward her and added, "Sweetly Smiling Aphrodite, if I must fill his bed, I pray you fill my heart."

Kerkolos paused near a group of seamen. Psappha heard one of them say, "A worthy prize."

"Aye," said Kerkolos. "A prize well worth a mid-season row."

Psappha seethed. A prize indeed, she thought, trying to get angry enough to squelch her fear as Kerkolos continued toward the foot of the gangway. She did not know whether to be relieved or peeved when he passed her without pause.

Psappha shifted on the cushions and parted the drapes behind her. Only then did she realize there were two chairs. The African lounged with curtains wide, grinning at Kerkolos' frown.

Psappha let her curtain fall. The Fates landed us here together, she thought. Why can't I enjoy the adventure of it, as she seems to, instead of wondering how they plan to torture me next?

She felt every sound like a bee sting to a nerve as the bearers bore her through noisy streets and alleys. After a while, the way became quiet. Every other turn led to a hill, and the swaying of the chair nearly lulled her to sleep before the bearers paused.

Hearing the sound of grating metal, Psappha stiffened, trembling as heavy gates clanged shut behind her. Where is Lycos? She wondered. Where is Kerkolos? It seemed hours since she had heard a familiar voice.

A woman ordered the chair lowered. The curtains opened. Psappha blinked, gasped, then felt a warm smile rise to her face. The woman was enormous -- the perfect image of The Great Mother. She extended a bejeweled hand, which Psappha gratefully accepted.

Psappha stepped from the chair prepared to love this woman as she loved The Lady. All resemblance to The Goddess faded when the woman spoke.

"I was told to make you welcome," the woman said, resentment dripping from her pursed lips. She turned and stumped toward the whitewashed stone house with no further word. The African stepped forward and took Psappha's hand.

Their hostess paused before a pair of ornate bronze gates, which she unlocked, with one of the keys almost hidden among the folds of fabric at her waist. Psappha felt like she was on the path to Hades and each clink of keys served to magnify the impression.

Gongyla bowed Psappha inside. Their hostess frowned, then led them down a long corridor with closed doors along both sides. At the end of the corridor, was a pair of inlaid cedar doors with a tiny grille eye-level to her guide, through which the woman spoke briefly before the doors swung open.

Curtained cubicles lined the next corridor. Each one draped with shades of one soft color, each different from the rest.

The corridor entered one side of an open pavilion, centered on a six-sided pool. Lush vines reached upward from marble planters to spread on trellises suspended from the transparent ceiling. Water poured from a large clay pipe above the greenery to cascade down an artificial landslide at one end of the pool. It drenched the pots of scented herbs growing in the crags then splashed from the rocks to gurgle among clusters of floating lotus.

The African took one look then shallow dove into the pool. Her cinnamon skin gleaming as she skimmed through the water. Around her, on cushions placed to avoid splashing, women whispered in quiet pairs. Others stood near the great pillars that supported the roof. More sat on the edges of the marble planters.

Psappha knew it was impolite to stare, but she could not resist. The gynakeoni's complexions ranged from the bluish-white of skimmed milk to the warm, rich shine of polished teak. Each wore a different color.

Psappha recognized many of the pastels from the corridor. Other, more vibrant hues matched glimpses of curtain in other corridors fanning from the pavilion. "There are so many," she whispered in awe.

"There were more when I came."

Psappha started. She had forgotten the woman at her side. "Forgive me," she apologized. "I know better than to stare like a pagan and ignore my hostess."

"It is expected," the woman sniffed. "Come."

Psappha

Blushing with embarrassment, Psappha followed her hostess around the pool, past the window arches and the corridor beside them, to a curtain of amethystine beads.

"My son insisted you be given this chamber," the woman grumbled. "I hope you appreciate it. Please don't blow your nose on the drapes."

Psappha could not speak. The floor of the chamber consisted of crushed and bonded limestone, set with the priceless iridescent mollusk shells from which men obtained the precious purple dye. Shades of precious purple decorated the entire suite, from the translucent amethyst of the curtain beads to the faint lilac-pink of the thick silk drapes that bracketed the window arches. Violet tassels on heliotrope hangings accented the ebony bed, and, through an arched doorway opposite the beaded curtains, she could see a tiny garden, resplendent in asters.

The effect was sumptuous beyond a Sybarite's wildest dream, disgustingly ostentatious.

"It is truly lovely," Psappha said as meekly as she could. "Thank you."

"Thank my son," the woman corrected. Her arm jangled with gold bracelets as she swept the air. "This is nothing," she said off-handedly. "His father had this built for me. My son could afford better. He finds more purple mollusks in a season than his father did in a lifetime."

A bit of drool at the corner of the woman's pursed lips and the blades in her yellowish eyes made Psappha feel as if the woman was about to spit in her face. She squared her shoulders, thrust her chin forward and prepared to say 'I am but a sojourner here --'

"My son wished that you call me Adriana," the woman said. The look she gave Psappha said 'you do, and I'll bite off your nose'. Then, like her exasperating son, she left the room without giving Psappha time to react.

Moments later, Adriana bounced back in dragging a wisp of a girl by the wrist. She thrust the child forward with enough force to send her sprawling.

"She will see to your comfort," Adriana said, as Psappha dropped to her knees beside the child. "You'll have to break her in yourself. She's stupid and ugly and I don't have time to train her."

Won't take the time is more like it, Psappha's inner voice declared as she brushed a wisp of hair from the child's forehead; she was beginning to detest the woman, in spite of her holy visage. The girl looked at her with vibrant purple eyes set in dark, sunken circles.

"She's not ugly," Psappha snapped, chucking manners in favor of the frightened child. "And, she looks hungry."

"Hardly," said Adriana sourly.

Clasping the girl's hand, Psappha was surprised to note that her own was smaller. "You've nothing to fear from me," she said. "It's I who am afraid. I've never been in a place like this before. You must help me get used to it." The girl's enormous eyes widened, although Psappha had not thought they could. "My name is Psappha," she offered softly. "What's yours?"

"Lyneachia," Adriana interrupted. Psappha's brow crimped. "Lyn-nay-ah-KHEE-ah," Adriana impatiently pronounced. "See how well her eyes match the chamber."

Psappha shot her a questioning frown.

"She stowed away on one of my son's ships last season and, knowing my love for the exotic, he gave her to me. She's a shiftless piece, but she does go well with the decor."

Running out of caution, Psappha let anger shine in her eyes.

Seeing it, Adriana said, "If you don't want her, I suppose I can take her with me. My husband's brother is building a house in Sybaris. She can serve in the guest chambers when it's finished. I suppose she'll pass in the dark.

"Do you always kneel to slaves?"

Psappha got to her feet but held tight to Lyneachia's trembling hand, warning, with her eyes and a squeeze of her hand, that she must not attempt to kneel in turn.

Adriana grunted her disapproval and decamped.

Psappha immediately sent Lyneachia to scout the kitchen. She returned with enough varieties of fresh baked bread to please The Lady, in all her thousand incarnations. Behind her, other servants brought trays heaped with vegetables and fruit. Still others offered dishes both hot and cold the likes of which Psappha had never seen on such short notice.

One thing is certain, she thought as she ate her fill of fine-textured bread and young mustard leaves bathed in herbed vinegar and olive oil. In this, my new abode, I shall not lack for fine cuisine. The crisp green taste of spring softened her memory of long weeks at sea.

She smiled as Lyneachia polished off much of the remaining food.

Psappha

"Where'd you come from?" she asked when they were again alone.

"I don't know," the girl answered shyly.

"Where were you born?"

"In a gynakeon."

"But, Adriana said you were a stowaway."

"I was." Lyneachia brightened. "I crawled out through a hole in the wall."

"What wall? Where were you?"

"I don't know," Lyneachia insisted. "It was a bad place. They were going to sell me to a procurer. I ran away." Psappha did not know what to say so she let the subject drop, for which Lyneachia seemed grateful. "It's all right now," she piped. "Now I belong to you." She ran her fingers along Psappha's cheek. "I'll never be afraid with you here."

Psappha sincerely hoped that was true. She did not want to think about the fact that she had little control over her own fate, much less Lyneachia's. "Where is Milord Kerkolos," she asked.

"At sea."

"When will he return?

"This winter or next." Lyneachia shrugged.

So long, Psappha worried. "I need to talk to him."

She did not know she spoke aloud until Lyneachia asked, "Why?"

"Never mind. It'll keep. Meanwhile, I'll do what I can for you, Lyneachia, but I won't own you."

"But you do own me," the child squeaked. "If you reject me she'll punish me and put us both out of these fine quarters."

"Don't worry," Psappha counseled, with a confidence she did not feel. "She answers to her son. You and I will be friends, Lyneachia, but no one will own you unless you want them to. Now tell me about the others. Are they also slaves?"

"Not all of them," Lyneachia said. "But, most are. Are you going to free them too?" she asked, her thin face scrunched in a worried frown. "They've no place to go."

"I can't free them," Psappha admitted with regret. "Where'd they all come from?"

"From everywhere." Lyneachia brightened. "Many of them belonged to the old lord, Lady Adriana's husband. He built his reputation on the number of beauties in his house. Milord Kerkolos brought the free women here, just like you, but all they got was a cubicle."

"If they're not slaves, why are they here? Why do they let themselves be locked away like this?"

"Why did you?"

"I had no choice," Psappha replied. When she realized she had answered her own question, she returned the child's impish smile, but her laugh was rueful. Tension gripped the muscles of her neck and shoulders.

"Lord Kerkolos is very kind," Lyneachia offered. "Though he ignores us once he's seen to our care."

"If he ignores you, why does he take in so many?"

"I've been told there are not as many as there were when his father was alive. I also heard his father did not ignore them," she added in a half-whisper.

Psappha was not surprised. "But why does Lord Kerkolos collect so many?" she repeated.

"Because he's kind. There is much hunger and sadness in the world, milady. He accepted many in trade for food for their father's people. The new one is a queen who gave herself to save her people, though she could have sent another in her place. Lord Kerkolos would not have minded."

Psappha felt a sharp pang at the thought of The African being a slave. "I'm sure the Lady Adriana enjoys having a queen for a slave," she said, rubbing the back of her neck.

"The African is not a slave," Lyneachia said as she led her new mistress to the tiled bath in a nook off the bedroom. "Lord Kerkolos would not do that to her. She is much too proud. Like you," she added with a smile. Psappha frowned.

Lyneachia clapped twice. Moments later, two serving women hurried into the chamber bearing amphorae of water, one hot, one not. Lyneachia sprinkled autumn jasmine into the tub. The fragrance of its petals rose with the steam. The closet filled with scent. She tested the temperature with her elbow before beckoning her new mistress.

Psappha stepped into the bath. She gasped, and then chuckled when Lyneachia dumped the contents of the second amphora over her head. Later, when she left the tub, Lyneachia wrapped her in a soft towel.

"The priestesses of Iphis will think you a tantalizing offering," Lyneachia said.

The words meant nothing to Psappha. She could hear the gynakeoni through the beaded curtains. Their laughter mystified her,

Psappha

considering their situation. They clapped their hands in rhythm with a song.

Psappha sighed and stretched belly-down on the lavender massage table. The music reminded her of a dancing golden girl-child and a wave of homesickness, apprehension and grief flowed through her, adding to her tension -- tension that gynakeon-born Lyneachia relieved with an educated talent Lycos could not have imagined.

~~~~~

Psappha was not ready to give herself over to the prison she believed the gynakeon to be. It represented everything designed to silence her. I am a poet, she protested. When I die, my words must live after me. The lack of lyre and tablet could not keep her from composing.

One pre-dawn, disgruntled because the poem she attempted would not behave, she threw a pitcher at a wall. It did not break. Instead, the lavender draped wall dented inward, letting the pitcher slide safely to the floor. Amazed, Psappha investigated and found a narrow flight of stairs behind several layers of tapestry.

At the top of the hidden stairs, she found her own secluded section of roof. Dazzling houses crowned the slope above the house, looming over the pretentious dwellings of new wealth like disapproving parents.

Pipes joined the house above to this one, then ran from Psappha's side of the roof to the next and the next and so on down the landscaped terraces, making a continuous viaduct. The homes and estates of the current elite stood on either side of the house and on the next terrace below. Other women gathered on their roofs to share cool morning air.

Far below, riotous Syracuse lay splattered along the shore like children's discarded toys. Dawn's shadows dressed the hovels on the outskirts, almost creating beauty.

Helios soon covered the roof with a steamy glare. Moisture trickled from Psappha's brow, but she did not retreat. Instead, she loosed her hair and shook it to catch the wispy breeze.

Directly below, Lyneachia picked irises in Psappha's private garden. The tiny courtyard looked cramped and crowded. Psappha ached for her lost home with its sweeping lawns and fragrant, unbound orchards. She longed to run again on the glistening beaches of Mytilene.

She heard a ripple of female laughter and felt a sharp pang of longing for her companions of old. She ached for the gentle beauty of children dancing in The Lady's park.

The gurgling of the fountain in the gynakeon filled Psappha with an ache she could neither explain nor dissipate. The music of women's chatter drew her across the roof. Rose scent floated up to her as she descended three steps to a lower roof. Below, in the women's garden, tiny silver and gold fishes chased each other in a small shaded pool. Women and girls clustered around a huge rose arbor, begging for a story. "There once was a young man of great cleverness," one of them prompted.

"Once, in his travels to Egypt, he stopped at an inn," said a low-voiced storyteller. Recognizing the African's vibrant tone, Psappha leaned on the low parapet, straining to hear.

"The inn-keeper had a wife and two sons and two daughters. At dinner, they brought five pigeons to the young guest to serve. He gave the innkeeper and his wife one bird. To the sons he served one bird, also to the daughters. To himself he served two birds and ate with relish.

"The innkeeper was surprised but, when they brought in a fat fowl, he again asked his guest to cut and serve, as the rules of hospitality demand. The guest served the head of the fowl to the innkeeper and his wife. To each son he served a leg, and to each daughter, a wing. The rest he kept for himself."

"Why, Gongyla?" a musical voice cut in.

"That is what the inn-keeper wanted to know," the storyteller continued, "so, he asked the young man, just as you have asked me, and the young man told him, 'I have done the best I could to be fair.

"You and your wife and one pigeon make three, as do two sons and a pigeon, and a pigeon and two daughters. Three, also, are two pigeons and I. As to the fowl, the reason is simple. You and your wife are the heads of your family and as such should have the head. Your sons support the family so, of course, they should have the legs. To your daughters, I served the wings since they will soon marry and fly away from your home. The body resembles a ship so I kept it for myself since it was on a ship that I came here and on a ship that I hope to return."

Psappha giggled. A bevy of faces turned upward. The dark-haired storyteller leaned from the arbor and called, "Did you enjoy my story, milady?"

Psappha

"A most clever young man," Psappha called, and then she drew back, cursing The Fates for their twisting of her life. The women sounded happy. She knew she would enjoy their company, if given a choice. But, no one had given her a choice, and it galled her. She was afraid that, if she allowed the women entry to her heart, she would never escape this luxurious prison, never again sing the praises of The Lady for the world to hear.

Nevertheless, she edged toward the stairs leading to their garden. Each step downward seemed a step toward oblivion, but she kept going. As she approached the fishpond, the women and girls scampered into the pavilion. She regretted their going but she understood. By assigning her the purple chamber, Kerkolos had set her apart, and she compounded it by hiding there, she realized.

The roses smelled sweeter when she neared them. At least I have the bees for company, she thought.

"I thought you would come." Gongyla sat deep within the arbor. Her wide-set, almond-shaped eyes glowed; reminding Psappha of dark ripe olives dressed in dew. Her head thrust slightly forward on her swan-like neck.

She could pass for Nefertiri, Psappha thought.

Gongyla's hair lay close to her scalp like sheared black fleece. Her face inscrutable, perfect, as if chiseled by a master's hand. Her sensuous lips curled in a hint of a smile. When she spoke, her voice enfolded Psappha like fur on a winter's day.

"Come," she invited, patting the bench beside her. "Sit with me."

"Do you wish to return to your home on a ship like the young man in your story?" Psappha ventured shyly.

"You are not of the gynakeon, Psappha, or you would have no need to question. You have kept to yourself so far, but you have months ahead with only memories to sustain you. One day, loneliness will bring you to the Sisterhood and we will gladly welcome you into the Temple of Iphis."

Psappha remembered Lyneachia mentioning that name. "Who is Iphis?" she asked. "And, where is this temple?"

"Iphis rules the gynakia when no man, not even a god, may enter."

"You're confusing me," Psappha snapped. "No one can keep Kerkolos from the gynakeon, not even a goddess. He owns it, just as he would like to own me. Explain yourself!"

"No, Psappha. You will come to know Iphis when you are ready to know the gynakeon."

"By Aphrodite's eyes, I know the gynakeon. I've seen it all. It squats like a fat toad waiting to devour me."

Gongyla's soft jungle eyes offered comfort, driving chinks in the armor Psappha had wrapped around her heart. "Your temper spoils the beauty of your eyes, Psappha. You have seen Lord Kerkolos' gynakeon, that's true, but you have closed your Self away from its spirit. I've watched you when you thought yourself alone. I've heard you, too. Your soul cries through your music. Eventually, you will come to us. I hear it in your songs."

Psappha slumped. She tried not to cry, but the African's arm felt warm around her shoulders.

"When you want to know the gynakeoni, you will come to us," Gongyla crooned. "Only then can you be initiated into the rites of Iphis."

"What would you have me do?"

"I want nothing from you, Psappha. Only that you open to what life brings."

"Life in a gynakeon brings only obscurity," Psappha said. "It is a luxurious prison: a hole from which my voice cannot be heard."

Gongyla's tender, black eyes promised comfort, but Psappha refused it.

"You may be content to use your stories for the entertainment of imprisoned women, but I am Psappha of Lesbos and I WILL be remembered."

Psappha

3

"Who is Iphis?" Psappha asked Lyneachia when she returned to her quarters.

"Iphis is not for you, milady."

"Why not? You were the first to mention her."

"That was a mistake," the child sputtered. "Lord Kerkolos has other plans for you."

"What plans?" Psappha felt a spark of temper.

"Just plans," Lyneachia whispered, her voice trembling.

"To Hades with his plans," Psappha said.

Lyneachia's enormous eyes filled with tears.

"Oh, stop that!" Psappha snapped. "Nobody's going to hurt you if I can help it," she said, knowing she was powerless even to protect herself: Kerkolos could kill her, if he chose, and no one would ever know. Whatever his plans, Pittakos and his exile left her no choice but to acquiesce. Taking a deep, calming breath, she said, "Tell me."

"All right," Lyneachia said. Her lower lip trembled as she plunked, cross-legged, onto the Persian carpet. "Iphis lived long, long ago," she began in a hushed and nervous tone.

"It is said that, before Iphis was born, her father extracted a hateful promise from her mother," Lyneachia whispered, her gaze darting to the beaded curtain that separated the chamber from the gynakeon. "Iphis' father made her mother vow that, if the child she carried was born female, it would be left in Zeus' cave to die. But, when the time came, his wife could not bring herself to kill their daughter.

"Instead, she swaddled the girl-child and told her husband he had a son. When he presented the infant to the gods, he named her Iphis."

"And?" Psappha prompted.

"And, his wife felt great relief. By giving the child a name that has no gender, there was less chance of offending the many gods.

"The girl-child, Iphis, grew into a very beautiful boy. Or, so her father thought," Lyneachia said with a merry twinkle in her eyes.

"At the proper time, her father announced that his son, Iphis, was now adult and that the beautiful Ianthe was to be his bride."

"Oops," Psappha giggled.

"Oops is right," Lyneachia agreed.   At this point, Lyneachia forgot she was supposed to be quiet. Her voice became strident and stronger as she continued. "Iphis and Ianthe were much together, as befits a betrothed couple, and it was not long before Iphis fell hopelessly in love.

"Iphis and her mother did not know what to do. If they told the father the truth, the mother would surely die. If they did not, they both feared Ianthe's reaction on the wedding night."

"So? What happened?"

"It is said that, on the eve of the wedding, Iphis' and her mother went to the Temple of Io to pray. It is said, the mother prayed for forgiveness, while Iphis prayed to be released, either from her masquerade or from her burning passion for Ianthe. But, in truth, Iphis prayed hardest to be allowed both."

"And?" Psappha prompted with increasing impatience.

"And . . ." Lyneachia mocked with a conspiratorial giggle, "after a time, Iphis and her mother left the temple. As they walked away from the altar, Iphis grew stalwart and handsome. Some say that, to this day, there is always a gift at the Temple of Io from the youth, Iphis, who came to the altar a beautiful woman and walked away a proud young bridegroom."

Psappha sighed, finding it hard to imagine a love strong enough to make the gods pay heed. "But, if Io transformed Iphis into a man, why do you and the African speak of him as female? And, why did Gongyla call Iphis a goddess if she was mortal? Does she still live?"

"Please, milady, no more questions," Lyneachia whispered, casting cautious glances behind her. "Let the gynakeon keep its secrets. Lord Kerkolos has special plans for you." That last was softer than a whisper, as the child hurried through the beaded curtains.

Psappha could hear talking and laughter, but she could not bring herself to follow. She still perceived the gynakeon as a prison. She was sure that, if she ever accepted it and its customs, she would never leave.

Homesickness nibbled at her. Loneliness ate her spirit. Banked fires smoldered in her veins. No amount of pillows over her head could shut out the happy chatter of the women beyond the beaded curtains.

When at last she drifted off from sheer exhaustion, she tossed and turned, tormented with sensuous dreams.

Psappha

~~~~~

Psappha awakened lying naked in her own sweat. Her body shook with unshedable tears.

"Get up," she commanded herself. "Your stubbornness is a tighter prison than the gynakeon could ever be. Get up, and share the cool refreshment of the pool."

Donning a loose robe, Psappha pushed through the beaded archway, dropped her robe at the edge of the pool and stepped into the fragrant water.

Lyneachia popped up in front of her, kissed her, then disappeared beneath the lotus leaves. By her impulse, the child evoked a flood of memories. Psappha's mind transformed the pool into the placid Bay of Mytilene. The women became her beloved companions. Her homesickness floated away in the midst of their splashing play. They passed her merrily from one to another as if she were a water ball, swimming in circles around her, kissing her as they passed. They formed a ring and gestured for her to swim by them.

Psappha swam in ever-widening circles. The women let their hands flow along her back as she skimmed by. There were more of them with each pass. Eventually, women rimmed the entire pool, caressing her beneath the water.

To tired to swim, but unwilling to leave, Psappha walked around the circle, pausing to kiss each woman and girl lightly on the cheek. They were not all beautiful, although some were amazingly so; some were mere children like Lyneachia.

"Ah! You are here," Gongyla greeted her. "Do you wish to join the Sisterhood of Iphis?"

Judging by her welcome into the pool, Psappha guessed the nature of the sisterhood, and it went against everything she had been trained to expect in her life, although she was not sure why. The men had their cupbearers, but they were young boys in need of a mentor; they grew out of it. Most of them, she reminded herself, thinking of Lycos.

"Psappha?" Gongyla prompted.

"I don't know."

"Perhaps it is too soon?"

"Perhaps."

Gongyla nodded to Lyneachia, who got out of the pool, picked up the robe Psappha had dropped and held it for her, giving Psappha no choice but to leave the pool, don her robe, and return to her lonely chambers.

~~~~~

The remainder of the summer went much the same. Psappha spent her days in the garden enjoying Gongyla's vast repertoire of tales, and her nights trying to shut out the sounds of the gynakeon – so near, yet so deliberately far away.

When the nights began to shorten, great hearths burned day and night around the scented pool. Now, warmth as well as laughter filtered through the beaded curtain. Lyneachia fastened the heavy double drapery over Psappha's garden arch and brought several braziers into the purple chamber, but no amount of heat had any effect upon Psappha's resolve.

On one particularly brisk evening, while trying to ignore the noises from the heated pool, Psappha sat before her mirror, studying her reflection, her mind awash with discontent.

Through the diaphanous folds of her wine-colored kiton, her nudeness hinted of gold, but it was only a hint. "Why couldn't I have been born all pink and golden like my mother," she argued with her reflection. "Why must I look like a peeled olive?"

"I like olives," someone said.

Psappha's hand jumped to her throat. In the glass, she saw the purple wall-hanging move.

Kerkolos untangled himself from the tapestry and said, "I'll be glad when we can take this down."

"Must you always sneak up on me? Why wasn't I told there was a door back there?"

"The door leads to my chambers," he said. "You were given adjacent quarters because I intend to make you my wife."

"You intend, do you? Did it occur to you to ask me?" There was no hint of supplication in his stance. He seemed calm and businesslike. "No. I suppose not," she answered her own question, recalling his earlier words. 'When I decide what to do with you', he had said. Apparently, he had decided. Her voice dripped sarcasm as she said, "Of course your intentions are to be obeyed."

"My dear lady, I am paying you a compliment." His tone reminded her of Pittakos. "Will you marry me?"

"You're more than a little late with the question," she retorted. "What will you do if I say no, put me up for sale?"

"You're not a slave, Psappha."

34

Psappha

"Women are all slaves here, are they not?"

Turning her back on him, she studied his reflection in the glass. He stood with his bandy legs planted as if on a rolling deck. His sinewy arms folded over his massive chest.

"Will you marry me?"

In the glass, she saw desire flare in his eyes as he watched her brush her hair. He wants me, she thought. Why won't he say so? "If you want me, I can't stop you," she said. "As for marriage -- " She turned to face him. All trace of emotion vanished from his eyes. His expression seemed cold, empty, his attitude haughty, disapproving, and an echo of his mother.

"Will you marry me?"

"No."

His eyes flared again, burning into hers like volcanoes of indigo flame. "You will be mine," he said with the mocking arrogance that she found so infernally aggravating. Then, he scooped her up, carried her through the doorway behind the tapestry, and dumped her onto a huge mahogany bed. "You will be mine."

Psappha rolled over, jumped up and scooted past him, to and through the gaping doorway, slamming the door behind her. "In a pigs eye, I will."

~~~~~

Weeks passed with no further exchange between them. Psappha avoided the women more completely than before. It embarrassed her that they had all known his intentions. It perturbed her that none of them told her.

In the evenings, she heard their laughter and imagined Kerkolos enjoying their charms. Not that she cared, but he had proposed. She wished she had not rejected him so rudely. What would a bandy legged oarsman who turned out to be richer than Croesus do with her now? His power over her fate reminded her of Pittakos, and she was afraid.

"Oh, maidenhood, maidenhood," she sang softly to herself, composing on a stormy autumn afternoon. "Where have you flown from me? Where are your sweet, cool dreams – your innocent nights of restful sleep?"

His proposal was just a convenience, she decided. He could take her any time he chose. It was all Pittakos' fault. Left alone, she would have been safely married now – at home in Mytilene. Where I belong, she thought, as her mind filled with memories of squandered innocence.

It was the night before departing Mytilene. Psappha was desolate at the prospect of leaving. Saying goodbye to Alkaios did not help.

Betrothed since birth, Psappha and Alkaios had never been more than a day's walk apart and, although Pittakos had exiled them both they would sail on separate vessels in the morning.

Grateful for the storm that delayed departure, Psappha had clung to Alkaios as never before. He smelled of home, and salt and wind. His bare chest scorched her cheek. He was her last hold on her beloved Mytilene and she wanted him. Now!

Oh, Lady, help me, she had prayed. Make him quiet the aching loneliness the Fates have caused me.

"Do you still think me a child?" she asked him in a tone she thought seductive.

"I told you long ago you were no child, Psappha."

"I am not yet a woman."

"You are barely sixteen, Psappha. Relax. There's plenty of time."

"There's no time, 'Kios. Pittakos wants to silence us, and he may succeed. Listen to Poseidon rage at Zeus' winds. The Fates are cruel, Alkaios. We could die out there."

Standing on tiptoe, she tangled her fingers in his beard and tried to pull his lips to hers. Her inner turmoil matched the fury of the storm outside. She clutched him, afraid that, if she let go, she would disappear. She wanted him to do something -- anything -- to fill the aching void inside her soul.

Alkaios pushed her away. "Behave," he said in a husky whisper.

Behave indeed! How dared he? She felt fury flame her face.

"I didn't mean to offend you," Alkaios said.

"Offend me? Fool! You refused me. What greater offense is there?" Tears streamed on burning cheeks.

"Stop it!" Alkaios shook her sob-wracked shoulders. "I didn't refuse you, you little idiot. You are to be my bride -- "

"Bride?" she shouted, "When, Alkaios? Where? Pittakos is sending us to who knows where. There may never be a time of brides for us. You save me to feed your pride with a public display of stained cloth," she accused him. "Don't you understand that tomorrow we leave all of the public that matters far behind?"

"You dare speak of pride?" Alkaios had growled through clenched teeth. "Where is yours? What is it that makes you ask this of

Psappha

me? You've come to womanhood untouched. Remain so until you are my bride. Or, find yourself another bridegroom. I won't ruin your wedding night to satisfy your curiosity -- or mine."

Oh, you won't, won't you? Psappha snuggled against him, fluttering her moist lashes against his chest. She almost giggled when her hand brushed his penis and found it attentive. In spite of her narrow hips and undeveloped chest, she knew he desired her and her spirit rose triumphant.

Alkaios shoved her to arm's length. "Stop it, 'Spha. You're behaving like a porna."

"Porna am I, Milord Righteous? Do you intend to smite me with that sword which threatens to cut through your loincloth? Wouldn't you rather put it in a sheath designed to hold it?"

"A bride must be above reproach," he scolded, his hands trembling on her shoulders. "The desecration of a virgin is abhorrent to the gods."

"Which gods, 'Kios? Surely, you don't mean Zeus. His penchant for rape is astronomical. The only gods we might offend are those who teach that men own everything. What they think abhorrent is that The Lady's Maidens own themselves. The gift of sensuality is mine to do with as I will."

She wriggled just enough to make him lose his grip. His hands slid toward her elbows before he hid them behind his back.

"You will come to our marriage bed a virgin," he said.

Psappha heard the tremor in his voice and fought to conceal delight. Lessons learned in the Maiden temple filled her mind. This time, when she grabbed his beard, she claimed his mouth. Her tongue became a serpent determined to destroy his will.

The infinitesimal remains of a growl escaped him as he scooped her into his arms. All thought of scruffy ships and exiles faded as he carried her to her cabin.

Psappha untied the ribbon from around her waist. She released the scarabs at her shoulders, a tiny smile teasing the corners of her lips. Her kiton fell away as he approached. She sighed, knowing she had teased him beyond restraint.

Alkaios tossed her onto her bed and mounted, becoming tentative when his penis met resistance. The lock on Aphrodite's most sacred altar held firm.

Psappha had refused to let him cheat her of her moment. Wrapping her legs around his hips, she crossed her ankles and planted her heels on firm moist buttocks. Then, with one determined heave, she forced her own birth into the realm of The Lady's chosen daughters.

"Nevermore will you come to me, maidenhood, nevermore will you come."

As Psappha completed her composition, fires of boldness too long banked returned to blaze anew. Her life was hers and she would make the most of it. She would not let frustration drown her.

"Lyneachia!" She shouted.

The startled slave-girl dropped her jar of scented oil. For no reason Psappha could fathom, Lyneachia began mopping the spilled oil with Psappha's favorite brocade wrapper.

Psappha snatched the glittering robe from her fingers, slapped her and immediately apologized.

Lyneachia looked at her and smiled with dawning comprehension.

"What are you grinning at? Clean up this mess!"

Lyneachia smiled sweetly. "Do you want me to take a message to the master?"

"Take a message? Where is he?" Psappha glanced nervously at the tapestry. What hideous plan was he conjuring now?

"The master is aboard his ship in the harbor," Lyneachia assured her quietly. "He will stay there until the wedding."

"There isn't going to be any wedding," Psappha insisted. "His offer of marriage was nothing but a way to meet the demands of society.

"Send word to him that Psappha of Lesbos commands his immediate attendance. We'll settle this." Lyneachia nodded but did not budge. "Well? Go on. What are you waiting for?"

"What you said -- " The child hesitated.

"Yes?'

"What you said about marrying the master --"

"I didn't say I would marry him."

"But --"

"But what? Are you still afraid of me?"

"No," Lyneachia said with a giggle. "Being afraid of a kitten would be easier."

"Kittens sometimes scratch," Psappha said.

"But they're also soft and cuddly," Lyneachia said, and Psappha hung her head, still feeling guilty for having slapped the child over something as trivial as a spoiled dress.

Psappha

"You're wrong about society, too," the child insisted. "Syracuse doesn't care how a man takes care of his women, only that he does. Kerkolos doesn't have to marry you, but he does have to take care of you and, since he wants you, the best way for him to take care of you is marriage."

"He has more than enough women."

"He isn't like his father, Psappha. He's never touched any of the women."

No wonder they worship Iphis, Psappha thought. Then she said, "I hear him among them at night."

"You couldn't have. He's been here only once since he docked, and that was in the daytime. Should I take your message now?"

"Take it? You can leave the gynakeon?"

"Of course," Lyneachia responded with a shrug. "In Syracuse, slaves are freer than their mistresses."

"Tell me the way out. I'll deliver the message myself."

"I can't do that." Lyneachia trembled. "The master would be very angry if anyone saw you on the street."

"He can get as angry as he likes," Psappha decided. "What more can he do to me?"

"Nothing," Lyneachia said. "But, he could turn me over to his mother. She's stayed out of the gynakeon since you came, but if he turns me over to her, she'll beat me. She likes that."

Horror chased disappointment from Psappha's mind. She chastised herself for letting thoughts of freedom temporarily rob her of good sense. Kerkolos could do whatever he wished with her, but she would not cause Lyneachia suffering. "You go, Child. Tell him I wish to speak with him."

~~~~~

Adriana flounced into the purple chamber like an avenging god. "So," she growled without benefit of greeting, "you've decided to accept the high honor my foolish son insists he must bestow on you."

Psappha nodded. "I have no choice."

"Of course you have a choice," Adriana sneered. "You can come to Sybaris with me. I have a new home there and you could serve my guests, and not be troubled with my son."

Her tone left no doubt in Psappha's mind what kind of service was intended. She felt the traps grow tight around her, but she knew of no way out. "As I said, Adriana. I have no choice." Better to be porna to one man than to many, she thought resignedly.

39

Adriana sniffed. "So you say -- very well. I will inform my son his foolishness shall not go unrewarded. Maybe we can get through with this nasty business quickly, so I can return to Sybaris, where I belong." With that at least, Psappha could whole-heartedly agree.

"You will be mistress here," Adriana said in parting. "While my son lives."

Psappha

~~ 4 ~~

Lycos marched through the hidden doors, destroying the pre-dawn quiet. "Wake up, you lazy girl. It's your wedding day."

Psappha groaned and rolled over, nuzzling her pillows, peeking surreptitiously when Lyneachia spoke.

"How'd you get in here, you preposterous little man? You are a man, aren't you?"

"Of course I'm a man, untrained one. You needn't bar the way to the gynakeon like an undersized mongrel. I have no interest in gynakeoni. I'm here to prepare Psappha for the wedding. Be a nice little girl and I might let you assist."

He nudged Psappha. "Everything is ready but you, slugabed. Since you have no family here, this house is to be considered your father's house for now," he said. "Kerkolos is aboard ship. The guests will escort him here for the feast. He'll pretend to steal you away and take you to his cabin," he said with wistful softness.

"Then, after First Night, he'll consider the ship your father's house and spend Second Night there. I've arranged everything. Adriana will meet you in the main hall to give you her keys. Then she will take up permanent residence in Sybaris under the protection of her brother-in-law, Lord Kerkolos' uncle," he concluded and he yanked Psappha out of bed.

"You'll see. It'll work out just fine," he said as he stripped her of her nightdress and hustled her through the beaded arch into the central pavilion.

The gynakeoni clustered around her, pouring warm, scented oil from ornate carafes onto her breasts, shoulders and back. Gongyla was conspicuously absent.

Lyneachia scrapped the oil off with an olivewood strigil then led Psappha to the pool.

Lycos permitted Lyneachia the honor of attending Psappha in the ritual bath. But, the instant she stepped from the water he wrapped her in virgin fleece and hustled her back into the purple chamber, where he dressed her in pale-rose, whisper silk. Over that, he draped

41

translucent veiling the color of an April sky. The two colors blended into a lilac fantasy every time she moved.

"Hold still a little longer, Adelphi. I've nearly finished."

Psappha sighed and relaxed against him, resting a shoulder on his thigh as he worked with her hair. What can even Lycos' mastery do for me? She wondered. No amount of paint and jewels can add color where none exists.

"Behold," Lycos commanded long minutes later.

Psappha's fingers trembled as she took the proffered mirror. He had braided her fawn-copper tresses into a high coronet that acted as a dry vase for a cluster of violets. Other than the flowers, her only ornaments were her eyes. She frowned as she returned the mirror.

"You there – girl – what's–your–name," Lycos called. "Where are milady's sandals?"

"Right where you kicked them, milord jackal," Lyneachia countered. "You've lost them in all your fussing. I should have taken care of my mistress myself. See how you've tired her, charlatan."

"You'd have had her painted like a Cretan urn," Lycos snarled. "She is the bride of Kerkolos of Andros. She must outshine all the beauties of Syracuse."

"How can she outshine anyone, you dullard? You've done her up as plain as an empty temple."

"That's what you think, you impudent snit. Psappha is so beautiful she needs no jewelry."

"Hush," Psappha interjected. "Have mercy. You're giving me a headache."

"It's not me giving you a headache," Lyneachia grumbled. "It's milord prissy's braids. I could have told him they were too tight."

"Hush, I said!"

Psappha led them through the mahogany and teak master chamber to an enclosed courtyard beyond.

~~~~~

Adriana met them in the private courtyard, her bulk encased in brocade, her keys half-hidden in the folds over-lapping her waist. When she saw Psappha, she sniffed and turned her back, preceding them into the public areas of the house.

Psappha's head reeled with excitement. The great hall threatened to explode around her as they entered. It seemed to her that all of Syracuse had crowded into it. People peered at her as if she was a jewel presented for appraisal.

Psappha

Kerkolos' eyes reflected her splendor, but all Psappha saw were Ocean's depths waiting to drown her. She posed at his side while her spirit ran like a trapped deer. The vintage Chianti in the marriage cup tasted like vinegar to her, but she sipped it anyway.

The servants placed one marvelous dish after another before them, but they all tasted like wadded papyrus to Psappha's nervous palate. Just when she dared hope for prompt release from her public misery, a parade of servants entered bearing a burnished platter resplendent with the traditional peacock of Hera, roasted full feathered and surrounded by fresh, ripe fruit.

When, at last, the ceremonies ended, Adriana relinquished the household keys with a half-hidden scowl. The newly wedded couple sat together and endured the ribald teasing of the guests, a universal torture Adriana took particular delight in.

Psappha hid her face against Kerkolos' shoulder, weak with strained emotions. To her immeasurable relief, he scooped her up into his arms and carried her from the hall amid a riotous chorus of cheers and coarse jests. She kept her face hidden until the doors to the banquet hall closed behind them.

Kerkolos stood her on her feet in the main corridor, which she had not seen since the day she arrived. Lycos draped an embroidered violet robe around her shoulders. The gold, copper and bronze threads in the embroidery might have come from her shining hair. Psappha raised the hood, keeping her face hidden and her thoughts to herself.

Kerkolos whisked her from the house and down the many terraces to the docks. Her hood fell away as he carried her into the cabin that had been hers for a little while. A down comforter covered the wide bunk. The traditional quince, supposed, when shared by the bridal couple, to insure sweetness of speech, waited on the bedside table.

Neither of them spoke as Kerkolos removed her cloak. Psappha removed the pins from her hair and combed her fingers through her braids, sighing deeply. The braids had indeed been too tight. At least, they felt so to Psappha, after hours of public display.

Kerkolos offered her the quince and they bit into it simultaneously as custom demanded. Neither of them broke the uneasy silence. He removed the clasp at her waist and let her double kiton flutter off the tips of his callused fingers to spread around her ankles like frothy pink and blue clouds, creating a variegated violet mound.

The ship rocked against the dock. Psappha heard the wedding guests chanting and singing on the deck outside. Kerkolos whispered something as he drew her closer to the fur covered bunk, but all Psappha heard were ribald jokes and Adriana's shouted suggestions. She knew why they waited so noisily and she trembled.

Oh, Aphrodite, you weaver of wiles, I've lost it. There will be no blood. He will surely cast me out, denouncing me as a porna, she thought as Kerkolos eased her onto the bunk with a tender kiss.

He entered her and she shrieked. Oh, Eros, you wondrous scamp, you've mated me to a giant! He'll never know.

In her triumph, Psappha's limbs became liquid, serpentine, twining. Her small body arched to meet his every thrust. The deepest recesses of Aphrodite's altar flexed, relaxed, reached and gripped. Her lips turned molten, fluid, expanding, devouring. Her body trembled as she bound him to her, enslaving him with passion she did not feel.

~~~~~

Next morning, after a brief, dreamless sleep, Psappha sat by a mahogany-framed mirror and brushed her hair, wondering why she felt so detached from what had happened in the night. She admired Kerkolos' reflection in the glass and knew she ought to be ecstatic.

Chagrined, she spun on the polished bench and winced. She had forgotten that he tore her. Eros, you traitor.

She smiled, remembering her bridegroom's proud grin when he tossed the stained sheet to the waiting wedding guests.

Laying her brush aside, she caressed the curve of his hip with her eyes and decided he was beautiful. He lay on the bed, on his side, facing away from her. She went to him, dropping her robe to the floor as she walked. Brushing her fingertips over his hip, she kissed him in the hollow where it joined the over developed muscles of his back.

He awoke and drew her to him. His voice was throaty and warm as he whispered in her ear. "I hope spring is long and stormy. I do not wish to leave you now that you are mine."

Later, when Psappha rested in his arms, he said, "You've been too much alone. When I sail, go to the women. They will welcome you."

"Why should your women welcome me? Especially now, when I have taken you away from them."

Kerkolos laughed. "They're not my women and you haven't taken me away from them. I wouldn't be surprised if they thanked you

Psappha

for being here. I've never been so attentive to the needs of this household. Did no one tell you?"

"If they're not your women, whose are they?"

"Oh, they're mine all right. Mine to feed, house and care for. Many belonged to my father. My mother has arranged many marriages for them since my father's death. They do well enough, considering they have no dower." He lowered his eyes.

Psappha had not intended to let him see how much his casual mention of dowries hurt her.

"The rest are merchandise," he said. "Don't look at me like that. I don't intend to sell them, much to my mother's horror. Most of them come from destitute kingdoms, traded to me for food and rough cloth. The African traded herself out of pity for her people. I didn't want to accept, but to refuse her would have taken her pride, and I must admit that having the best of the tribes grace my house has not harmed my reputation."

~~~~~

Although Kerkolos expected Psappha to learn to manage the house and servants in preparation for his mother's departure, Adriana refused to teach. Psappha became a showpiece for the entertainment of an endless stream of guests. Conversations soon forgotten filled her evenings. Adriana typically excused her early to await Kerkolos' pleasure in their chamber. A pitiful lyre of inferior quality was all the music she could find in Adriana's sprawling house.

On the day of the fleet's departure, Psappha strummed the lyre as Lycos helped Kerkolos pack his already bulging trunk. "Kerkolos," she said, laying the lyre aside. "May I keep Lycos with me?"

"Why do you want me here?" Lycos asked. "Adriana is leaving, but the gynakeoni will keep you company."

She ignored him and touched her husband's arm. "Please."

"Why?"

"We're to have a visit from Hera," she whispered so no one but he could hear. Kerkolos looked stunned. She could feel a tremble in his fingers as they lifted her chin.

"A child? When?"

"After the leaves fall, I think."

He scooped her up without warning, whirled with her in his arms and laid her, like an infant, on the great bed. "I will tell my mother she must stay to look after you."

Psappha felt a sudden wave of nausea, unassociated with her condition. "That will not be necessary," she said. "Adriana has delayed her voyage much too long already. She loves Sybaris and, as Lycos said, I have the gynakeoni. But I would feel more comfortable if you would let him stay."

"I need Lycos with me," Kerkolos said. "You must wait 'til we return."

Psappha giggled. "Hera waits for no man, you great black bear. She comes at her appointed time."

"She will wait for me," he insisted.

"And, of course, since you decree it, it shall be so," she said, ruffling his hair.

He scowled. She took his face between her palms, and kissed his nose.

~~~~~

Psappha had not expected to miss Adriana, but she did. When full management of the household fell to her, she quickly came to rely on the older servants. They trained Lyneachia and the other girls and taught Psappha what she needed to know in order to establish a comfortable routine.

Psappha filled her days directing the servants in binges of unnecessary cleaning and polishing. At night, she tossed on the great bed with banked fires smoldering in her veins; a throbbing being with no one but herself to bring her quiet sleep. Her body mocked her. The feel of Kerkolos' hands seemed branded on her flesh.

She could no longer resist the magnetism of the gynakeoni's happy chatter. Donning a loose robe, she stepped toward the torch–glow that filtered through the beaded curtain, shining like a beacon in the fog of Psappha's mind.

A hush fell over the women when she entered. The effect was ethereal. The garden-like pavilion was familiar to her, but she had been so careful to enter it always alone that now it felt as if all the nymphs of Olympus gathered to examine her.

There were not as many as before. Psappha decided many of those she had seen about the house had been servant's wives. She did not see them here.

The water gurgling from the conduit high in the wall sounded loud in the silence. Torches, blazing in their sconces, sent billows of smoke high into the vines overhead, pulling the heat with it and creating

Psappha

a pleasing draft when combined with air from the open arches. Psappha smiled when Lyneachia stepped from between the islands of light.

"Why are they all so quiet?" she asked.

"They're afraid," Lyneachia whispered. "They don't understand why you've avoided them, nor why you come here now."

"They have no reason to fear me. I'm small and they are many."

"That is not the sort of hurt they fear," the child explained. "You are their mistress now. You could sell them if you chose."

"I wouldn't sell them. This was their home before it was mine."

"I know that," Lyneachia said. "But they don't. Lady Adriana sold all the young concubines to farmers in the outback before she left, and took the prettiest serving women with her. Those left are afraid you will think them too expensive. Especially the old ones, now that they've outlived their usefulness."

"Outlived their usefulness! What kind of place is this? Wisdom is to be revered. To lock life's creators away from the world is bad enough. To turn wisdom out is beyond belief."

"Lady Adriana would agree with that as regards her own person, but not in reference to slaves."

"We're all slaves here," Psappha said, looking around. The gynakeoni returned her gaze silently, cautious and curious.

"Tell them why you're here," Lyneachia prompted.

"I have come to the Temple." Psappha's voice trembled as she spoke.

The gynakeon became a sudden rhapsody of sound. The women chattered like all the ports of the world. Psappha barely noticed Lyneachia's deft hands peeling away her flimsy robe. When she felt their many eyes upon her nakedness, she plunged beneath the surface of the pool and swam underwater as long as she could. Good-natured laughter greeted her when she burst the surface, sputtering.

Gongyla strode from the shadows. She walks like a lynx, Psappha thought, and swims like a dolphin, she added when Gongyla cut the water like a glistening ebon knife.

Psappha smiled as the ritual of circles began again. This time, no one invited her to leave. When she completed her last circle, Gongyla entwined a lotus blossom in her hair, and then disappeared beneath the lily pads, surfacing a few feet away, laughing. Psappha almost reached her before she dove again.

Psappha followed, swimming strongly, but Gongyla continued to elude her. If Psappha went underwater at one side of the pool, the lustrous African was taking the air at the other.

Exhausted, Psappha stood, breathless, near the waterfall. Gongyla propped her elbows on the opposite edge and sent droplets flying with a quick shake of her close-cropped ringlets, then she winked and dove again. Seconds later, she appeared inches from Psappha, floating on her back.

Psappha felt as if her heart had floated through her body and escaped through her toes. Gongyla's sinewy body glistened beneath a thin sheath of scented water. Slurping waves lapped high, conical breasts. Their nipples accented perfection like inlaid mahogany. When she stood, the water dipped into a tiny navel set like a jewel in contoured, supple, well-oiled leather.

Gongyla crinkled her nose as if tired of scrutiny. She took Psappha's hand and they swam together to the marble stairs where Gongyla swept Psappha into her arms and carried her, limp and dripping, from the pool into the purple chamber.

Gongyla placed Psappha on her massage table where Lyneachia wrapped her in snowy linen. The gynakeoni crowded in around them, arranging themselves on the floor, their multicolored kitons spread like wildflower petals. Gongyla flashed a gesture and they rose as one and vanished through the beaded curtains.

After a few whispering moments with Lyneachia, Gongyla followed, leaving Psappha bewildered, speechless and wanting, with no idea what it was she wanted. She sighed often while Lyneachia brushed her hair.

When the brush was laid aside, Psappha accepted a cup of fragrant tea, then she shrugged off her sheet and reclined, face down, on the table. "I wish they would all trust me as Gongyla seems to," she said when Lyneachia began kneading scented oil into her tense muscles.

"Gongyla is a queen and fearless, but you can make the others trust you."

"In the name of Aphrodite how?"

"In the name of Aphrodite," Lyneachia said, bearing down on relaxing tendons, working the oils as if she wished to drive them into the bones themselves. Her hands eased a little as she anointed Psappha's feet, rubbing the oils between toes that wriggled beneath her touch.

"Will you join the Temple of Iphis?"

Psappha

"I thought I already had," Psappha mumbled, drifting in the euphoria that always accompanied the massage. The pressure of Lyneachia's busy hands became more insistent, almost painful, as she dug her fingers into firm buttocks.

"Will you allow the initiation?"

"All right, all right, anything" Psappha said. "Just leave off the unnecessary digging."

Lyneachia's touch gentled instantly.

Psappha drifted into the nether world of erotic visions. She felt the hands plying the muscles in her calves, caressing the tingly hollows of her knees. There was an almost imperceptible moment of neglect and then the feeling changed.

Lyneachia's hands seemed larger somehow, their purpose more pronounced.

Fingers whispered over her thighs, sending fiery messages to every follicle on her body. Strong hands circled and shaped her buttocks, invoking sensations familiar yet subtly strange.

Psappha lifted her hips toward their arousing touch. As the gentle pressure spiraled toward her heels, she squirmed with delight. At the gentle urging of a playful twist on her right great toe, she rolled over in the darkness without rousing from her sensuous euphoria.

Disembodied hands began their journey from her ankles, massaging upward, finding and stimulating every nerve along the way. Psappha reveled in the tongues of flame that radiated from the searching fingers. They wandered over her slightly rounded abdomen, tracing nerve lines to delicious delirium. Psappha moaned and wriggled away from their delightful torment, then writhed toward them again.

Her own hands had never come close to arousing such wild sensation. Long nails delicately teased her breasts. Like serpent's tongues, they warmed and cooled the tender tips then trailed slowly down the length of her arms. Oily fingers snaked around and between her own.

The moist touch of a flicking tongue on her alert nipples added dimension to the trance. Warm lips and cool tongue revisited all the places the fingers and the nails had found, blazing trails of breathy coolness on molten skin.

Relentlessly, the persistent tongue invaded Aphrodite's most sacred temple. Hot rivers of blood coursed through her veins. The fever of veins erupted like lava from the mightiest of Poseidon's volcanoes, filling her brain with honeyed fire. The child in her womb stirred and stretched as wave after wave of aftershocks trembled through her body.

Slowly, ever so slowly, the lapping tongue eased frustration's fire and led her tenderly from unsteady earth and lava pools to deep and dreamless sleep.

Psappha

Psappha drifted awake, stretching languidly, enjoying the fluidity of her satiated body. Her mind lingered in the afterglow of sensuous fantasy. Her body tingled as she ran fingers over her breasts, her stomach and her thighs.

Suddenly, she swung her legs over the edge of the table and sat up. It was no dream. My mind cannot imagine what it has never learned, she thought. But, if not a dream, then who?

The question rang cracked bells in Psappha's brain. The echoing bells were themselves echoed by the jingle of the curtained doorway.

Swaying amethyst beads cast flickering shadows on the purple tiles. Psappha looked up and blinked. Gongyla stood just within the chamber clad in cinnamon-satin skin and a tiered collar of gold disks. A smile played at the corners of her lush mouth.

Psappha stared in spite of her nursemaid's careful training. The African was more glorious every time she appeared. When she spoke, her husky, possessive tone evoked Psappha's imaginings, in embarrassing detail.

"And how does my lady feel this morning?" Gongyla asked.

Psappha flushed with her racing pulse. The nudity in which she had luxuriated moments earlier became an embarrassment of nakedness beneath the scrutiny of eyes as deep as jungle pools.

"Since when does a queen call me milady? I am Psappha," she said, feeling her soul slip beneath the hypnotic spell of Gongyla's haunting eyes; eyes so dark they seemed to have no iris.

"You are my lady," Gongyla said with a note of ownership that should have infuriated Psappha.

Instead, Psappha felt protected and bedazzled as a single emotion.

"My lady." Gongyla repeated.

Psappha watched the vibration of sound on the surface of Gongyla's swan-like throat, and found nothing to say.

Remembering that Gongyla had said she was dedicated to Cybele, Psappha's gaze roamed the splendid body before her, searching for the scar of sterilization, which always marked the priestesses of the Great Mother. Her fingers reached toward unmarked flesh like curious kittens. At the touch of warmth, they darted back to her lap.

"My people have skills of which the priests of Asklepios dare not dream," Gongyla explained as if Psappha had spoken her question. "The dedication surgery is completed through the vessel from which the sign of fertility flows."

"Did it hurt?"

"No more so than your wedding night," Gongyla said.

Psappha hung her head, remembering a night in Mytilene instead. "I'm to be initiated to Iphis today," she said, changing the subject.

"Thou innocent, gentle-voiced monkey," Gongyla said with a soft chuckle. "I made you a devotee of Iphis last night. Do you now wish to become her equal?"

Psappha felt blood rush to the surface of all her skin; her body flamed with the memory of a dream that was not a dream. Did she want to be the equal of Iphis?

Chagrined, yet intrigued as never before, Psappha wondered what it might be like to perform such delightful ministrations on radiant cinnamon-hued skin. Again, inquisitive fingers reached. This time, when they touched flesh, they hesitated, but they did not withdraw. They walked over dark silk like gulls treading lava sand.

Gongyla did not move. Her bemused expression seemed to encourage Psappha's exploration.

"Gyla," Psappha whispered as she slid from the massage table and stepped closer. Her nostrils flared to the scent of sweet musk as she ran her fingers over wing-tipped brows then down over wide, high cheekbones, across lips as soft as rose petals in the morning to stroke Gyla's long, sleek neck. Breathing more quickly, she drew the stoic warrior nearer with her lowered gaze.

Gongyla embraced her prize and lowered her to the floor. Their bodies intertwined as they settled among the cushions. Their hungry spirits melded tighter with each shared caress.

Psappha's fingers wandered Gyla's body, in echoes of touches on her own. The alien sameness evoked a tempest in her senses, evoking an emotional storm that became a cyclone of feeling, feeding upon itself until, at last, it consumed its center.

~~~~~

Psappha

Summer danced in splendor. Mornings were an unending frolic. In the evenings, while Psappha composed verses and songs, Gyla whittled. She kept her long-bladed skinning knife honed so sharp Psappha was sure she could have shaved the down from a day old gosling without causing a peep. Most evenings, she alternated between a Lydian style lyre for Psappha and a bow she wanted for herself, while teasing Lyneachia until she revealed her secret escape route.

After that, Psappha and Gongyla spent most afternoons exploring Syracuse hand in hand. To hide her identity, Psappha dressed in Lyneachia's clothes before joining Gyla at the vine–hidden postern gate.

They found a treasure trove of Cretan relics in a tiny out of the way shop. They returned to the gynakeon loaded with Ophidian statuettes and a large sacred labyris; a double-edged Cretan axe that Gyla could not resist sharpening.

With the enthusiastic help of the gynakeoni, they dismantled one of the vacant cubicles and turned it into a shrine full of tiny snake priestesses surrounding the polished labyris. Behind the shrine, Gongyla constructed a hidden passage to the public rooms.

"Just in case," she said, but she never bothered to explain.

~~~~~

One morning, a week or two after the autumnal equinox, Gyla toyed with Psappha enough to get her interested, then rose to leave. Psappha jumped up and ran after her. But, without clothing, there was nothing to grab. Instead, she dashed in front and planted her hands on Gyla's chest hissing, oh no you don't, you marvelous despoiler of innocence. You started this. Now finish it.

Gyla did, with her usual splendor, making them late for their usual excursion into the city.

On this particular day, Psappha concealed her advanced pregnancy with a heavy cloak that also served as protection against a brisk wind. Only her servant's sandals showed as she and Gongyla slipped out for another try at finding a statuette of The Mother to grace their makeshift temple.

They returned at sunset, empty-handed, and found the little gate barred from the inside. Gongyla shooed Psappha into a recess in the wall. "Wait here," she whispered.

A thousand possibilities racing through Psappha's mind and none were welcome.

"Psst," Lycos hissed; it seemed like hours later.

"I'm here," Psappha whispered in a panic. If Lycos was here, so was Kerkolos. What would he do? How would she keep him from punishing Gyla?

Lycos offered no clues. "Put these on," he said, handing her a bundle of gynakia clothes.

"Here?"

"Yes, here," he said. "Unless you want to face your husband in servant's garb. He was furious when he couldn't find you. Lyneachia told him you went to see the Asklepian priests about your condition.

"I would never do that," Psappha protested. "Men know nothing of Hera's work."

"Argue theology later, Psappha. You barely have time to change. We were terrified until Gongyla scaled the wall and told us where you were. Kerkolos must never know you went out, on foot no less.

"Quickly, Psappha, change! I've got to run hire a chair."

Psappha scrunched as far into the nook as she could, barely feeling the cold. She changed her dress beneath her cloak, struggling to control her fears. When Lycos returned, she shivered as she stepped from the shadows into the seclusion of the rented chair.

Psappha somehow managed to control her breathing and compose her face by the time the bearers set it down inside the main gate. Lyneachia shooed them away. She was pretending to assist a very weary expectant mother into the house when Kerkolos spotted them.

"You should not have left the compound," he growled. "What if you had been seen?"

"I wasn't," Psappha assured him.

"But you could have been," he grumbled. "Give me your keys."

"I need the keys to manage the household," she protested.

"I've seen how you manage," he said. "Give me the keys."

Reluctantly, Psappha handed them over, feeling like a scolded child.

"Go to my quarters," Kerkolos ordered.

When Psappha got to the master chamber, she found the door to her purple chamber locked and bolted, and there was no key around. Thank The Lady, he did not know that Gyla had been with her.

~~~~~

Two days later, it was as if Hera had indeed awaited the master's return. Psappha tossed in a stiff-backed birthing chair, its

Psappha

straps cutting into her wrists and ankles. She felt like she was a slop rag being wrung out by a giant.

Kerkolos paced and growled. The priests of Asklepios, god of medicine, considered him an intruder. He had turned everything over to them when Psappha's labor began. She had no time to wish for the gentle attendance of The Lady's Crones.

The room was filled with the smoke of torches, braziers. Psappha sobbed and ranted, shrieking irreverent prayers. "Eros, you lascivious bastard, what have you gotten me into? -- Lady, Lady, -- Mother of All, help me now in my hour of need. -- Let go, Poseidon! -- Misbegotten Eros, you traitor -- your aim was faulty. -- you mated a doe with a stallion and expect her to birth a horse."

With each spasm, her body stiffened, arched and strained against her bonds, bashing her head against the unresisting birthing chair, her hair hanging in loose, limp tangles.

Lycos slumped by the wall, his strength lost in an ocean of helpless tears. Kerkolos hovered over her like an angry bear unsure which way to spring. The priests clustered around the high-backed chair shaking their heads, stroking their beards and wailing incessant invocations.

Psappha's scream cut the air, then seemed to hang there.

Gongyla burst into the chamber and brushed the priests aside like yapping dogs. When one grabbed her arm, he landed in a corner like a discarded puppet.

Psappha screamed and arched again.

Gongyla strode to the birthing chair, ripped the straps loose, picked Psappha up and laid her on the great mahogany bed. Gently, she peeled the sweat-soaked gown from Psappha's pain-ravaged body, easing her knees up to provide herself with a clear view of the birth canal.

The child was jammed against the temple gate, the life-giver intact. Drawing her blade from her hair, Gongyla held it in the torch-flame until it glowed. Then, with one deft stroke, she punctured the sacred membrane, soaking Kerkolos' bed with bloody fluid.

Ignoring the drenching, Gongyla reached her gentle hunter's hands to turn and draw forth a slippery squalling scrap of female indignation.

~~~~~

Awakening in her own bed, Psappha took several minutes to reorient herself before noticing her feet, beautiful feet, wonderful feet

55

that could be seen while lying flat on her back. I've missed you, feet, she thought as Lyneachia placed a swaddled bundle in her arms.

Psappha gazed upon a minute red face framed with wispy yellow down, and she trembled. She held her breath as she folded back the final cloth. "Beloved Mother, thank you," she whispered as her anxious fingers examined tiny hands and perfect toes. She had a daughter. A perfect golden girl, she thought.

In memory, she saw a giggle of children danced among the trees, following a lithe girl whose ivory-cream skin and long, silver-gold hair perfectly defined the generally accepted concept of beauty.

"Who is she?" Psappha remembered asking.

"I don't know much about her," Alkaios had said. "Her coloring is Athenian, like your mother's, but it is assumed she is from some far country, since she knew no Hellene when they found her."

"Found her? Where?"

"Washed up among some wreckage on the beach," he said.

"What is she called?"

"Atthis -- after the Goddess of the Rugged Coast. Some say she is the goddess. She certainly dances like one. And, judging from the way Poseidon-Earthshaker raged the day they found her, she must at least have his protection."

Psappha remembered following Alkaios from the park, her heart forever tangled in the girl-child's golden hair. Unawakened, she had not recognized her feelings. Now that she did, the pain of exile deepened.

The lovely girl-child, Atthis, danced in her memory as her newborn daughter sought her breast. She remembered the girl-child's golden hair and a glow began deep within her gut. She recalled the moment Atthis whirled near, her kiton clinging to long clean limbs, and the glow took fire.

The infant found the nipple and the fire sent sparks through Psappha's inner thighs. In memory, she saw Atthis circle close, and the sparks coalesced into a cauldron of molten lava on the altar of Aphrodite.

~~~~~

Lyneachia transferred her loyalty to the infant. Lycos served the Master's chamber.

Psappha thought of the months she had remained in the purple chamber, holding herself aloof from the gynakeoni, haunted by the siren call of their laughter. Now, she ached for the sound. Her spirit fumbled

Psappha

toward it as her infant daughter fumbled toward her distended breast. However, she could not hear the gynakeoni from the master's chambers.

She longed to see Gyla but, with Kerkolos nearby, she was afraid to send for her. Winter's first storm howled outside the day she decided she had tolerated confinement long enough.

Psappha scarcely waited for the servants to finish removing the dinner tables before she began pacing the overly warm room.

Kerkolos stretched on the bed and patted the space beside him.

"Come here. It's too soon for you to be up so long."

Psappha made a great show of stirring the embers in the brazier. She puttered with her jars and repeatedly sorted her jewels.

"I said come here."

"I'll be there in a minute," Psappha said. "I want to straighten this tray."

"Leave it. The servants will do it -- if it still needs doing. Now -- come here."

Psappha perched on the edge of the bed; her fingers busy with the scarab at her waist as she searched for words. When he touched her, she fell back onto the bed without having opened the pin, her feet still on the floor; her eyes fixed on the canopy.

Later, he maneuvered their bodies until they were lying in the middle of the bed with her head cradled in the crook of his shoulder. "Now -- don't scowl -- tell me what is troubling you."

"The gynakeon," Psappha whispered.

"Do we go through that again?" He raised himself onto one elbow and turned her to face him. "I told you the gynakeoni are as nothing to me. Do you disbelieve me?"

"No. But, what about me?"

"What about you? You can continue ignoring the gynakeon or spend all of your time there when I'm at sea. It doesn't matter to me, as long as you're here when I want you."

"I'm a servant of Iphis," she whispered.

He laughed.

Psappha stared in amazement. "You're not angry?"

"Why should I be angry?" Even so, to her he sounded annoyed. "The rites of Iphis may be older than time. Your summers will be less lonely now."

"You don't mind?" Psappha could not believe his indifference.

"Of course I don't mind. I had assumed your initial aversion to the gynakeon was because such customs have not yet reached Lesbos. I was pleased when I learned you were an initiate. It might make you more responsive."

Psappha was totally confused. She had expected rage, had primed herself to counter it. Now, he left her speechless.

"If it weren't for Iphis you'd be dead," he said. "And I would have no daughter. Your warrior queen brought the babe when the priests of famed Asklepios were ready to forfeit your life to Hera."

"My life can't be forfeit to Hera," Psappha said, grateful for a topic she could understand. "I'm destined for Poseidon," she told him. "But, tell me more about Gyla?"

"Gongyla, magnificent savage that she is, stormed in here like a demon fresh from Hades, sending Asklepians flying into corners. She punctured the stubborn membrane with one jab of that lethal hairpin she wears and delivered our child with the inborn skill of one tuned by nature to the love of helpless animals.

"She loves you, my poor almost broken toy. She loves you as greatly, I think, as I."

~~~~~

It took Psappha several days to absorb the fact that her husband loved her, in spite of everything. Because of everything, she corrected herself, although she could not understand. A Lesbian husband would be furious, she thought. Imagine the damage to his pride.

Psappha sat in the purple chamber, writing their daughter's dedication, being careful to fashion it in accordance with her husband's beliefs. When she finished, she hurried through the connecting door to share it with him.

Kerkolos had his back toward her.

Psappha giggled at the sight of Lycos who, with a mouthful of pins, was trying to fit an ordinary sized toga around Kerkolos' massive chest.

"Such a proud father," she teased, "so swollen with pride his clothes don't fit."

Kerkolos yanked off the unfinished garment and tossed it over the head of his valet. One glance at the man's struggles to free himself and he doubled with laughter, his hands on his knees. Psappha kicked his bare bottom and retreated to her room.

"You overgrown bear," she protested as he summarily dumped her onto the bed. "I'm all dressed. You're getting me all mussed. Stop it." She squirmed as he nuzzled her neck with his beard. "Stop it! The babe is to be dedicated and we're already keeping everyone waiting."

Peggy Ullman Bell

~~ 6 ~~

Kerkolos' strode from the house, his furs flaring as he walked, his buskins making convenient indentations in the early snow. He charged the hill below Aphrodite's temple as if it were a bastion to be conquered. Lyneachia followed, stretching her legs to step in the hollows he had made with his feet, all the while holding the fleece-wrapped babe tight against her breast.

Psappha shivered from the icy wind, thinking that today her husband really looked like the great bear she sometimes called him. Hearing a soft crunch behind her, she smiled over her shoulder at Gongyla, who had abandoned the slippery path to march in self-made tracks along the side; every curve of her body straining against soft doeskin.

The inside of the temple was bright with torches that gave off no heat. Psappha clutched her mantle and yearned for summer.

"Hail to thee, Oh Illustrious Aphrodite," they said in unison.

Kerkolos put his huge hands around his infant daughter's ribs and lifted her nude from the fleece. "Behold Klies, daughter of Kerkolos of Andros by Psappha of Lesbos," he recited as he held her toward the altar. "Behold Klies," he called to each of the four winds in turn.

Psappha gulped pride. In spite of the chill wind whistling through the open temple, her brave little daughter did not cry.

Kerkolos raised Klies above his head to present her to unseen Artemis. Next, he would introduce the child to The Fates in her mother's arms. Psappha stepped forward.

Kerkolos ignored Psappha's anticipation and prayed to Artemis in words she had not written. "Take heed, Dark Lady, and watch her well lest The Foam-Born One lead her into mischief."

Psappha was not sure if his impromptu prayer was for their daughter or for her. He finished the dedication as written.

As they were about to enter the house, Kerkolos scooped her up, Klies and all, and carried them both across the threshold. Psappha was so filled with mixed emotions that "I love you" was all she could say,

Psappha

although she knew she could never give him the kind of love that he desired.

Later that night, Psappha slipped out of the master's bed, lifted her daughter from her cradle and hurried through the dark tunnel to Gongyla. Together, they collected every spare lamp in the gynakeon and placed them around the makeshift temple. The tiny shrine was rich with the fragrance of incense and spice scented oil.

Gongyla removed the tiles and bonded limestone, baring a small patch of Earth's breast for Klies to lie on.

"Behold your daughter, Klies," Psappha began as she placed her daughter before their tiny altar. "Accept her, Gracious One, as you accepted her earthly mothers. Daughter of Psappha, is Klies, granddaughter of Klies, your priestess."

The Lady demanded no more. She knew the rest. Psappha, however, was not finished. Picking up her daughter, she carried her to the garden and lifted her high overhead. "Behold! Artemis, Queen of the darkened moon, I pray thee accept Klies, daughter of Psappha, brought to life by a hunter's blade. Take heed, Divine Huntress, Lady of Wild Things, and watch her well."

Turning, Psappha laid her nude and wiggling infant into Gongyla's hands. "Your spiritual daughter," she said. "May The Lady Cybele watch over us all."

"I will guard her well, my lady. As I have always guarded you."

~~~~~

Klies filled much of their time during the long winter. Her first real smile was for her father. She was barely out of swaddling the day he tossed her in the pool.

"No!" Psappha dashed to the rescue. Kerkolos caught her at the edge of the pool.

"Relax," Gyla said. "She was in water when she came. Watch and learn. She has not forgotten."

Psappha felt herself about to drown as her daughter coughed and spurted. Gongyla walked into the water, got a firm grip on Klies' ribs and held her with her tiny feet dangling inches below the surface. Klies gurgled and her father roared with laughter.

"Stop!" Psappha jerked away from his restraining hand and rushed into the water, angry when her kiton slowed her down.

"What a way for Poseidon's daughter to behave," Gongyla teased as Kerkolos snatched Klies from her mother's hands.

"She must swim," Kerkolos called. "Do you want her to drown the first time she meets the sea?"

"She's not going to sea," Psappha snarled, clutching her struggling infant close.

"Hush," Gongyla cautioned. "Be still and let me remind her of what she knows."

Psappha knew Gyla wished no harm to the child she helped into the world but, as she handed her back, she thought her lover as dictatorial and demented as she thought her husband.

Minutes later she stared in awe as her pudgy little girl paddled around the pool like a jubilant puppy, never more than a few centimeters from Gyla's protective hands.

~~~~~

Klies soon learned to swim from lotus to lotus like a pink and gold water nymph. She toddled after her father one minute, Gongyla the next, while Psappha laughed from the comfort of the arbor. As soon as Klies was steady on her feet, she began copying the steps when Lyneachia danced to Psappha's tunes, her giggles reminding her mother of Lesbian sheep's bells.

Unlike their busy days, Psappha's nights became a puzzle of loneliness. In her husband's bed, she found a measure of peace that vanished seconds after love's final flare. When he slept, she lay awake, wondering why she felt so incredibly detached.

Would it have been this same way with Alkaios, she wondered, thinking of another lifetime: A time when she spent long afternoons beneath an apple tree above her home in Mytilene, listening to the shepherd's ribald tales. She recalled being there the day Pittakos ordered her arrest. She remembered shielding her eyes from the mid-day sun, watching a dust cloud move along the winding road from Mytilene. In her mind, she relived the precarious ride into the city, clinging to the rim of the chariot, her legs aching as she fought for balance.

They had ridden in silence, the driver busy with the fractious team, Psappha terrified of what might lie ahead. As they crossed the bridge to the old city, she felt the guards' lascivious eyes on her back and was grateful for the cloak her nursemaid had draped about her shoulders as she left the house. She remembered wondering if the guard lusted after her, or her mantle.

Psappha

Praxinoa had chosen to drape her in ankle–length ermine in spite of the warming weather. It lent her courage as she entered the citadel.

She would have marched directly to the audience chamber had a sentinel not barred her way and directed her toward a bench-lined wall, where she perched on the edge of a splintery plank, back straight, chin up and eyes front, determined not to show the hornets buzzing in her gut.

"I came as soon as I heard you'd been arrested," Alkaios said when he joined her. "He wants me. Not you."

"He won't harm me," she had told him. "What can he possibly fear from one small girl?" she remembered asking. Oh, the naïveté of youth.

"Pittakos is capable of anything," Alkaios had warned, but she had not truly listened. "You baited him rather efficiently last summer."

"Not nearly as rudely as you," she countered firmly. "You must get out of here before you're recognized."

"Too late," he said, and he was right.

The sentinel motioned for Psappha and she strode forward without looking to see if Alkaios followed.

Inside the audience chamber, she stopped at the foot of the dais and glared up at the newly self–declared Tyrant of Lesbos.

"Nice of you to bring your lover with you," Pittakos smirked. "It saves me the trouble of tracking him down."

"Psappha didn't bring me, Crack-toes," Alkaios said from behind her.

Pittakos stepped down and stalked back and forth before them, appraising Psappha, his thumbs hooked in his belt, his dingy hair contrasting sharply with his gleaming breastplate. Rich court greaves topped buskins stained with what looked like the grime from a dozen battlefields. As always, his eyes made her feel unclean.

"Leave Psappha alone, Shufflefoot. Your battle is with me," Alkaios said. "My opinion of you is well known."

"Your opinion is too well known, Street-poet. You will leave Lesbos on the first ship out of port, and your mouthy betrothed on the next."

Psappha's hands shot to her stomach as she relived her feelings from that moment. She had been appalled. She remembered thinking she would rather die than leave Lesbos. Leave Mytilene? "No!"

"What is it?" Kerkolos inquired groggily.

"It is nothing," Psappha lied. "Go back to sleep."

But, Psappha could not sleep. Every time she closed her eyes, she saw Mytilene receding. She could not forget the way the sunbeams dressed the bridges in gold as she boarded the squat travesty of a ship that Pittakos had chosen for her journey into exile. While the crew made ready to sail, she had watched the sunlight leave the crowded streets, stinging her with the knowledge that she might never walk on them again.

She remembered clutching the railing until her knuckles ached, knowing Alkaios was already gone, striving to hold on to her beloved city a little longer. In her mind, she saw again that final sunset over the Lesbian Mt. Olympus. In memory, she envisioned golden beams streaming through a break between the hills; passing gently over the home Alkaios had planned for her.

When she had looked again the following morning, Mytilene lay shrouded in a low fog, as if the city mourned their going and had clothed itself in loneliness for the occasion. Tears dampened the pillow beneath her head as she recalled the sound the oars made, dipping into dawn-dark water, drawing her away from everything she loved.

~~~~~

Psappha felt a growing discontent. She wanted to feel close to her husband, but she could not. Each night, she stayed in her purple chamber as late as she dared, talking softly with Gongyla, listening to the music of gynakeoni laughter, and looking toward spring as if it were a beacon in the dark.

In the spring, she was dumfounded when Kerkolos sent his ship to sea with Lycos at the helm. Together, he and Psappha watched as their little daughter rode through the blossoming garden on Gyla's shoulders. The dark warrior cavorted as though the world was as new to her as it was to the child.

In the passing weeks, Psappha found her fondness for her husband growing in proportion with his fondness for their child.

In her second winter, Klies built imaginary roads on the hearth with kindling while Kerkolos taught Gongyla and Psappha the intricacies of Sennet. Whenever Psappha grew tired of losing, she let Klies steal a die and end the game. Klies pretended they were chariots.

Klies' second spring arrived and Kerkolos prepared for his voyage to the trading centers of the Aegean, unable to trust his fortunes to hirelings for another season, despite his inexplicable faith in Lycos.

Psappha

On the morning he was to sail, Klies rode to the docks on the front of her father's saddle, waving her chubby arm at everyone they passed. Klies would be two before he returned and Psappha regretted all that he would miss.

~~~~~

With Kerkolos at sea, warm nights drifted by in Gyla's willing arms. Hot days brought a whiney daughter ever pestering for her father. Psappha welcomed the rains of autumn as a herald of his return.

She stood by her window one day, watching the wind drive multicolored leaves westward, listening to the click of dice behind her where Gyla and Klies played Sennet near the hearth. She did not look around when Klies' merry chatter stopped.

The scrape of a chair and a sharp intake of breath made her turn, and she gasped. Lycos stood two steps inside the room, his face as dark as the impending storm. Lyneachia hustled Klies away as Lycos opened his mouth to speak.

Psappha clamped her hands over her ears. Her eyes begged him to say nothing. Without the words, the truth she read in his eyes would not be real.

Gongyla knocked her chair aside and rushed to enfold Psappha in her strength. Psappha's fury spilled its salty self onto Gyla's comforting breasts. They did not notice when Lycos left them.

Psappha's fists pounded Gyla's back. "Kerkolos is dead," she raged at offending gods. "Where were you, Hermes, protector of traders, when your salty uncle stole my protector? Were you sleeping, God of Commerce, while my Kerkolos drowned in Poseidon's greedy pool?

"Poseidon, my father, is this the price you place on my life? You sent me to a safe harbor, Father of Ocean, now you've claimed the harbormaster for yourself.

"I will accept no more of your temporary gifts, Earthshaker. They cost too much."

~~~~~

Psappha sat in the shadows of the arbor, twisting her bedraggled hair, ignoring Lycos' calming voice. Her tearless eyes began to sting when she felt his tender strokes upon her back.

Two-year-old Klies sat at Psappha's feet steeped in her mother's misery.

Lyneachia ran from the gynakeon, shouting incoherently, her eyes wide with terror.

Peggy Ullman Bell

Psappha jumped up, grabbed her shoulders, spun her around and then caught her close in her arms.

"Lyneachia," she crooned, setting aside her grief in the face of the child's fear. "What is it?"

"Adriana," Lyneachia blubbered, pointing behind her.

Psappha sighed, glad for the distraction. She felt she could handle her mother-in-law. "Look after Klies," she said, hurrying toward the house with Lycos at her heels. Glancing back, she saw Lyneachia and Klies disappear at the top of the roof-stairs.

Inside the gynakeon, a burly man marched toward the exit corridor, the arm of a struggling gynakeoni in each hand. A second brute emerged from a sleeping cubicle with a child slung over his shoulder. Psappha rushed toward him but Adriana blocked her. "Stand back, Psappha!"

"Stand back? How dare you bring men in here? This is my home." Psappha tried to push past Adriana's substantial bulk.

"It may be your home," Adriana said with obvious satisfaction, "but it is no longer your house. Since my son did not return to claim it, it belongs to his uncle, my husband's brother. You can thank him for the roof still over your head: he convinced me the pleasure of denouncing you was not worth the damage to my reputation."

"I don't give a fig about your reputation."

"You made that clear with your behavior," Adriana sneered. "I know all about your jaunts into the city. Kerkolos should have put you, and your bastard, on the street where you belong!"

"Your rapid rise from porna to Sybarite has warped what's left of your mind, Adriana. Klies is your grand-daughter."

"Sheep dung," Adriana said. "My grandchild would be a boy and he wouldn't have piss-colored hair. No doubt some wine-sluggard you and your black bitch found in the gutter sired your spawn."

"Klies is Kerkolos' daughter and your grand-daughter, more's the pity. How long do you think it takes a seed to sprout?"

Adriana sneered. "I merely came to collect my brother-in-law's property. We could have removed the slaves easily if not for -- well -- you see."

A clutch of men-at-arms milled near the entrance to the exit corridor, unwilling, or unable, to continue. Adriana signaled and the largest of the men stepped back allowing Psappha to see Gongyla standing with her lovely legs spread and braced, her strong white teeth bared, and her bow drawn.

Psappha

Gyla held men at bay with the sight of gleaming female flesh, unadorned from fire-spitting eyes to firmly planted toes. Her only attire, the ostrich plumes that crowned her crimped hair and hid the skinning knife Psappha knew she kept hidden there. A full quiver leaned against the nearby wall.

Psappha heard Lycos' chuckle behind her. Gyla winked. She looks so small compared to them, Psappha thought, with a shiver of apprehension.

"There is the disturbance," Adriana said, drawing an exasperated arc in the air with one flabby arm, jerking her hand back when it narrowly missed the point of Gongyla's ready arrow. "You men are imbeciles," she growled, retreating. "Shall we return to your master and tell him you failed in your assigned task because of a woman? Get on with the removal!"

Gongyla bared her teeth and the men took a half step backward.

Psappha saw the gleam in Gyla's eyes and she sighed. "Gongyla protects what's mine," she informed her sputtering mother-in-law.

"The slaves are not yours." Adriana pulled a sealed scroll from her sleeve and handed it over.

Psappha passed it to Lycos. "What'll you do with them?"

"They will be sold, of course."

"No," Psappha protested.

"You have nothing to say about it," Adriana gloated. "My husband's brother has more than sufficient slaves and, unlike my son, he is not willing to keep those whose sale could bring him profit. He will have enough added expense maintaining this house and those here who are not slaves until suitable husbands can be found for them."

Psappha flinched, afraid Adriana numbered her among those in need of husbands.

"Fortunately," Adriana continued without missing a beat. "Most of the slaves are breeders and will bring good prices."

"You've been planning this," Psappha accused.

"As you please, Psappha. Nevertheless we will sell the slaves, and the others will be married to whoever will take them without a dowry. Don't worry helpless one. There are enough old and ugly ones to ensure your comfort, if you choose to remain here. The house is part of Klies' dower and will therefore have an adequate staff as propriety demands."

"Very well, take them."

"Will you order the African to at least clothe herself, so the men will get on with it?"

"But, Adriana," Psappha said with feigned innocence. "Gongyla is a queen, as you well know. One doesn't issue orders to a queen"

Adriana gave the men a wilting stare. "In truth, the African may save my brother-in-law some gold. He will not need to pay men who fail in their charge."

The slavers suddenly remembered their trade and rushed the warrior queen as one. Gyla met their assault with a cat-like snarl. Her bow twanged and a man fell back, an arrow quivering in his shoulder. Two others threw themselves at her, tearing the bow from her hands and pinning her arms. As she struggled, a man ran at her. He fell back, screaming from a fractured pelvis.

The men holding her shifted their grip on her oiled skin. Gyla used their movement to free herself, breaking the nose of one in the process. The other stepped out of range, eyeing her carefully, as if stalking a wild she-cat. Adriana screamed in futile rage.

"Gyla! Stand back," Psappha shouted as Adriana's brawny chair-bearers rushed into the corridor. Warrior queen she may have been, Psappha thought, but she's no match for Adriana's brutes.

"Hold," Psappha called.

Gyla shrugged, and leaned against a pillar, disgustedly allowing Adriana's bearers to perform the task she had not allowed the slavers to do.

Psappha watched through tears as the frightened younger slaves trailed past her. She had promised to protect them, yet here she stood, helpless, with Gyla glaring at her, while Fate and inheritance stole them from her.

"Are you leaving none of them, Adriana?"

"Of course," Adriana preened with success, "even you must have servants. The old and ugly ones can stay," she allowed. "They will serve you well enough without the need for hirelings. The purple-eyed one is yours," she added with obvious regret. "She was deeded to you when my son ordered you assigned the bridal chamber. It's on the scroll I gave you." She licked her lips as if clearing a bad taste from her mouth.

Psappha reveled in her tiny victory, drawing a modicum of satisfaction from the sense of substantial loss of profit written on Adriana's face.

Psappha

The remaining servants drifted quietly away. Klies' chatter filtered from the roof, sounding loud in the near empty gynakeon. Lycos watched Psappha, his face ravaged by grief and guilt. She lifted his chin with the tip of a finger, offering him a comforting smile. "What could you have done, Little Fox?"

"I could have tried."

"She wouldn't have let you," Gyla grumbled, laying her bow aside.

"Get her!" Adriana shrieked from the entrance.

Fresh men-at-arms rushed into the pavilion.

"Take her!" Adriana screeched.

Five men grabbed Gongyla from behind, and wrestled her to the floor.

"Bind her!" Adriana growled. "Use the chains!"

Psappha could stand and watch no more. Grabbing the razor-sharp labyris from their makeshift-temple wall, she charged the men struggling with Gongyla.

"Psappha, no!" Lycos shouted.

Psappha paid no attention. She caught one of the men on his hip, but her arms were not strong enough to sink the blade. He snatched the labyris with a snarl. When she lunged for it, he bashed her nose.

She awoke on the gynakeon floor with Lyneachia holding a slab of raw meat to her eye while Klies wailed nearby, unattended.

"They're gone?"

"Yes."

"Everyone?"

"Yes. Lycos and Gongyla too."

~~ 7 ~~

Psappha brooded in the arbor, twisting her bedraggled hair. Weak sunlight whispered through vacant trees. Klies scampered among crisp leaves on dull, brown grass, chirping happily. Psappha gave her half a smile then looked away.

Lyneachia's dragging feet stirred the stones on the path when she approached.

When Lyneachia thrust the Lydian lyre into her lap, Psappha jerked her hand away. The lyre looked as lovely as it had the day Gyla first polished it, the carving intricate with love and patience.

Psappha took the lyre between two fingers and sat it on the bench beside her.

Lyneachia shook her head, picked up the lyre and put it back into Psappha's lap.

"You must sing," she said.

Psappha let her hand fall against the strings as if to silence them, though they made no sound. Soon, her practiced fingers plucked the strings as if directed by some other being. After a time, they found a melody and chords came uninvited.

"Black, the world," she sang. "No light has my garden. In shadow I walk, but do not move. I see, but do not look. My light, my life, my sight is gone. Alone, I cease to be. Time is --"

Lyneachia snatched the lyre. "No, Psappha, that is not your song. Look at your daughter."

Psappha raised her head to meet tear flooded, sea blue eyes. Klies took her cues from her mother. If Psappha cried, Klies must cry, though she did not know the reason. Feeling a twinge of guilt, Psappha took up the lyre and forced a smile.

"A little daughter have I," she sang. "Like a perfect flower is Klies. No ribbons have I for her shining hair. It needs none. It glows on its own. A sparkling bubble of music is Klies," Psappha continued, picking up the beat.

Psappha

Klies scrambled onto her mother's lap, wriggling a place for herself between Psappha's softness and the magical lyre. Psappha could not help chuckling.

"Now, that's what I like to hear."

Psappha dropped the lyre, sat Klies on the bench and bolted to her feet, running before she shouted, "Gyla! How?"

Catching Psappha with a huff, Gongyla shrugged. "A little swim," she said as she grasped her close.

"A little over two leagues," said Lycos, strolling toward them.

"You, too," Psappha exclaimed. Looking at him over a warm shoulder, from her vantage off the ground in Gyla's arms, she thought he looked no different from when he left. A bit less arrogant, perhaps, but unaffected by his adventure. "How did you escape?"

"Quit climbing Gyla as if she were a tree and I'll tell you."

Gongyla chuckled, unclasped Psappha's arms from around her neck and eased her down.

Psappha's eyes widened the moment she was on her feet. "You're hurt!"

"It's nothing," Gongyla grinned.

"Nothing! They cut your beautiful face."

Gongyla touched a finger to the festering gash above her eye. "Hmmm," she murmured, "so they did."

"It's a mess," Lycos said with a touch of amusement.

"A mess! Is that all you can say, you donkey? Gyla, sit so I can reach you. As for you, you grinning incompetent, go fetch a physician."

"She doesn't need to be physicked," he said. "Oh, don't ruffle up so, Psappha. Take a good look at her."

"I am looking at her, fool. She has an oozing wound."

Psappha tore a strip from the end of her kiton, dipped it into the fountain then reached to clean the wound. Gyla shrugged away from her hands.

"Leave be, Kitten. You'll spoil the scar."

"Warriors," Psappha huffed, hurting from the thought of a vicious mark on Gyla's beautiful face.

"Come, Little-one, sit. Your daughter is weeping and Lycos is tired."

"I'm tired," Lycos scoffed. "You're the one who should be tired." When they settled in the arbor, Gyla took Klies into her lap then consented to having her wound cleaned while he explained. "I sneaked aboard Adriana's ship," he said. "About two leagues out the witch caught me and decided I should serve her tea, which was a big mistake. I took the old porna her tea well laced with crushed poppies. As soon as she nodded off, I slipped out and undid Gongyla's locks.

"Gyla kicked two of her guards overboard and dove in after them. I volunteered to catch her in the dinghy and here we are."

"Adriana will come back for you," Psappha worried.

"And miss the social season in Sybaris? Not bloody likely. We're safe 'til spring. What's for supper? It's been a long row."

~~~~~

Winter in the near empty house was long and spring came late. Each morning, Psappha scanned the harbor from her roof. She did not get around to serious worrying until the day she saw the ships in the Port of Syracuse preparing for the trading season.

"If she's going to return and make more trouble, it will be soon," Lycos echoed her thought when she joined him later.

Psappha's gaze flew from the arbor to the garden path where Gyla stood sprinkling Klies with hyacinth petals. "What will Adriana do to her?" she worried.

"Thank you very much, Adelphi," Lycos mocked. "I thought it was my hide you were concerned about."

"I'm worried for both of you."

"Um hum. Of course you are." He waited until she took a seat beside him.

"What can we do? Adriana must be livid."

"Of course," Lycos chuckled, "but she won't do anything that endangers her precious reputation." Suddenly, he jumped to his feet, staring at her as if someone had just kicked his shins. Then he laughed. "If we roll the dice right, none of us need worry.

"The beloved and talented widow of the renowned merchant, Kerkolos of Andros must open an academy of the Muses and Graces. It's the only way to protect everyone. If we can attract the daughters of the Council of Elders, Adriana wouldn't dare harm us. She'd be barred from the port for eternity if she tried."

"An academy! You're not casting dice, Lycos. You've lost yours. I'm no philosopher, no Solon. What do I know of teaching?"

"Everything. Admit it, Psappha. You can make a lyre defy the gods. Why keep your skill to yourself and your songs locked in this garden? We can open this big empty house to students. You teach your poetry and music. Gyla could instruct them in the use of the bow. The

Psappha

young women of Syracuse would love that. They never get enough diversion."

"My bow is not a diversion," Gongyla said.

"It is here," Lycos said, ignoring her as she poured herself onto the grass in front of them. "Think about it, Psappha. Your house and purse are empty. Open your home to the young ladies of the city and I guarantee it will fill your purse."

"I think the sun has fried your brain," she scoffed. "How can I open my house when I'm forbidden to open my gate?"

"Forbidden by whom?" Gyla asked, propping her chin on her fists. "Kerkolos is gone and the foxy one is right. It's selfish of you to keep your genius hidden. You once said you intended to be a professional poet. This may be your chance."

"It is. It is," Lycos agreed, obviously thrilled to have an unexpected ally. "At sixteen, you aspired to greatness. Has marriage and motherhood changed you so much you no longer desire it? When are you going to stop sitting around waiting for The Fates to decide what game they want to play with you? Take your fate into your own hands. Why let this house be your prison, when you can use it to save us all?"

Before Psappha could answer, a ball bounced in front of the arbor and rolled beneath the bench. Klies scampered after it. Psappha swatted her plump posterior as she dove between Lycos' legs to retrieve her toy. Gyla grinned as Klies clambered into her mother's lap to play with Psappha's lips as she continued the discussion.

"We've barely enough servants to care for us," she said. "You are a fool to suggest we invite guests."

"Not guests, Adelphi, pupils; pupils who will bring their own servants. Say the word and I will fill the gynakeon with the daughters of respectable families. We'll make taking care of the house a part of their education. Lyneachia could see to that."

"Lyneachia can see to what?" Lyneachia called as she hurried toward the arbor. "What disgusting task are you planning for me now, you obnoxious rooster?"

"Hush," Psappha insisted. "Peace. Lycos has suggested that I turn my home into a school --."

"School?" Lyneachia entered the arbor with her eyes full of skeptic hostility.

"Yes, school," Lycos grumbled. "What did you think I would propose, you bothersome twit? A brothel?"

73

"It wouldn't surprise me," Lyneachia said. "Except for Psappha, who likes you for some unknown reason, nobody but a porna would give you the run of the gynakeon with that fire-grass on your chin. What's an overage cupbearer doing growing a beard anyway?"

"Hush you two."

"Lycos claims you could teach the spoiled young ladies of Syracuse the art of keeping house," Gongyla said. "The way you taught Psappha."

Lycos chuckled. "Can't you just see the little snip bossing aristocrats around?"

"I told you to hush," Psappha snapped. Lycos hung his head, but she could see the corner of his smile. "Lyneachia, please take Klies inside," she said. "She's fallen asleep and she's heavy."

When she was gone, Psappha turned to Lycos and said, "Tell me, Little Fox, how could I gather pupils for this mythical academy? Aren't all women of family confined to gynakia?"

"Then you're thinking about it?"

"I'm considering it, but I am a stranger here, and not yet twenty. Why would anyone send their daughters to me?"

"Syracuse may be strange to you, Adelphi, but you are not without standing in the city. Kerkolos was well thought of and the populace still bristles at the shame of Adriana's treachery. Their sympathy is with you.

"Gynakia women are permitted to reside for a time in the homes of friends, or family," he explained. "They would be encouraged to reside with a renowned teacher."

"I'm not renowned," Psappha demurred.

"Not yet, but your fame has spread farther than you know. Your verses already sail the seas. Kerkolos bragged everywhere about his beautiful talented wife. Your pupils will come eagerly and will bring a sizable tuition with them."

"But no one has seen me since Kerkolos died, and I don't remember anyone who was here before."

"They remember you, Adelphi."

"Hmm, well, I suppose it could work."

"Just leave the details to me, Psappha. All we really need are some criers and a good cook. I've got enough put by to hire the criers and I know where to buy a cook."

"No!"

"No? Psappha, be reasonable."

Psappha

"I haven't said no to your idea, Lycos. But, I won't buy a cook."

"Damn, Psappha. We need one. I'm going to starve if I don't get something to eat besides Gyla's boiled bread."

Gyla gave him a mock glare. Psappha pinched his chubby middle and said, "I know you're suffering terribly, but I'll allow no more slaves in my house. If I agree to this scheme of yours, we'll have to find someone who's willing to come and cook for a decent wage. Perhaps a widow or an old sea-cook would be interested.

"But I'm still not a teacher."

"You'll adjust."

~~~~~

Soon the crier's voice could be heard from beyond the wall. "Come, thou, gentlemen of Syracuse. Bring your daughters, the sisters of your heart, to Psappha of Lesbos that she may instruct them in the graces.

"Daughter of Agamemnon is Psappha, also of fair Minea. Guarded by Mighty Poseidon is she, beloved sister of the Muses, widow of famed Kerkolos, blessed daughter of Aphrodite.

"Lovely are her songs, oh lords of Syracuse, great are her many gifts. Make haste, gentlemen of Syracuse, that The Lady of Lesbos may have time for thee."

And, the gentlemen of Syracuse came, a few, then a trickle, then a stream. Soon a flood of women and girls filled the house with beauty and laughter.

The school and Klies grew and flourished and, as Lycos' had predicted, Adriana did not bother them. Gongyla suggested she was probably laying claim to her daughter-in-law's success.

"I must tell Lycos to dismiss the crier soon," Psappha reminded herself one late autumn afternoon. The contracts he had told her of that morning were more than enough. Any more and the students would have to share their cubicles, not that many of them would mind.

Gyla's rich voice drew Psappha's attention to the other side of the garden where she taught the use of the long bow to a cluster of chattering maidens. Klies perched on a rock nearby. The girls were clad in the type of abbreviated kiton Lycos used to favor. Gyla wore an arrow quiver and a smile.

Psappha plucked her lyre strings absentmindedly. "Sing for us," her pupils chirped almost in unison. "Do sing for us, milady." A few others hurried near.

"Sing the happy song," Klies chirped as she ran to take over her mother's lap.

"Which one?" Psappha asked, although she already knew.

"The dancing one," Klies said.

"Which one," Psappha repeated.

"You know," Klies huffed indignantly.   She wriggled off Psappha's lap, plunked her tiny fists on her hips and said, "The dancing one. You know -- dancing." She tried to demonstrate, holding her arms straight out from her sides as she dipped and swayed to imaginary music. Then, she brought her feet together; bent her knees outward and dropped to the grass with her legs already crossed. Propping her elbows on her ankles and her chin on her fists, she said, "You know. Dance."

Psappha could not keep from laughing. "Perhaps this will do," she said when she was able to control her giggles. Her fingers flew over the strings in a wild introduction that sounded like children's laughter. "Dance, Terpsichore, dance," she sang, remembering another girl-child. "Make your electrum tresses fly. Whirl, dancer, whirl, twirl to the rhythm of my heart. Dance, Terpsichore. Spin heartstrings into kitons of passion.

"Do not depart, Fair Dancer. Return, return, I implore thee, in your milk-white kiton. Your dance is the titillation of a goddess. No one could resist trembling from its sensuous seduction."

"Another," the maidens encouraged. "Another."

Glancing down, expecting to see Klies parked at her feet, Psappha searched the garden with her eyes and saw her daughter climbing back onto her observation rock. Handing her lyre to her brightest student, she went to watch the archers from a bench near the fountain.

Gongyla pulled the bowstring without strain. A blink later, the arrow quivered in the center of the target. She flashed a 'that's-how-it's-done' smile at her pupils and handed the bow to an inattentive, dark-eyed brunette.

The maiden pulled the string, released the arrow, and sent it up -- and down. The watchers twittered. Psappha tried not to smile, but failed. Her snicker brought Gyla across the little pond like a gazelle fording a narrow brook.

"Don't laugh," she commanded. "They try."

"But they look like puffs of wind trying to blow away a mountain," Psappha chuckled.

Psappha

Gyla leaned over her. "Can you draw my bow?"

"No, but I can pull your hair."

"Who will protect you if you do," Gyla murmured, her breath ruffling the new hair by Psappha's ear.

"I won't need protection if I pick the right time."

"And what time might that be, Songbird?"

"When you are my playful cub," Psappha purred. "Bdrrrr. Where is your fierceness now, my cat?"

"Right here," said Gongyla. She scooped Psappha up, slung her over her shoulder, stalked through the pavilion, through the purple chamber and dumped Psappha onto Kerkolos' great mahogany bed.

"Not now," Psappha cautioned; mindful of the twitter they left in their wake.

"Bdrrrr," Gongyla responded, nuzzling Psappha's shoulder, her fingers busy unpinning scarabs.

Psappha shivered with pleasure. "Stop it," she whispered. "They'll know."

"Of course they'll know," Gyla mumbled against the nerves just below Psappha's right earlobe. "They were born in gynakia. Hold still. . . ."

She sprawled onto the bed empty-handed as her captive wriggled away.

"Hold still, indeed," Psappha said from her relatively safe distance. She reached for the pull cord that would summon Lyneachia.

"Touch that and pay the price," Gongyla drawled. She relaxed onto her back, put her hands behind her head and gave Psappha a defiant 'go ahead, I dare you' look.

Psappha let go of the cord and went to the chamber door. Her kiton fell to the floor as she returned from securing the bolt. She stepped away from it and stood nude, on the small Persian rug, inches from the beauty stretched before her on the carved and polished bed.

Gyla grinned. Psappha snatched the pins from her hair. Her braids unwound against her back. Gyla crooked her finger. Psappha tossed the hairpins aside and made a running dive.

The great bed groaned under the weight of their frolic. Gongyla cupped Psappha's breasts and buried her face between them. "Bdrrrr," she purred, shaking her head from side to side. "Ouch! Two can play that game." Lycos was not the only one who had dispensed with depilatories.

~~~~~

77

Peggy Ullman Bell

Psappha's fame spread, season by season. Wealthy families throughout the trading world sent their young women to The Poetess. They became so many that, in the third year, Gongyla relinquished her post at the gate to an accommodating eunuch and assisted with the teaching full time.

Nevertheless, Psappha still watched the harbor on the first warm day of each new season. Once, when she came down from her rooftop vigil, she found Klies attempting to use a miniature bow. Psappha recalled long, late night, winter carving sessions by a blazing hearth. The bow was a present for Klies' sixth birthday. Gongyla had finished it with barely a week to spare.

This day, while Gyla showed Klies the rudiments of archery Psappha retrieved her picking basket from the arbor and strolled to where Lycos gathered purple hyacinths. He handed her the flowers with a grin that reversed itself when he got a clear view of her face.

Psappha was homesick. Her garden overflowed with merry maidens whose very presence was a constant reminder of what she had lost the day Pittakos ordered her from Mytilene. Each time she entered the gynakeon or the garden, they fluttered to her like a fountain of multi-shaded rainbows daintier than rosebuds. But, today she felt like an observer, unassociated with her life.

"Come, milady. Sing for us."

Psappha sighed as two of her students clasped her hands and drew her along the path to where Lyneachia waited with her lyre. She accepted the lyre but rejected the inviting pile of cushions in the rose-shaded arbor. Instead, she retreated to the broad base of a window-arch that reminded her of home. She patted the sill and Klies came to sit beside her. The girls arrayed themselves on the grass near her feet like iridescent peacock feathers.

Gyla saluted her from across the garden. Lyneachia hovered near, but not so near as she had when Klies was younger. Lycos frowned as Psappha began to sing.

"Mytilene, thou lovely Mytilene," she sang in plaintive contralto. "Your daughter's eyes strain vainly toward your sun-burnished citadel; your hills that shine like heavens of green dotted with clouds of grazing sheep. Psappha of Lesbos yearns for orchards where once she walked with her companions, composing paeans to your beauty.

"In memory, I hear your bubbling streams in winter, singing their way to spring. I long to breathe air so pure, like crystal, adorning an azure sea, to see your cliffs of pure and beautiful delight, kissing

78

Psappha

Poseidon with joy. Even thy raging winds and trembling mountains would I welcome, to be once more with thee.

"But, no more shall I see your fragrant hills dressed in spring's gay 'broidery; no more Earth's brocade pajamas on your frosty trees; no more your snow-sheeted snoozing beneath a wintry sky. Call no more to Psappha, Sweet Island. Psappha of Lesbos cannot come."

"You may return one day," Gongyla said, having come to her side unnoticed. "Is there someone there you love?"

Psappha looked up, startled by the question. "Perhaps I could have learned to love Alkaios," she said. "But we were parted before I got the chance."

"Was there no one else?"

"No," Psappha said then, on second thought, she added, "There might have been someone. I don't know."

"Tell me about him."

"Not him, her," Psappha said, thinking of a golden girl-child dancing in The Lady's park.

"But you knew nothing of Iphis before Syracuse," Gongyla sputtered.

"No, I did not, you jealous cat. But, Iphis did not create the feelings. The feelings were there long before I became an exile. Dormant, until you forced me to accept them. But -- Lesbos is far away and I may not return."

"Nor do you need to," Gyla said. "She's probably a fat matron by now anyway."

"Dancers seldom run to fat."

"Nor do hunters."

Peggy Ullman Bell

Klies sat on the small Persian rug, leaning against Psappha's knees, her hair flying to meet the brush, golden waves springing tighter with each stroke. I'll soon have to stand to brush her, Psappha thought.

"Be still!"

Klies fidgeted like any eight-year-old slowed by the demands of her elders. Her adolescent face pinched into an impatient frown.

Psappha smiled at the startling resemblance to Kerkolos. She is the bright reverse of his dark image, she realized. How proud he would have been to see her flower.

Uproar outside released Klies from the pestering brush. She was gone before Psappha was sure where the shouting came from.

The gatekeeper's falsetto tones cut through the quiet evening. "You cannot enter here, I say. The House of the Muses is inviolable."

Psappha hurried toward the front courtyard. As she neared the tiny circle of torchlight, the gatekeeper's voice grew louder.

"This is no house of joy," he said. "We have no pornas here."

"You evil-minded mound of dung." A vaguely familiar male voice sounded from beyond the gate. "I have legitimate business here."

"No decent business could bring you here at this hour," the gatekeeper screeched. "Come back in the morning."

"I will enter now!" the intruder insisted. "I bear a message of great importance to the daughter of Scamandronomos."

"I don't care whose daughter you have a message for. You can come back in the morning or you can put it through the look-out."

The tiny peek-through at the top of the gate swung open and Psappha forgot to breathe. Torchlight from the street illuminated a face she had never expected to see again.

Alkaios grinned through the lookout as if they had parted the day before. A flaxen beard covered most of his lower face. His azure gaze sparkled with mischief. "So, milady of the velvet voice," he teased. "Have you no song of welcome for your betrothed?"

Psappha stared. The voice he once called velvet hid in the pit of her stomach.

80

Psappha

"Well, Psappha? Have you grown so famous you've no time for poor petitioners?"

"Open the gate," she cried.

Alkaios strode toward her with his hands extended in greeting. She grabbed them and swung him round and round, high stepping merrily until she ran out of breath.

Gongyla stepped between them.

"Gyla," Psappha pleaded, "don't scowl so."

Gongyla frowned as Alkaios whistled and wiped his beaded brow with his thumbs. Touching his heart with his fingers then extending his arm, palm upward, he honored her with an archaic Cretan salute. "The Lady's blessing," he offered with a smile. He glanced at the worried look on Psappha's face and grinned as Gyla adjusted her stance to block his view.

Psappha's view of him was also blocked. Remembering her own initial attitude toward the gynakeon and its customs, she did not expect the Lesbian mercenary soldier to accept the situation casually. It had been different with Kerkolos. He was not Aeolian.

"Hail, oh Iphis," he said. Psappha wished she could see his face.

"Kios is the dearest friend of my childhood," she said to Gongyla's back, hoping to break the tension.

"Childhood?" Alkaios sidestepped to wink at her. "What happened to the Psappha who demanded to become a woman?" he asked with eyes dancing with mischief.

"Oh, hush, Kios, that was when I loved you."

"You don't love me? My life is worthless." He grimaced at her with such a parody of grief even Gyla had to laugh.

"Kios, thank you," Psappha said. "It's been too long since I've been this amused."

Amused or not, Psappha was mystified by his attitude. She could not help wondering if she had ever truly known him. "How did you find me?" she asked, for lack of something better.

"You've become rather famous," he said. "The entire world has heard of your school, much to Pittakos' embarrassment."

Pittakos! Psappha spat the name in her mind. Nausea born of anger cramped her gut.

"It's said pupils come to you from all the greatest households," Alkaios continued without noticing her pained expression.

"Hardly all," Gongyla put in. "Although we have seven from the Persian royal family and two of Croesus' granddaughters."

"Nice work." Focusing on Psappha, he said, "Your skill has grown, Little One, although I wouldn't go so far as to say, as the Athenians do, that you write like a man. Did you know they have dubbed you Sappho Masculo?"

"Sappho the masculine indeed." Gyla chuckled, her arm firm around Psappha's small shoulders.

"Her work surpasses mine in every way," Alkaios said.

"The Great Alkaios? Humble? This is new," Psappha said. "I remember when you called my verses infant scribbles."

"That's what they were," he insisted affably. "But, no longer. Today, all know that Sappho of Lesbos is The Poetess, worthy peer of The Poet, Homer. Old Crack-toes is so impressed, he sent me to fetch you home."

"So," Psappha snapped, beginning to understand. "Pittakos wants The Poetess to add luster to his ignoble rule." In an aside to Gongyla, she added, "He's a pig who wants to profit from my fame."

"What do you care why he summons you?" Alkaios asked. "Don't you want to come home?"

"Would she be safe?" Gongyla asked, drawing Psappha close. "This Pittakos person may have already changed his mind."

"Old Crack-toes would not dare raise a hand against The Poetess," Alkaios said. "You will be honored at home, as you are here, Psappha. New pupils await you. Many had already made plans to sail for Syracuse when Pittakos published your amnesty."

Psappha laughed. "Of course," she said as her understanding grew. "He will tolerate my presence to prevent the exodus of Lesbian maidens. But, will Poseidon permit me to reach Lesbos?" she worried aloud, remembering her last experience at the Father of Ocean's mercy. "Dare I tempt The Fates again?"

"I'll leave you to consider your decision," Alkaios offered. "If someone will show me where I can divest myself of the grime of travel?"

"Forgive me, Kios. I let surprise supercede manners," she said, belatedly noticing that their reunion had drawn a crowd. "Lyneachia, have a guest chamber prepared," she said. "As for you, my sleepy daughter, it's time you excused yourself as well."

Klies pouted at her mother but did not move.

"Your daughter?" Kios said, noticing the child for the first time.

"Yes, Kios, my daughter, Klies. Her father died at sea," Psappha answered the question in his eyes.

"She is named for your mother?"

Psappha

"For my mother," Psappha acknowledged, "and she grows more like her every year."

Alkaios winked at Klies. She blushed and darted from the room.

"A fine little rabbit you have there."

"No rabbit that one," Psappha chuckled. "More like a pampered Pekinese. You must forgive her rudeness. She has seen no man except Lycos and the gatekeeper since she was a toddler."

"Lycos?"

"We'll talk more tomorrow," Psappha said, noticing Gyla's exaggerated yawn.

Smiling, she tucked her hand companionably in the crook of Kios' elbow and walked with him to the guesthouse, his presence still hard to believe.

~~~~~

The next day, after lunch, Psappha led Alkaios to the tiny room in the gatehouse where Lycos hunched over the household accounts. Barging in without knocking, she said, "Lycos, put by your figures and come visit with a friend."

"You know I don't like leaving my work to help entertain your guests," Lycos grumbled. Nevertheless, he brushed his fingers through his tousled red hair, pushed his chair back and turned. He blushed and fumbled with his clothes when he realized she was not alone.

Alkaios gazed at him as she had expected him to gaze at her.

Eyeing them both, Psappha said, "Come. We'll share wine in the shade and talk of times past."

Lycos blanched and turned away. "You go on," he muttered, shuffling a stack of wax tablets containing her recent work. "I have all of these to transfer to papyrus. And, don't expect me for dinner," he said. "I'll have something brought to me here."

Psappha was stunned. Such rudeness to a guest broke every rule of hospitality, rules more sacred, she believed, than those decreed by gods. "You finish what you're doing and we'll see you at dinner," she said, leaving no room for debate.

"I must apologize for Lycos," she said as she and Alkaios crossed the garden. "He isn't usually so churlish. He can be a delightful companion when it pleases him."

"I know --"

Klies chose that moment to join them.

"Ah-h-h, the nubile daughter," Alkaios said, causing Klies' face to flame. But, Psappha was not so easily put off.

"You know?"

"Later, Psappha. I'll explain when we're alone."

Klies clung to the space at Alkaios' elbow throughout the afternoon. Gongyla remained mute through dinner. Lycos did not join them. Psappha could hardly contain her questions until after the final course. After which, the adults adjourned to the master's sitting room, while Psappha settled Klies for the night.

By the time that she rejoined them, Psappha's curiosity crackled like the small logs in the fireplace. Taking her usual seat near the hearth, she motioned Alkaios toward the opposite chair. He nodded to Gongyla and pulled up a stool instead, not lowering his eyes as she studied him.

Gyla's dark brows arched above penetrating onyx eyes as she took a seat in her usual chair.

Alkaios chuckled. "This calls for a touch of the grape."

"Alkaios, Alkaios," Psappha sighed. In memory, she had deleted the part about his fondness for Dionysus. She blinked happy tears from her eyes as Gongyla summoned a servant.

When each had a full flagon, Alkaios raised his and said, "To friendship."

"Friends?" Psappha tasted the word as she sipped her wine. "Yes," she decided. "We are friends, Alkaios. Much has happened to change us both. Where have you been? How long ago did you return to favor?"

"I went to Egypt and the continent," he said, turning his head from side to side as if explaining as much to Gongyla as to Psappha.

"I must say I was surprised to hear that Psappha of Lesbos was teaching in Syracuse. I wanted to take the first ship to investigate, but there was the matter of a small war that needed finishing. By the time that was done, you were rumored to have returned to Mytilene so -- I petitioned Pittakos and here I am."

"You petitioned Pittakos? What happened?"

"He said, 'come home', of course -- else I'd be pining in some temple longing for you instead of sitting here with a broken heart."

"Be serious. What, exactly, did he say?"

"He said, 'come home,' and some nonsense about forgiveness being better than revenge. What does it matter? The important thing is that when I arrived home and you were not there, I came to find you. Are you sure you don't love me?"

Psappha

"I'm sure," she said. "But why is it you never married? There must have been someone in all this time."

"I've been in exile," he said. "Men without estates get few offers of marriage."

"Without marriage then. Don't tell me you've been celibate all this time."

"Hardly. And you?" He arched a brow toward Gongyla.

"We're talking about you," Psappha insisted. "Was there no one you wanted for your own?"

"Other than you, my lovely, there was one, long ago before we --"

"Never mind that," she said, glancing surreptitiously at Gongyla. "There was one?" She prompted.

"There was one long ago, but it takes a bit of explaining. As a youth, my companions and I often had nothing to do but gamble. Sometimes, when our gold was gone, we wagered slaves. Once, I won a flame-crowned stripling --"

Psappha's gaze darting toward the gatehouse.

"Yes," Alkaios said, confirming her suspicion. "Now you know why he refused to join us."

"Did you treat him badly? Did you beat him?"

"No, of course I didn't beat him. He loved me."

She studied him, but saw no hubris in his expression.

"Did you return his love?"

"Only in the usual fashion of dilettantes," Alkaios admitted sadly. "I was very young. I didn't find out how he felt until he left, leaving behind a box of lyric poetry."

"If he loved you, why did he leave?"

"I lost him on the turn of the dice," Alkaios said. "I know. It was thoughtless of me, but he was a slave, don't you see? Anyway, he vanished. Hades has no wrath like that of the fellow I lost him to. I nursed bruises for a month."

His smile never reached his eyes. "How did you acquire the flaming fox?" he asked. "Has his taste in lovers changed?"

Psappha did not answer right away. She refilled the goblet he waved in her direction, then returned to her chair, having chosen to ignore his arch expression.

"I call him Little Fox," she said at last. "Strange that we chose such similar names for him."

"Not so strange," Gongyla said. "Considering that unruly mane of his, I suspect his mother was the first."

Silence reigned while Alkaios drained the goblet.

"Is Lycos why you never married?" Psappha asked as she again refilled it.

"I never married because I was already married to my memory of you," he slurred, waving his goblet nonchalantly, spilling a drop or two onto the carpet in deference to Dionysus.

"Oh, be serious," she said. After a time, she added, "He still cares for you."

"Nah-h-h . . ." he said through a yawn. "He hates me. If he cared, he'd be here."

"How simple it must be to be a man," Gyla said.

Psappha nodded in silent agreement. "Lycos thinks like a woman," she said. "If he didn't care for you, he'd flaunt his beauty to remind you of what you lost. Beauty, which has been heightened by maturity, in case you didn't notice."

"I noticed," Alkaios admitted, scratching his beard.

~~~~~

"You will sail in the spring?" Lycos asked, his expression oddly pensive.

"We will sail in the spring," Psappha said with emphasis on 'we'. "Alkaios left to take word of my decision to Pittakos lest some Lesbian maidens depart Mytilene for Syracuse before word reached them that The Poetess was coming home.

"You must come with us, foxy one. I couldn't manage without you."

"You have your betrothed to look after your interests," he said.

"How could you think that would make a difference?"

He stared at the fire, shuffling his feet. "I thought perhaps I would go home myself."

"You have no home to go to, and you know it. Why are you trying to deceive me?"

"I don't want to be a burden to you. Things are very different on Lesbos. You must remember some of the outdated ideas you had when you came here. I don't want to be a burden to you."

"Oh, Lycos, my dear sweet friend. The love I have for you is no burden. When I first saw you, it was as if the loveliest of Lesbian cupbearers had appeared before me." She opened her arms to him. He came and knelt, snuggling his head in her lap. "You are part of me," she

Psappha

said, weaving her fingers in his russet hair. "You will always find welcome in my home. You'll be my business manager in Mytilene, just as you've been here. No proper school can function without its chief administrator."

She stroked his back until the muscles relaxed before she spoke again. "Come, now," she said sharply, with a smile. "There's much for you to do. All the travel arrangements must be made." She urged him to his feet. "You're going to love Mytilene."

"Of course, of course," he warbled, taking on an exaggeration of her enthusiasm. "The criers must be informed that The Poetess will be in Mytilene next season. The pupils will need time to prepare."

Psappha laughed as he scurried from the room. Turning, she saw Lyneachia watching her with veiled eyes. "What is it, my purple-eyed friend? Surely you don't think we will leave without you."

"I hope you do, milady. I want to stay here. Please, milady, don't look so hurt. I don't want to be apart from you, but I think I should stay here."

"Nonsense. You'll come to Mytilene with us. You are needed to look after Klies' interests."

Lyneachia hesitated a moment as if unsure how to proceed. She glanced toward Gongyla and flinched from her disapproving glare. Returning her attention to Psappha, she squared her slender shoulders and said, "It is in Klies' interest that I wish to stay. Gongyla will be better for Klies now; with her stern face and her stories she can teach what I cannot. But, this house is Klies' dower. It could be stolen from her if she has no representative in residence."

In her excitement, Psappha had forgotten Klies' greedy grandmother.

"You may wish to use the house again yourself one day," Lyneachia suggested. "It would be best to keep it open."

Psappha shook her head.

Lyneachia returned the gesture. "When you came here, you thought you would never return to Mytilene. You may come back to Syracuse one day. Your home will be ready to receive you when you do."

"Very well, Lyneachia. If you really want to stay behind, you shall be Klies' steward. Tomorrow I will prepare scrolls putting her dower into your hands." She would miss Lyneachia's smiling attendance, but she could not help being pleased by the girl's concern for Klies' future.

Peggy Ullman Bell

~~~~~

Winter crawled on ancient knees. Psappha packed and re-packed a hundred times before the first crocus finally appeared. Of those who were going, only Gongyla had no trunks waiting on the docks. The minimal clothes she seldom wore lay tucked into a corner of Psappha's smallest sea chest.

"Is it true that women walk freely in Mytilene?" Lycos asked one balmy afternoon.

"Women do," she quipped. "Men and boys mind their manners." Lycos ignored her jibe. "If women are free," he said, "Gongyla must come with us."

Sweet Thalia's ghost! Where did he get the notion she was not? Psappha fixed her gaze on her hands to cover her surprise. He could not be more wrong, but she could not resist so good a chance to tease him.

The years seemed to melt from Lycos' face when he pouted, and she loved to see it. It reminded her of their early times together. The more serious he became, the more he pouted and the less she could resist tormenting him.

"Be sensible," she said. "Gyla is free. She can do as she pleases." She almost choked on the effort it took to keep from laughing. "Gyla wouldn't be happy in Mytilene. Lesbian women mingle freely with men. Iphis wouldn't find so ready a welcome without gynakia for support."

"Iphis finds welcome wherever women are," Lycos pronounced indignantly. "She no more confines herself to gynakia than Eros fails to fling his arrows outside of the marriage chamber. Like him, Iphis is everywhere, by whatever name.

"Look at me when I'm talking to you, Psappha. I insist that Gongyla come with us. Why isn't she packed?"

"You insist, do you?" She got up, plunked her fists on her hips and glared, knowing she had carried the joke too far but unable to stop. "You insist? I thought you'd be glad if I forsook her. You enjoy ordering me around so much. Why aren't you smiling? If she's not happy, she can go home. The famine there is over. Isn't a separation what you've always wanted?"

"Gongyla's home is where you are and you know it," he growled. "She has no home but you."

"Now you're making more of me than I am, Little Fox. Gyla is my friend, my companion, yes, all right, she is my lover, but we don't depend on each other for life. We wouldn't die if we were parted."

Psappha

Lycos glared. "Perhaps she doesn't need you to live, you heartless she-goat. But, she does need Lesbos, or the freedom of Lesbos. She's a creature of the fields. She needs something to occupy her bow besides a block of fodder. If you leave her here, she'll die inside, because she will not want to live."

Psappha was stunned speechless. Lycos did not ordinarily call her vile names. Watching his eyes, she realized that somehow, without her noticing, he had come to care more for Gyla than he intended. His angry expression added to the tenderness she felt for him.

"What are you grinning at?" he snarled.

Psappha dropped her tiny smile.

"Did you really think I would abandon my champion? Would any respectable woman travel without a proper guard? Who would protect me on my journey home if not Gongyla? Who would defend my honor? You?"

Lycos grimaced, smiled halfheartedly, then he shook his head.

"Psappha, Psappha, what am I to do with you?"

"You, worker of wonders, are going to design a wardrobe for Gongyla. She can't sail in what she doesn't wear here. The crew might like it, but we might never reach Mytilene."

"There is nothing to design," he said. "You call her your champion, dress her that way. Have Lesbian armor made for her. I'll make the molds myself."

"You will not," Gongyla piped, having entered the room unnoticed. "You may be a womanish fop, but you aren't a woman yet. I'll make the molds myself. If I have to cover myself, sir maiden, I'll do it with my own designs."

Lycos ruffled slightly then smiled. Psappha chuckled.

"She's not insulting your ability to create beauty, my cagey fox. Only what's left of your masculinity. Let her do as she wishes. Whatever she decides upon, she'll be magnificent."

Peggy Ullman Bell

9

Magnificent was too small a word. From doeskin buskins to jaunty white ostrich plume, Gyla was radiant. She wore a gold breastplate that looked as if it had been put on warm and allowed to cool around every seductive curve. She stood like Artemis awaiting the hunt, her long bow resting on the floor, its tip half-hidden in the feather on her helmet. Her midnight eyes sparkled with teasing affection.

"Oh, Gyla," Psappha exclaimed. Enthusiasm bubbled through her like sparkling wine. "You've never seen the equal of Mytilene. In spring, she dresses her hills in flowers. In winter, her winds sing Zeus' songs, both terrible and marvelous," she said, intoxicated by the prospect of returning home.

"We'll walk among her trees, you and I, among the apples with their pastel garlands, the olives with moonlight-bladed leaves, the oaks with squirrels dancing on their uplifted arms. We'll stroll together in the marketplace. The world meets in the markets of New Mytilene.

"We'll have our school, but it won't be locked behind garden walls. We'll roam the scented hills and valleys with our pupils, as free as the clouds of grazing sheep. The girls will gaggle in open fields like the many flocks of geese. You'll hunt the woodland game and fish in crystal streams."

"It sounds like my green land," Gongyla said with skepticism marring her patient face. "Such liberty was known where women ruled," she said, "but men will not permit such freedom."

"The men of Mytilene will allow whatever I demand," Psappha assured her. "The Poetess is not some snit of a girl to be intimidated by outmoded custom."

"Come then, little tyrant," Gyla purred. "The Poetess must not miss her ship."

~~~~~

They spent the journey alone together in their cabin, undisturbed by the bustle of the many ports of call. It was in the third week that a shout from the rigging brought everyone on deck. Psappha ran to the bow, where she gripped the rail with one hand, shaded her eyes with the other and stared at the horizon, straining her eyes to see the speck that had been home.

"Gyla, Lycos, Klies," Psappha called them all to the starboard rail. "Look!" She pointed. "Lesbos," she shouted. "She sparkles like an emerald cameo on the sea."

Gyla tightened her arm around Psappha's slim waist as if to help contain her bubbling happiness. Psappha's impatient eyes blinked as Helios kissed the citadel with morning, his light resting on it like an extended caress.

Each stroke of the oars showed her more of her beloved city. Squat white houses dozed within their alabaster walls. Streets yawned in the crisp spring air. Docks and warehouses hunched in cleanliness, waiting for the start of the day.

Mytilene awoke as they approached. By twos and threes, men stumbled along the quay. Merchants raised tent flaps and set their wares on display. The chanting of the seamen rang anthems in her heart as they furled the sails. Her pounding heart echoed the coxswain's drum. From behind and below, she could hear the oarsmen straining. She watched and listened as, to duet of stevedore and boatswain, ship and dock were wed.

~~~~~

Psappha sauntered down the ramp dressed lavishly in purple, copper, ivory and onyx. Pittakos bustled to meet her. His appearance had not changed much. Except for looking older and a bit shopworn, he still combined the splendid with the shoddy to create a grotesque parody of grace and leadership.

"Welcome, Lady Psappha," he bellowed, hurting her ears. Smiling this way and that, he added, "Your city is proud to welcome you home," speaking more to the crowd than to her.

"Proud, Pittakos?" Psappha spoke quietly, forcing him to bow in order to hear her. "Has so much changed since last we met?"

"Nothing has changed so much as you," he murmured.

The echo of lascivious invitation in his tone threw Psappha's thoughts into the past. He sounded just as she had heard him the week before the banquet that was her undoing.

That morning, she had scarcely settled beneath her favorite tree when Pittakos roared into the garden below, lumbering toward the house like a great clumsy ox. What a fine Cretan priest he would have made, she remembered thinking. He would not need the ox head mask to look like the Minotaur.

Pittakos stayed with her stepfather all that day, while Psappha watched his horse munch dill by the kitchen gate. Eventually, the setting sun warned her that time for procrastination had passed. Her lyre seemed unusually heavy as she trudged downhill.

Upon reaching the house, reluctant to enter while Pittakos remained, she sat on the threshold and cuddled her great cat. Stroking the soft Persian, cooing to him, listening to him purr, she failed to hear the door open behind her. She flinched as a shaft of candlelight crept across her lap. The cat dug in his claws then leaped off into the night.

"What are you doing here in the dark?" Pittakos had asked.

She almost told him. But, whatever else he was, he was a guest. "It's very late," she told him with venom dripped from her words despite all effort to remain polite. Rising slowly, struggling for composure, she had started into the house.

He stepped between her and the open door. "You are so beautiful, little Psappha," he said in the same lascivious tone that had plunged her into the memory. He had laid rough hands on her shoulders and stroked toward her elbows. She cringed internally as she recalled what he had said when she wrenched free of his grasping hands.

His words echoed in her mind. "Later than you think, Miss Arrogance." But, today is a new morning, Pittakos, although you have apparently not changed.

"You have grown lovelier in your absence," he said, in the fawning tone that churned her stomach.

"An absence you caused, sir satyr."

"An error, milady, which I have come to regret."

"Such gallantry must tax you," she said. "Or, has the burden of your office stolen the sting from your tongue?"

"You wrong me, gentle lady," he said, watching those around them from the corner of his eye. "I have no quarrel with you," he claimed with a smile for his simper of sycophants.

"Quarrel enough to have kept me in exile these many years." Psappha seethed with resentment.

"You would have been sent for long ago had your whereabouts been known," he claimed. "It was assumed you had perished."

"You would have liked that, you old pirate," Psappha whispered. Noting the building tension in his taut neck, she thought, he would exile me again if he dared.

Psappha

Taking a deep breath, she vowed he would not use her to further his reputation. She spoke from low in her diaphragm, projecting her trained voice to the outer reaches of the hushed crowd. "Do you expect me to believe I am renowned in Babylon and unheralded in Mytilene?"

"We heard long ago of the Illustrious Sappho of Lesbos," he hedged for the benefit of the crowd. "We just recently learned that The Poetess spoke Aeolian. Your betrothed was immediately dispatched to fetch our beloved Psappha home."

His groveling sent a familiar shiver the length of her spine. She did not try to hide her disdain when she spoke.

"Is it that you no longer fear my innocent verses, crack-toes, or has my small success softened your resolve to deprive me of my home?"

For the world, Pittakos looked like a merchant trying to sell something wonderful at a bargain no one wanted, but Psappha saw his anger and she smiled.

"It was not from fear that I sent you away, Psappha. There simply seemed no logic in allowing you and your mouthy betrothed to stay here worrying at my heels in troubled times."

"Have you forgotten that I am no cur-whelp to demean myself by worrying at the heels of a gutter-climber? I was never a danger to you, yet you sent me away. Now you deign to welcome me with honor. Why?"

"Perhaps I missed the sharpness of your tongue," he whispered as people clustered close.

"I doubt that," she said, keeping her voice hushed. "More likely your greed for fame drove you to reason in spite of yourself."

He veiled his porcine eyes as she waved to the gathered throng.

"It is true," he admitted, his words barely audible above the roar of welcoming cheers. "Some of our best maidens were preparing to journey to Sicily. However," his voice rose as he added, " you could have returned at any time."

"Somehow, I doubt that, Pittakos. Now, if you will excuse me, I would like to get under cover before the sun gets much higher."

He bowed before her.

"I will escort you to your home, Lady Psappha. I have had your father's house prepared for your return."

"I will reside with my betrothed, thank you, Pittakos," she said.

"Alkaios' house is quite fine, Lady Psappha, but it is not fitting for a teacher of your stature. Surely your pupils would feel more at ease among the upper aristocracy."

"I was not aware you fit the category, Pittakos. On the other hand, I am an aristocrat wherever I reside. My students will feel at ease with the simple pleasures of earth and sun -- or they will not be my students."

"As you wish," he conceded. "I will escort you."

"I prefer my own escort, thank you."

At Psappha's signal, Gyla disembarked. Psappha suppressed a chuckle as she watched Pittakos gape, blink, and cough then gape again. Gongyla strode past him and paused. Psappha took her arm. Together, they waited for the others.

The ornate sedan chair Pittakos had intended for Psappha served Klies. She looked like a nubile princess, waving grandly as she was borne through the expectant crowd.

Psappha had to laugh at Lycos' wide-eyed perch astride a magnificent chestnut stallion. When he had passed them, Psappha skip-stepped to keep pace with Gyla's easy stride, waving from time to time to acknowledge the cheers that followed her and her resplendent protector.

Everything seemed smaller, but no less beautiful, than she remembered. As they left the marketplace, she tugged at Gongyla's hand, drawing her along the shore, while the others continued up the road. As soon as they were out of sight, Psappha removed her sandals. The blue water tickled as it sucked the sand from beneath her feet. The trees in The Lady's park had just begun to bud. Their branches cast filigreed shadows over hyacinth beds. The grass felt cool and slightly damp from lingering dew.

The culverts beside the hillside path trickled with remnants of melted snow. Psappha climbed with unexpected ease. My legs are longer now, she thought.

"The house is full," Lycos shouted when they crested the hill. "There are maidens everywhere. Kios says if more come we will need a larger house."

"If we need one, we'll find it," Psappha said, hurrying past the gate.

~~~~~

94

Psappha

Gongyla had gone on ahead and was already spinning tales in a corner of the garden. A bevy of girls adorned the lawn around her. Psappha waved to some and smiled a welcome to the rest.

"M0-ther," Klies huffed when Psappha met her on the stoop. "This WOMAN says I must do as she tells me. I never had to do what Lyneachia said unless I wanted to."

Psappha sighed and smoothed Klies' undisciplined hair. "Lyneachia was not as wise as Praxinoa, my love. Praxinoa was companion to my mother, the grandmother for whom I named you. She suckled me. Of course you must do as she tells you."

"The daughter of Kerkolos of Andros takes no orders from slaves."

"Klies, please. You need to learn what is expected of a Lesbian lady." And, none too soon. "There is no better teacher than Praxinoa. She will teach you as she taught me." With great difficulty, as I recall, she thought, casting a tender glance at her aging nurse, and releasing a rueful sigh.

Klies frowned, an unasked question in her angry eyes.

"Yes, willful one," Psappha confirmed. "I will do as Praxinoa advises and so will you."

"I'm nearly ten-years-old. I don't need a nurse," Klies sulked.

"We all need a nurse sometimes, little one," Psappha consoled. "We never get so grown up we don't need someone, sometimes, who loves us in spite of ourselves. Now -- go with Praxinoa, dear heart. I want to be alone a while."

"But . . ." Klies pouted.

"Go," Gongyla put in, pointing to the door.

Praxinoa nodded to Gongyla with approval in her eyes. Then, she followed the child's flouncing parade-of-one, shaking her head from side to side and wearing a rueful smile.

Alkaios met Psappha in the main corridor. "It is not as confused as Lycos thinks," he said. "All of the maidens are situated. I sent their guards and married servants to my mother's house.

"You will need more room soon though, judging from the number of petitions coming in."

~~~~~

When the house filled to overflowing, Alkaios gave her the one that was to have been their wedding gift. Commissioned lyrics had earned her more than enough gold to finish it far beyond its original plans. "Gyla's going to have to leave the hunting to the foresters and help me with the school," she murmured as she watched the workers toil to complete their new quarters before the winter winds.

The house lay like an amphitheater below the orchard where she sat. Mid-summer breezes played hide and seek in the folds of her kiton. Her fingers danced unattended on the strings of her lyre. She felt as if her soul might break free and fly off to Olympus at any moment. All seemed perfect in her world.

Klies had grown as fond of Praxinoa as she, herself, had always been. Roaming free had made Gyla lovelier than Psappha had ever imagined she could become. The criers called for teachers now yet each week brought petitions from fathers intent on getting their daughters into Psappha's exalted circle.

~~~~~

Psappha picked the scroll from her dressing table glared at it a moment, then let it fall, forgotten.

"Why don't you have Lycos meet with Pittakos?" Gongyla suggested. "He handles all other petitioners. Why not this one?"

Psappha walked to the sideboard and reached for the water jug. Changing her mind, she picked up a flagon of wine and filled a large goblet to the brim.

"He's a plague," she grumbled, kicking the petition under the bed.

Gongyla snorted, letting Psappha know that her infinite patience was wearing thin. "You are The Poetess," she said. "He would not dare harm you."

Taking Psappha by the shoulders, she turned her toward the sheet of silvered Phoenician glass that covered half of one wall. "Look," she said. "Is that Psappha, the helpless orphan?"

What Psappha saw in the mirror bore little resemblance to what she saw in her heart. The woman in the glass looked confident – mature – the mother of a blossoming adolescent. But, within herself, Psappha was fifteen, frightened and unloved.

"You shouldn't need me to remind you of who you are," Gyla scolded. "You are The Poetess, The Teacher, respected throughout the world. Now -- Teacher, prepare to receive the pretender and remember, my lady, Pittakos, the usurper, is beneath your concern."

~~~~~

It was late afternoon before Pittakos stomped into the main hall. Psappha received him standing, making no effort to hide her revulsion.

Psappha

"You have orders for me, milord?" She addressed him with exaggerated courtesy.

"I have a request, milady."

"A request from you is an order in effect, is it not? I heard you have given new meaning to your title, Tyrant."

She motioned him to the only chair in the room, a low Egyptian affair intended for a menial. When he was seated, she reclined on the chaise Gyla had placed on the dais for her.

Pittakos squirmed. "I do not come as Tyrant," he said. "I brought no orders, merely a humble request."

"Have you some back-alley daughter you dare put forward for my group? Surely, you would not presume to that extent. Perhaps, a, um, niece?" The connotation she placed on the word niece made it clear it was not her first choice.

He stood to meet her challenge eye to eye. "Not a niece," he assured her, giving the word the same disparaging connotation, "a ward, an orphan, but worthy of your company. An exceedingly clever maiden with a talent so great I sometimes think she is Terpsichore, pretending to be mortal just to tease me."

"She sounds delightful to have gained such praise from you while remaining a maiden. Unfortunately, I have no room for another pupil."

"Excuse me, Lady Psappha, I'm afraid I did not make myself clear. Atthis . . ."

Psappha trembled. Pictures from her childhood flashed behind her eyes. Golden Atthis! The vision seared her brain. He could not be referring to her Atthis. Not the dancing girl-child whose memory she'd come to love. Her Atthis could not have remained a maiden all this time. She was far too beautiful. Yet, he said she dances. Atthis danced. Like Terpsichore, she danced. But, a maiden? After so many years?

"Lady Psappha?"

"Excuse me, Pittakos. You were saying?"

"I was saying, dear lady, that I was not suggesting The Lady Atthis . . ."

The Lady Atthis! He presents a woman. But, of course, she thought. When I left Mytilene, Atthis was younger than Klies is now. The impossibility of it made her catch her breath. Catching her breath allowed her to hear Pittakos again.

" . . . But as an instructor. Her capabilities as a dancer would compliment your songs and add to the joys of your pupils."

Psappha wanted to refuse him on principle. However, since Lyneachia stayed behind in Syracuse, she missed watching her pupils dance. And, if it were the same beautiful Atthis . . .

"Very well," she said with apparent calm, "send her to me. If she is as accomplished as you say, I'll accept her."

After he left, Psappha consumed a goblet of wine to wash away his presence before seeking the fresh air of her garden.

Alone in her outdoor arbor-pavilion, she closed her eyes, letting her mind's eye gaze fondly on the girl-child Atthis, dancing among the flowers in The Lady's park. Could she be? She left the question dangling on the edge of nothing, allowing the busy buzzing of the bees to lull her into a peaceful doze. Listening to their droning, she imagined herself a dull brownish moth flitting from blossom to blossom drinking ambrosia in the company of a glorious gold and blue butterfly.

Evening shadows had lengthened long before Gongyla sprinted into the garden. Her brief kiton pressed against her as she loped up the path, bow in one hand, and a brace of bright-feathered birds in the other.

Gyla tossed her bounty to the ground near Psappha's feet, leaned her bow against the arbor and poured herself onto the grass, resting her chin on her fists.

Gazing into her dark, far-seeing eyes, Psappha quickly grew impatient for the night.

~~~~~

"May I go to the city with Alkaios tomorrow?" Klies asked, smiling at him, but not meeting Gongyla's eyes. "Lycos said to ask you," she said as she plunked cross-legged onto the hearth at her mother's feet.

"Did he say to ask me or did he say no?"

Klies' flinch betrayed her.

"So, little imp. Lycos said no and you wish me to over-ride his judgement. For shame, Klies. If Lycos said no, he had a reason."

"Please, Mother, Alkaios wouldn't let anything happen to me. Lycos is such an old maid. He doesn't want me to go because Daphnos is going. He thinks I'm still in swaddling."

Her choice of words found their echo in Psappha's memory. She did not need Alkaios' smirk to remind her. Not trusting her voice, she nodded to Klies who jumped up and vanished before she could change her mind. Alkaios chuckled. Psappha blushed. She knew the scene he was remembering.

Psappha

"Who is Daphnos?" she asked.

"Just a boy I'm mentoring," Alkaios assured her.

"Will Lady Atthis be coming here?" Gongyla asked suddenly, ignoring the conversation in progress.

"She will come for an interview," Psappha said, matching Gyla's gruff tone. "I will decide if she is to join us."

"I didn't know Atthis had returned from Naucratis," Alkaios said with puzzling gravity. Psappha was so excited by the thought of his knowing Atthis she did not question the tightness in his tone.

"Do you think she would accept a place here?"

"Atthis would be honored to be accepted here."

"Hardly honored," Psappha demurred, again overlooking his omission of the honorarium. "Would she be happy here, do you think, after her travels? We live a very simple life. It can be a dismal life for an attractive maiden to live solely in the company of women."

"Atthis would consider this a perfect setting," he replied, drawing a sharp look from Gongyla.

Psappha squirmed in her chair, suspecting they were deep in a conversation that did not include her, though neither of them uttered a sound.

"What is it?" she grumbled, irritated by their silence. "Do you think I should invite Lady Atthis to join my staff?" she asked, bringing the subject back to its beginning.

"If you're sure you want her," he responded with a trace of tension in his voice.

"Would she accept?"

"She has no choice in the matter."

"No choice?"

"Not if her guardian wishes it. Obviously, his reasons for sending her to Naucratis no longer apply. You and your school have turned fashion in Atthis' favor and Pittakos will follow fashion no matter where it leads."

As in the past, the Tyrant's name halted their conversation. Psappha and Alkaios drank their wine in shared silence. Gongyla leaned down and brushed Psappha' cheek with her lips before she left them.

"Send more wine," Alkaios slurred, but Gongyla had already closed the door.

Psappha hurried to catch her, but, as she reached the door, she heard Praxinoa's voice. Not wanting a lecture on the evils of Dionysus,

Psappha started to close the door. She stopped to listen when she realized whom her old nursemaid was talking to.

"Why do you slump so, Gentle Warrior?"

"Why are you here, Old Woman? It is late," Gongyla said. "You should be in your bed."

"This is a chair my bones are used to," Praxinoa told her. "Many nights, when Psappha's mother was alive, I never saw my bed. She was the demanding sort. Ever aware of her own importance, like her young namesake."

"I thought you were Psappha's nurse," Gongyla said.

"That, too," Praxinoa said. "But, my Psappha was far less demanding than her mother or her daughter. Never wanted a thing but her mother's love, that child."

Psappha felt a lump in her throat.

"Her mother did not love her," Gongyla said, with a note of incredulity.

"Klies the elder loved only herself," Praxinoa told her tiredly. "Although she doted on her son, Charaxos. Spoiled him, I suppose. Perhaps that's why he could not stand it when she married so soon after her husband's death. She married Alkaios' older brother; did you know? Charaxos went away right after that, he did. Hasn't been home since."

"He cared nothing for his sister?"

"They were not a caring family, after the master was taken, and Psappha was already promised to Alkaios," Praxinoa sighed.

"Promised from the cradle. Her future was assured, or so they all thought. Too bad they never asked her." She chuckled. "She'd have told them a thing or three, I'll warrant. Wanted nothing but to make her music, my Psappha. Had no use for marriage or for men, even then. Don't look so surprised," she said. "Did you not wonder that I wasn't shocked to see you in her bed?"

"I did," Gongyla admitted.

"Well," Praxinoa winked. "Praxinoa always did know what was good for her Psappha."

How dare she say those things about my mother? Psappha mused. And, my daughter? None of it is true. If she weren't so old, I'd send her away for her lies.

"Spha?"

"I'm sorry, Kios. I'll be with you in a moment." Listening, hearing nothing, she eased the door the rest of the way open. Gongyla was nowhere in sight. Praxinoa nodded in a chair. "We need more wine," Psappha growled. "See to it."

"Ouch! Take it easy on my head," Alkaios groaned when she slammed the door.

Peggy Ullman Bell

10

The girls clustered around Psappha, trying to copy a melody that she would never be able to duplicate because her mind was not on it. Letting her fingers strum the familiar strings without conscious guidance, she watched Klies play handball not far from the arbor. The ball flew over Klies' head. She jumped for it, missed, and fell laughing onto the grass. Psappha frowned as Alkaios' young friend, Daphnos, snatched a handful of flowers and showered them over her daughter.

Klies stood to brush petals from her skirt then tucked the hem into her girdle before returning to the game. She's too old to be showing her ankles, Psappha thought. The idea stunned her and she thought, if she's too old, then what, pray Hecate, am I?

Pondering her own maturity, Psappha watched Daphnos toss the ball. Klies dove for it and would have crashed into a bush had Alkaios not caught her and set her on her feet. In the midst of their raucous laughter, Psappha plinked her lyre for attention and began the lesson again.

Klies joined them, frowning when her mother yanked her skirt loose. Nevertheless, she draped it demurely over her feet when she sat. Her clear, sweet soprano blended and harmonized with Psappha's rich contralto as she added swirls to the vibrant fullness of her mother's song.

When they finished, Gongyla called from the opposite side of the garden where maidens grouped themselves at her feet, awaiting her latest story. All save Psappha joined them. She loved Gyla's ability to weave elaborate tales, but sometimes she preferred the solitude of her arbor. She did much of her composing there.

Psappha let her eyes drift shut to listen to the lyrics in her mind. She was deep in thought when the hum of Gyla's monologue dwindled to nothing. Opening her eyes, she saw a tall woman in a stark white peplos and skirt, whose sole distinction was her swinging dancer's gait. Psappha's body quivered as the woman knelt to touch the poppies by the path, her long hair falling forward like a shimmering, saffron veil.

Psappha

A year had passed since Pittakos presented his so-called request. Psappha had long since concluded that the Lady Atthis had dissuaded him from ordering her to teach at the growing school.

Yet, when the woman entered the arbor, there was no further doubt. This fair young woman, warming her being with a radiant smile, was the golden girl-child, Atthis, grown and flowered into an opulence of femininity.

Psappha felt the muscles beneath her clench. The moon, she thought, with midnight in her eyes.

"Lady Psappha?"

Atthis' voice fell on Psappha's ears like the whisper of a goddess. The imagined texture of her skin made Psappha's hands itch. She wiped her palms on her skirt.

Atthis frowned and Psappha felt as if the sky had clouded over.

"Please excuse me for my lack of hospitality," she said.

"It is I who should apologize for coming upon you unannounced. I only, just yesterday, arrived in Mytilene. I had assumed my lord, Pittakos, would inform you as to when I was to dock. Forgive me, Lady Psappha. I should have communicated the information myself. If you would have me audition for you, you have but to begin the tune."

Psappha's fingers found a melody almost without her help. She scarcely noticed as the others gathered close. Normally, she would have smiled when the younger students vied for openings among the roses through which to see. This time, she did not even comment when Klies returned to her seat beside her, her skirt hiked well above her shins.

Lycos, Alkaios and Daphnos formed a line across the arbor entrance. Gongyla pushed between them and came to stand near Psappha. Atthis swayed in time with the music. On the third refrain, she began to dance.

Her feet made patterns new to all those who watched. Psappha's muse sang within her mind. Golden siren – tantalizing, she composed in her mind. Sea-blue eyes entrap me, inviting me to Hades, making me know that I'd find Elysium there. Golden siren –- dancing -- every fiber rhythmic -- in tune with the cosmos. Golden siren – Enchantress, my body sparkles as I watch, fixed, grounded by thy hypnotic gaze.

Psappha ended her tune with a flourish that Atthis translated into a pirouette, gracefully collapsing as the music softened, settling to the grass, her head bowed between outstretched arms like a dying swan. The song left a deafening silence in its wake.

There was a distinct whoosh as the watchers remembered to breathe. Atthis raised her torso, extending open palms.

"Will you accept me, milady?"

Psappha nodded, unable to find her voice. The maidens rushed past those in the opening, fluttering into the arbor, surrounding Atthis, competing for her attention, talking simultaneously and so fast no one could decipher half their words. Atthis laughed and indicated that – yes - she would dance again.

"No," Psappha said. "The Lady Atthis is fatigued from her journey."

"I am never too tired to dance for beautiful maidens," Atthis said and Psappha felt a twinge of jealousy.

"They'll see more dancing than they want when they begin to learn the movements," she insisted. Turning to Lycos, she said, "Have a chamber prepared."

"Next to yours?" Gongyla asked.

"No, my love. The one next to Praxinoa's, Lycos. Lady Atthis may wish to use the nursery for classes in inclement weather."

By twos and threes, the maidens drifted away. Klies and Daphnos followed; her hand tucked neatly into his. Alkaios offered to show Atthis to her chambers. Lycos scurried to the gatehouse and slammed the door.

As soon as they were alone, Gongyla pulled Psappha to her feet. "This dancer is the one you would have called to Iphis?" she asked none too gently.

"You know I did not know of Iphis before we met."

"Would you have called her if you had?"

Psappha refused to meet her eyes.

"You want her," Gongyla accused.

"It's you I love."

"You answer too quickly. She's bewitched you with her dervish twirling."

Psappha hung her head. Desire and loyalty warred within her mind. Her soul caught in a memory, she could still see golden Atthis dancing in the park, a wonder of innocence she longed to educate.

Gongyla laid a hand on her shoulder.

Looking up, Psappha let her eyes wander over dark beauty and she nearly strangling on confusion.

"My precious Ianthe," Gyla whispered, capturing Psappha gaze with her dark-eyed spell. "I am your Iphis."

Psappha

Psappha nodded, picked up her lyre and let Gongyla draw her into the house.

~~~~~

For Psappha, summer became a theatrical spectacle, resplendent with music. Though she seemed to be teaching chords to reluctant students, Atthis held most of her attention.

Each afternoon, Atthis led the maidens in intricate choreographs on the lawn with Klies echoing her every gesture. Not far away, Gongyla instructed archery. Seeing the two of them so close, Psappha felt sundered -- shattered by a throbbing dichotomy of desire.

One night, her work reflected the splintering of her soul. She spoke the words softly to herself as she cut them into the wax.

"In my loneliness, I feel her kitten fingers on my breast and wonder what sweet fragrance tempts me now. I feel her web entrap me, as my fingers tangle in your raven hair. My lips reach, dry and flaking, to taste her pungent flavors and wander, oh so lightly, across the ebon satin of your thighs.

"With each passing moment I can hear your languid whisper, 'let me love you, My Lady.' And, gently do you carry me, on waves of sensation, to volcanic peak of feeling, then tenderly escort me safely down, while all the while I watch her dance behind my eyes.

"Tomorrow is as nothing. Yesterday is gone. There is only you and now and dreaming to fill my empty hours. Though people crowd around me, demanding my attention, I still float, within my soul, into her arms. You are. I am. We are. All else is mere charade. Why was I not born singly, like others that I know? Duality lies heavy on my soul."

Later, after Gongyla fell asleep beside her, Psappha tossed with frustration. In her dreams, need tore at her like rampaging vultures with wrenching claws of missed opportunity. Awake, it was worse. Each morning she lay rigid in their bed, trying to block visions of a dancing golden girl-child from her tormented mind.

Summer grew hotter and Psappha's misery grew easier to bear. The dancers confined themselves to the coolness of the many-windowed nursery while she spent her afternoons alone in the arbor, no longer forced to watch Atthis -- so near -- so far -- so beautiful.

By the time the asters began to bloom, the garden felt like the pit of Hades. The roses hung limp on thirsty branches that failed to supply relief from the heat. Their drooping leaves shut out relentless sunlight but they excluded the breeze as well.

Peggy Ullman Bell

Lycos' hair hung in damp tangles on his creased brow when he joined her late one afternoon. A hint of silver accented its fox-fur tint. Alkaios came to lounge on the grass. Gongyla came to sit beside Psappha as the dancers filed into the garden despite the heat.

Atthis gyrated in the center of the circling girls, the focus of Psappha's attention. She did not notice the growing restlessness around her until the midday sun stopped adding glimmer to Atthis' flowing hair.

Atthis fell to her knees, screaming in terror as Helios slowly disappeared. Gyla stood like the queen she was; her students clustered around her. A slim wing of brightness, attached to an even slimmer band of light remained in Helios' accustomed place.

After one brief, painful glance skyward, Psappha stood unmoving, her head down, her eyes closed, not caring that her body ached from tension, certain some worse catastrophe was due her.

Oh blessed Olympians, she prayed in silence. Forgive my vagrant desires. Blessed Mother, return thy shining son to the sky and I swear I will forsake that which I most desire.

Oh, brilliant, brightly shining Helios, do not forsake me. Holy Mother, my vow shall ever be my bond.

It seemed an eternity before she felt Helios again caress her back with warmth. She opened her eyes cautiously. The flowers at her feet shone in the normal brightness of early afternoon. Raising her eyes, she saw Alkaios reach to help Lady Atthis to her feet.

Lycos took the lyre from Psappha's motionless hands and laid it at her feet. "She follows him with her eyes," he said as he straightened up.

"What bothers you, Little Fox, the fact that she watches, or that he might look back with interest?"

Lycos retrieved the lyre and plucked at its strings as if he had not heard. Psappha recognized the song as one Alkaios had used in his youth. He had composed it in his romantic period. Before all his verses turned to marshal musings, she recalled. Feeling a burst of empathy, she touched Lycos' arm.

"I'm afraid, dear brother of my heart, we are more alike than we have ever been before."

"I'm sure we are, Adelphi. Have you watched them together?"

"They've been together?"

"Not like that. He watches her dance and she watches him when he sings after supper. Soon they will catch each other's eyes. What then?"

106

Psappha

"You don't need to settle for watching, though I must or close my eyes. Atthis is forever lost to me."

"How can she be lost? You've never had her, though you could easily enough. You are The Poetess. You have but to ask and she will come to you. If not for Gyla, she would probably have come without an invitation."

"No, Little Fox. She would not come. She knows nothing of Iphis. Perhaps there was a time I could have taught her, but that is no longer possible."

"She needs no . . . " he began, then appeared to change his mind. "Why do you think it would be impossible?"

"I vowed to forsake my desire for her."

"Vowed? To whom? Gongyla?"

"No, dear friend. Gyla would never ask a sacrifice of me. I promised The Lady I would forsake all thought of Atthis if Her son, Helios, would return with his sacred light."

Lycos slumped. "Psappha, you silly, love-besotted fool. Helios did not go away. The Lady Moon passed between Helios and Earth. There was nothing to be frightened of, much less anything to cause you to bind yourself with a vow which I dare say you've already broken in your lustful little heart."

~~~~~

Winter closed them in together. Cold winds seemed warm compared to the storm Psappha saw in Gongyla's eyes.

They lingered in the dining hall one night after the household had retired. Gongyla stalked like a trapped panther. Guttering candles spurted in their own smoke before she yanked Psappha to her feet.

"If you want the shallow one, take her." Gyla's voice rasped through clenched teeth. Psappha stood quiet until released. "Why won't you take her, little one?"

Psappha wondered at her change of tone. "Everything seems so simple to you, thou splendid cat. Some things can't be had just for the taking."

"And, some things can," Gongyla said. Smiling wryly, she pulled Psappha onto her lap.

Psappha nuzzled Gyla's shoulder. "You handle me easily enough, sweet warrior, but even your strength would be taxed by Atthis. Terpsichore has blessed her with a dancer's agility. She is no wisp of air to be subdued by a raindrop."

Gongyla dumped her on the bed and stretched beside her, leaning on one elbow, cradling her chin with one hand while the other played with Psappha's hair.

"Must we always talk of Atthis? If you want her, take her," Gyla said, stroking Psappha's cheek. "Take her so we can ignore her, at least some of the time."

"I don't think I shall ever forget Atthis," Psappha sighed.

"I am not asking you to forget her," Gyla grumbled against Psappha's ear. "I said for you to get her, completely, so we can get on with our lives. Sing for her and she'll be yours in an instant."

"If you only knew how I sing for her," Psappha sighed. "Aphrodite must be weary of my songs. If I pray to her again I fear she will say, 'what is it that upsets you now, Psappha? Whom, now, must I tempt to give you her love?'"

"Why sing to Aphrodite?" Gyla muttered against the curve of Psappha's throat. "Will she quench your fires for you?"

"Aphrodite has been good to me," Psappha whispered against Gyla's smooth, warm shoulder.

"Aphrodite has done nothing, my dove. The magnificence of your poet's soul has won you glory. The fire of your music keeps it bright."

"What has kept thee, patient warrior? You know how I yearn for Atthis, yet you don't turn from me. Instead, you tell me to seek her out. Why?"

"Psappha, you are my soul's mate. I'm happy being where I can help you gain whatever you desire. I love you."

"I'm sorry," Psappha whispered, mystified by the pain of it.

~~~~~

"We'll have a banquet!" Klies danced around her mother.

"Stop!" Psappha demanded with a chuckle. "You're making me dizzy. Why should we have a banquet? Surely a simple dinner would be enough."

"No, it has to be a banquet. I'm getting married."

"You're what?"

"I'm getting married," Klies repeated.

"You are not!" Psappha shouted. "You're a babe! Who is this seducer of infants? I'll send Lycos to have him prosecuted."

Klies giggled. "Don't do that. He doesn't know about it yet. If you must prosecute someone, summon Eros before the magistrates. I'm not an infant, Mother. I love him. I cannot work nor sleep for love of him. His beauty taunts me. Yes, and I want to bear his children. Does that shock you?"

"No, it doesn't shock me. It's good to feel such things. But, these feelings are not love. Love is more lasting than desire. No. Don't speak. I can see in your eyes that you won't listen. You'll refuse to hear anything that might thwart your wish to taste the fires of Aphrodite. I know. I was once the same."

A sharp "Harrumph" from the corner reminded them that Gongyla was there, polishing her bow. When Psappha glanced her way, she turned her back.

"So?" Psappha said, returning her attention to Klies. "Who is this young man you've decided to marry, and when do you plan to tell him?"

"Daphnos," Klies said in a tone more suited to Apollo.

Of course, Psappha told herself. I should have guessed. She was always trailing after Alkaios. If I were not so enthralled by repressed passion, I would have known she focused on his handsome friend. Fool, she chided herself. Why weren't you watching?

Still, she thought, it could be worse. His family is noble enough in spite of their poverty. With industry, the union might gain some small measure of success. But, is my pampered Pekinese capable of the necessary zeal, she wondered, but she did not voice her doubts.

"Well, Mother?"

"All right," Psappha said with her usual indulgence. "Run tell Lycos we're having a party." Klies was gone before Psappha completed her sentence.

The banquet followed within days. With the entire household running in response to her brisk commands, Klies had everything except her mother ready for the day when it arrived. Daphnos' perpetually thunderstruck expression amused them all.

Klies' wedding day dawned brisk and clear. Throngs of people choked the streets. Klies dripped in the center of Psappha's chamber, letting the holy water of her ritual bath dry on her lithe body.

Psappha watched angrily. A superstitious servant had told Klies her grandmother had angered Hera by having had the sacred water wiped away before her wedding. She said Hera increased the pain of her grandmother's appointment to punish her and that that was why she died. I should have sold the foolish woman to a eunuch.

Lycos stood by with his paint pots like an artist waiting for apprentices to finish preparing his canvas. "Hurry, you pack of sluggards, the sun will sink before you get her dressed."

Most of the maidens rushed to the window to confirm his statement. Their delighted squeals brought Psappha, the rest of the maidens, and Klies, to peer over their shoulders at the spectacle below.

"Oh, why must Alkaios drive so slowly," Klies pouted.

Psappha looked her up and down and said, "It's a good thing for you he does. Go. Get dressed. Your bridegroom comes." She hurried her away with a swat on her bare behind.

Klies yipped but Psappha ignored her. Instead, she devoted her attention to the pageantry below. It was hard to tell whether the prancing white mules drew a cart or a garden, so bedecked were they and their burden with boughs and blossoms. She shook her head, thinking Daphnos' father must have loaded every seagoing tub he owned with southern flowers.

The populace lining the street chorused a ringing paean as Daphnos climbed down from his fragrant perch. Dancing children littered the ground before him with petals. The scent of crushed chrysanthemums rose to the window as he walked. He and his groom's men found a sumptuous spread on long tables set beneath an evergreen shrouded canopy in the courtyard. The bride and her maids would dine in Psappha's great banquet room before joining the men.

The prenuptial feasting was nearly over before Psappha escorted her nervous daughter from the hall. Daphnos grabbed Klies' hand and gaily pulled her to the waiting cart amid a rising chorus of ribaldry and laughter.

Psappha soon became breathless from the songs and jesting that followed them, her throbbing voice easily distinguishable in the rollicking procession. As they sang the bridal couple into the bridegroom's home, she sang her own rousing hymeneal. Gongyla led a rollicking flower throwing contest.

Psappha's heart lurched when Daphnos presented Klies to his household gods. Tears dampened her lashes when it was his mother, and not she, who led Klies into the bedchamber. Her eyes misted as she joined the singing outside the nuptial door.

Even so, her voice was strong among the revelers encouraging Daphnos when his friends escorted him to his bride. Her voice rose above all others as the songs and jests grew loud and bawdy. But, when Daphnos waved the stained linen from the doorway, Psappha's voice was missing from the cheers.

Gongyla took her hand and led her through the quiet streets.

The great hall slumbered in shambles, as if mourning the ribald throng so recently departed. Through a curtain of stale smoke, left from hastily extinguished torches, Psappha saw Lycos sleeping near the hearth. Alkaios sang softly in one corner with Atthis at his elbow, seemingly entranced.

Psappha slumped into her usual chair and sipped the wine Gongyla brought her. She tried to think of Kerkolos, of their wedding, of Klies' birth, what she remembered of it, of Klies' face when last she saw it, both happy and frightened -- but -- all she really thought of was Atthis and Alkaios cozy in the corner. Like a shade, she slipped from the hall into the garden.

"Why run, Adelphi? There's no escape."

"Lycos! I thought you were asleep. Why'd you follow me? Don't you know I want to be alone?"

"You want to be alone about as much as Klies does right now."

"They'll be happy," Psappha said when they reached the arbor.

"Atthis and Alkaios?"

"Them too, I suppose. I was thinking of Klies and Daphnos."

"I'm sure you were."

Psappha turned away from his obvious disbelief. "I feel so alone," she confided.

"You have Gongyla. Do you remember the night Klies was born? It was a remarkable sight. Gongyla . . ."

Psappha gave him a wry smile. "Even then, there was a spot within me Gongyla could not reach," she murmured.

Hearing footsteps, she looked up to see Atthis and Alkaios a few feet from them, apparently unaware of their presence deep within the secluded arbor.

The Lady Moon slid behind a lonely cloud. Psappha squeezed the hand holding hers. The cloud passed. Now, Atthis sat on the grass near the fountain. Alkaios' head rested in her lap.

Psappha's tongue drove into the roof of her mouth as if to lock the pounding of her heart from her ringing ears. Her jaw ached from holding her breath lest an explosion from her lungs betray their watching.

Lycos kissed her cheek. She saw the desolation in his eyes through the tears in her own. She did not hesitate when he tugged her hand. When next a cloud obscured the moon, they slipped away.

Inside her chamber, Psappha rushed to her couch and her precious, comforting lyre. Her heart throbbed in her music as she sang.

"Peer of the gods he seems to me, as he sits before you, and close beside you listens to your sweet voice and lovely laughter. My heart trembles. Seeing you blinds my eyes. In my ears a roaring sounds. Sweat invades my clothing. My being quakes with tremors and the fluids of my vessel pour. I am paler than the winter grass. Death rides near.

"My muse deserts me and my tongue is broken. Even so, I must endure."

Psappha

11

Storms heralded an end to autumn. Psappha's forbidden thoughts clamored for fulfillment. The unseasonable cold chilled her flesh in sharp contrast to flames that blazed within. The hearth fire hissed and crackled as the door burst open.

Alkaios stumbled into the hall on a gust of wind, looking like a pile of ruffled fur. His great, imported bearskin robe covered him to the eyes. It filled the chair where he tossed it, overflowing onto the floor.

"What a magnificent day to decide to go to Egypt," he said, rubbing his hands together like an avaricious merchant.

"Egypt? But that's so far," Psappha exclaimed. "If you would travel, why not Crete or Syracuse? You could use my house. Lyneachia would enjoy the company, I'm sure. What would you do in Egypt?"

"Fight, of course. They've always got a merry little war underway." He winked at Gongyla then plunked his lean frame onto a couch. Stretching his long legs beneath Atthis' limpid gaze, he crossed his ankles and clasped his hands behind his head. "Lesbos is much too tame since old Crack-toes turned into the people's pet. There's nothing like a war to shore up the ravages of boredom."

"Lesbos is far from tame today," Atthis reminded him. "If you crave excitement so badly, go tell Boreas to stop blustering and let autumn stay a little longer."

"I've already done that, my love. He laughed at me. Can't you hear him?" He absently rested his hand on her hair. "Will you miss me, Androgyne?"

Atthis' eyes darkened at the label. She glanced at Psappha and seemed pleased by her obvious confusion.

"Of course I'll miss you," Atthis said. "Your music is very dear to me."

"And your sense of the ridiculous," Gyla put in.

Psappha decided to ignore what they were not saying. Instead, she asked him, "Who will tempt laughter with you gone?"

Alkaios studied each of them in turn, his face stern at first and then he grinned. "You need my sense of something," he said. "You seem to have misplaced your own. The blindness in this room is enough to send the God of Ridicule into ecstasy."

Psappha jumped to her feet, plunked her hands on her hips and glared at him. "What do you mean I have no sense?"

"Sit down. You look like a ruffled goose. I have a better gift for you this time."

Psappha blushed and subsided, remembering the last gift he gave her. She was fifteen. Alkaios had just returned to Mytilene from one of Pharaoh's "little wars".

She remembered lying in wait for him beside the mirror pool above the orchard. When she heard his footsteps on the path, she began singing what was then her newest lyric.

Picking up her lyre, she sang it now, wanting to be sure he too remembered.

"Oh, Lady Earth, with bright-feathered birds singing in your hair, how tenderly you draw your hills of embroidered green velvet around you. Father of Ocean stretches strong arms to embrace you. Poseidon's pulsating voice joins Earth's own in passionate duet to life."

"Passionate duet," Alkaios echoed. "I like the sound of that."

"Oh, hush," Psappha admonished, blushing. She remembered laying her lyre beside her on the grass and leaning over the mirror pool. The sun had added burnished highlights to the reflection of Alkaios' silver-blond hair. His prominent chin was as bare as an Athenian's and tanned as dark as an Egyptian's.

Not like now, she thought. He's been too much indoors. His eyes, however, retained their perfect, blue-sky color; their whites as clear as milk. The golden fringe that shades them would be the envy of any woman. Even now, he wore an abbreviated tunic, belted at the waist.

She remembered averting her gaze from his leather-sheathed sword. Her nose twitched in recollection of the sharp, cinnamon smell of him, her nostrils flared as she recalled his youthful beauty. She remembered fighting the urge to spring to her feet and run to him when he said he brought a gift.

"Don't you want to know what it is?" Alkaios asked.

Startled into the present, Psappha shook her head. "No good came from the last gift you offered me," she said.

"Well, if you're not interested . . ." he drawled in the same tone he had used to lure her then.

114

Psappha

A young woman must maintain her dignity, Praxinoa's oft-repeated admonition echoed in her mind as she remembered watching him swing his arm as if to throw the gift away. In her rush to rescue it, she tripped on her hem. The memory of his gentle laughter warmed her thoughts, but at the time, it was not funny.

She remembered trembling, angry with herself beyond baring.

"What is it, child?" He had worried. "I didn't mean to frighten you."

Child is it? Psappha smiled; recalling how, in her injured adolescence, she had fumed. I'll show him who's a child, she had decided. Looking up, she reached as if to remove his helmet. Instead, she had raised herself on tiptoes and used the helmet straps to pull his head within her reach. Her curious lips met willing response and the sensations of the kiss intrigued her. She wanted to see where they led. But, as she moved toward him, Alkaios handed her a tiny cedar chest.

Confused but curious, Psappha had opened the lid to reveal a painted figurine, much like those she and Gyla later ensconced in their private shrine. Its smooth ivory had warmed in her palm, as if the ancient goddess still lived and wrestled her upthrust snakes especially for her. The seven tiers of Ophidia's gown fit perfectly between her fingers. She remembered blushing when her gaze fell on the goddess' naked breasts.

Replacing the statuette in its silky nest, she had snapped the chest shut and hurriedly returned it. "It is a bit early for fertility goddesses," she had told him. "Perhaps you should keep your gift until our wedding," she said, hoping her brisk tone covered her embarrassment.

How could I have acted like such a child? She mused. A silly, simple child, she remembered thinking. Thank Zeus the troth is already spoken, else he wouldn't have me and I'd be forever maiden.

Psappha smiled, thinking that maidenhood no longer seemed as terrible as she had thought it at the time. She remembered trudging home smudged and crumpled from her crying. Her stepfather, Alkaios' elder brother, had met her at the door. "Have you seen Alkaios?" he asked.

"Your brother is a blind, arrogant bull," she told him, wiping her nose with the back of her hand.

"Oh?" He chuckled. "So you have seen him."

"Yes," she said. "I've seen him. "The soldier's life has made him anxious to fill his bed."

She cringed, remembering his laughter. "A full bed is probably the one thing Neccho's troops didn't lack," Eurigios said. "From what I've heard, Nebuchadrezzar took more women than prisoners.

"Now go, Innocent One, and prepare to serve our guests." He swatted her tenderly and she scooted down the corridor.

That was the night she, and Kios, had taunted Pittakos until he had little choice but to exile them both. Now Kios proposed to leave of his own volition and she was not sure how she felt about it. His promise of a gift made her more nervous than curious. She could not help wondering what trouble his meddling would bring her this time.

"Will we see you again before you sail?" she asked.

"I think not," he said. "If I go overland, I can get aboard a Phoenician trireme loading bread in Eressos. That way I can sail directly to Egypt without having to stop at every port along the coast. But, I have to hurry. The trails will soon be closed."

"May Poseidon carry you safely on his back and Apollo bless you with fine weather," Psappha said, pouring a small libation to the gods.

Gongyla also poured a libation before raising her glass. "May The Lady Cybele greet you with kindness."

"Thank you, priestess." Alkaios took the flagon when Atthis would have returned it to the sideboard. "Don't look so sad, Spha. I'm leaving you a special gift and I'll send you all something from the caravans. Gongyla can carve the little trinket for Klies that we discussed. Lycos, come with me. I'll find you a good commander."

Lycos glared. Alkaios grinned. "Let me know if you change your mind," he said. "Meanwhile, if I stop at Syracuse, I'll give your love to little purple-eyes."

Lycos stalked from the room. Psappha frowned. Alkaios gave her an enigmatic smile. "You're missing all the points, aren't you, Spha? It serves you right, you know? Write me a song sometime when you get out of the clouds in your mind long enough to see your pretty nose." Turning to Atthis, he said, "May you get what you're after without causing too much damage." Atthis moved her stool over by the blazing hearth. Alkaios snickered. "Tell me, Androgyne, what can I bring you that would set your frigid little heart aflutter?"

"Bring yourself, you trickster. May Eros smile on you and Priapus be ever at your beck and call."

"And you, dear lady."

Psappha

To Psappha, he said, "On you, I am sure Eros shall grin most satisfactorily. May your lady continue to serve you unselfishly when he does."

He unwound himself from the couch, retrieved his vast robe from the chair and strode to the door. Atthis threw on a robe and followed.

"Kios. Wait," Psappha called. "Don't leave without telling me what you mean. Why should Eros grin at me? What present do you leave?"

"Ask Iphis," he said as he disappeared in a flurry of flying leaves with Atthis at his heels.

Gongyla stretched onto the couch Alkaios had vacated. Crossing her ankles and clasping her hands behind her head in the same pose Alkaios had used, she looked far more sensuous than arrogant. Her pointed breasts strained the seams of her doeskins.

The wind howled through cracks unnoticed in the summer. Psappha huddled close to the fire. Gongyla showed no sign she knew the wind existed. She uncoiled from the couch, took her bow from the wall and flexed the string. Bracing her rear against a table, she polished the bow with a length of chamois.

"He means nothing to her," she said after a time.

"How do you know?" Psappha scoffed. "She is always at his side."

"His genius draws her. She follows him as a daughter. She never knew her father, did she?"

"No." Psappha's teeth chattered.

"I thought so. She -- Psappha, you're freezing!" She whipped the cover off a couch, tossed it over Psappha's lap and reached for the wood box. "Is there no way to warm this mausoleum?" she grumbled, as she stoked the fire. "One day I will take you to my green land where you will never be cold again."

When she had the fire roaring to her satisfaction, Gongyla knelt to remove Psappha's buskins, rubbing her feet between strong, hunter's hands. Looking up, she asked, "Why don't you take her, Psappha?"

"I can't," Psappha whispered. Then, voicing a thought she had been hiding from herself, she said, "I don't know how."

"Let me take her for you," Gyla challenged.

Psappha balled her fists and pounded Gongyla's shoulders. "You stay away from her."

Gongyla chuckled and pulled her tiny adversary down onto the fur hearthrug. "You want too much, Psappha. It is time you knew the agony of Iphis. You think you want Atthis. All right. I'll teach you what you think you want to know."

She did not get the chance. Someone knocked persistently on the inner door.

"Come," Psappha called.

"No, you come," said Timas, a sparkling bubble of mischief from Phokaea. "The Lady Atthis wants you in the nursery. They're dancing a story, milady. Do come."

Minutes later, Psappha and Gongyla settled together upon a pile of cushions in the old nursery. Psappha concentrated on the dancers.

Atthis wore her hair pulled back and twisted into a coil at the base of her neck, forcing her chin to a regal height. Her pale gown matched her hair, causing Psappha to think of rich cream touched with peach blossoms.

The choreography evolved into a typical deception of the gods. Atthis danced the part of innocence. When she had been dramatically subdued, she glided over to Psappha and parodied a sweeping bow. "Did you enjoy the dance?"

"It was beautiful, Lady Atthis, as are all your dances."

"Thank you, milady. Alkaios said you would appreciate it. My dance is the gift he promised."

"Tell us the story," Klies said, having come in late.

Atthis turned to her like a gentle goddess granting special favors. Though she spoke to Klies, her gaze remained on Psappha as if to decipher her reactions.

"It is the story of a cruel and vicious man," she said. "A man who forced his wife to vow that, if the child she carried was born female, it would be given to Death. The . . . "

Oh, Alkaios, Psappha groaned within her mind. Dear, demented demon, with what parting gift of furies have you presented me?

~~~~~

"What am I going to do?" Psappha asked one evening as she and Gyla sipped after dinner wine. A gusty draft threatened their candles. Gongyla shuttered the windows while Psappha guarded the flickering light.

"Go to her," Gongyla said, returning to the hearth.

"I can't." Psappha slumped onto the edge of her chair, elbows on her knees, her face hidden by her hands.

Psappha

"Go to her or send her away."

Psappha's head jolted up. "What are you saying? I can't send her away. I'd rather let Helios die in the sky."

"Then go to her, or I will. I won't stand by and watch you burn for her any longer. Go to her or let me go to her or find me a ship to Africa. I've had enough of holy rivals."

Psappha's eyes brimmed with panic. Send Atthis away? Lose Gongyla? No! "All right," she said, "since you insist, I'll go to her tonight."

"I thought you wanted me to teach you what to do," Gongyla teased.

"It's too late for that now," Psappha told her, snatching up a lamp and starting for the door before she had time to change her mind. As the light passed Gongyla's face, the war of emotion she saw in the tender warrior's eyes seemed but a small echo of her own.

"Sometimes the disease is the only cure," Gongyla whispered.

Psappha did not pause to consider what she meant. Fear and desire burned her soul. All the years she had yearned to teach Atthis the wonders of Iphis blended into a tapestry of emotion that threatened to strangle her.

The wind in the corridor heckled her as she walked. It darted around her reluctant feet, lapped at the shutters, and threw raindrops against the side of the house. Psappha's lamp cast a tiny circle on the tiles as her buskins whispered across them. She had often used this corridor to reach the kitchen but tonight it seemed to stretch with each forward step.

Her knock on Atthis' door resounded in the taunting silence. It went unanswered. Psappha knocked again, louder, her fist tight, her nails grinding into her palm.

"Enter."

Psappha's fingers trembled on the latch.

"Enter," the call came again.

The hinges creaked when she opened the door.

"Come. Share my fire." Atthis huddled beneath silk coverlets, the light dimmer than her smile, the fire cooler than her voice.

Psappha's spinning soul refused direction. The room reeled with the madness of a youthful spring. Her knees felt weak. Her body limp with tension and desire. Numbly, she dragged a chaise to the hearth, placing it opposite the one upon which Atthis was enthroned.

"Will you share wine with me, Psappha?"

I'll share my life, Psappha thought, but all she managed was a timid smile. Atthis nodded then rang the tiny serving bell at her elbow.

Gongyla did not knock. She marched in with the serving table balanced on one hand like a tray with legs. The anger in Atthis' eyes startled Psappha. What am I doing here? She wondered. Gyla, my love, she wanted to say. I don't want this any more. But, Gongyla did not look at her.

"Please join us," Psappha invited. "I'll have my wine unwatered. Atthis?"

Atthis shook her head, but she accepted a brimming goblet.

Gongyla flashed her a sardonic grin as, with one hand, she lifted an Egyptian chair and swung it into position between them, setting the small table beside it with her other hand. Seated, her back to the fire, she smiled as Psappha sipped her wine.

The wine had an odd, acrid taste but the warm echo of Gyla's fingers on the glass abated caution and Psappha drank deeply, mystified by the way the softness left Gongyla's face when she turned toward Atthis.

A mask of dignity covered Gyla's face. "The choreography for the story of Iphis and Ianthe must have been very difficult for you, Lady Atthis. The tale is a familiar one in my country."

"I thought it might be," Atthis said.

"I assume it is also well known to you?"

"The dance of Iphis has been part of my repertoire for many years," Atthis said.

Gongyla's cool laugh was as nothing Psappha had ever heard.

"By Thalia, Gongyla. Why are you acting so weird?"

"Ask Iphis," Gyla said, upending her goblet before placing it beside the others on the table. Filling two of them, she handed a brimming portion to Psappha, the other to Atthis. Then she rose and melted into the darkness beyond the firelight. Mocking laughter trailed behind her as the door creaked and slammed.

Psappha sat for several minutes, sipping bitter wine. "How much do you know of Iphis?" she asked at last.

Atthis reached for the flagon, refilling her cup, and Psappha's. "I know the temple well," she crooned.

Her satiny tone shot through Psappha like molten metal, making her struggle for breath. Her gaze fell on the throbbing pulse-beat visible on Atthis' throat and she sighed with longing.

Psappha

Atthis brushed her coverlets aside and stood, nude except for a span of saffron cloth twined and tied around her loins.

Oh, Sweet Aphrodite, Psappha prayed. My soul is in danger. Not even on Olympus is there a fitting match for that which stands before me now.

Atthis began to sway, as if listening to some hidden music. Firelight flickered on her body. Psappha could see the rise and fall of pale breasts in its glow, creamy mounds half-hidden by silver-gold hair.

Heaven poses on ivory toes, she silently composed. Oh, what insipid songs I've sung to beauty without imagining such quality as that which sways before me now. To call up every word I've ever heard would only prove how pitifully impoverished language is. For the glory that is Atthis, a new word must be found.

The unheard music increased in tempo. Atthis depicted a flower unfolding, a leaf tossed in the wind, a snake giving homage to the sky then searching garden paths as she slithered ever closer to Psappha's tingling toes.

Psappha's mind conjured remembrances of a childhood garden. She welcomed innocence, pure and beautiful. She reached out her hand, desire driving her beyond caution, wine coursing through distended veins.

Atthis slithered between Psappha's lax knees, proficiently exploring with her flicking viper tongue.

No! Psappha thought. It's not supposed to happen like this!

Atthis' undulated expertly, her tongue commanding, demanding, foraging; manipulating.

No! Wait! Psappha's spirit protested. I must be Iphis in this, she vowed. I've waited for it far too long. Oh, Aphrodite, you deceptive porna. Have you been mocking me? Have I wasted years in aching dreams of innocence, while you laughed at my thwarted desire?

"Relax," Atthis insisted, claiming her with unprecedented skill, but without Gyla's exquisite tenderness.

This woman is not my Atthis, Psappha decided. This woman is cruel. Her touch is painful. Stop! This is not love.

But, it was past too late. Her traitorous body responded to Atthis' experience. Reluctantly, Psappha gave herself over to the demands of postponed desire, consummate skill and the hypnotic spell of herbed wine.

~~~~~

The rasp of raised voices drew Psappha from inebriated dreams. She awoke thinking Zeus and Ares competed for her brain. Her tongue tasted copper-plated. She lay on hard carpet instead of in her usual cocoon of covers.

"You drugged the wine!" someone accused.

No wonder gods are raging in my head, Psappha thought as she dragged her aching body toward the door.

"You heathen bitch," she heard Atthis shriek, "if you did not want me to have her, why did you send her to me?"

"She wanted you." Gyla's voice was soothing even through the oak.

"I need no drugs," Atthis said. "My skills are great when I choose to use them."

"Exactly." Gyla chuckled. "She thought of you as an innocent girl. How long did it take you to cure her of that false notion?"

"Not long," Atthis bragged.

Indeed, Psappha thought, remembering. My world is full of traitors. Kios knew! Androgyne he called her. Man-woman indeed! They set me up. Was I deaf as well as blind? I should have --

The latch clicked and she backed behind a column, pushing memory aside.

"You drugged the wine," she said when Gyla stepped into the room with Atthis at her heels.

Gyla nodded. "I wanted you to learn the truth. I was afraid you would back away from it again."

"I told you I didn't want to go. You should have trusted me. You had no right to mishandle my emotions so. Never mind." She held up a restraining hand when Atthis tried to interrupt. "No harm was done. The night was everything I ever dreamed it could be. It was perfect."

Shame piled on disappointment made each lie come easier. "Next time will be even better," she said.

Atthis smiled sweetly. Gongyla frowned.

"Next time, I'll drink none of your concoctions," Psappha told her. "Because of you, I've forgotten all that happened after the dancing. But, I know it was wonderful, and next time will be the same," she added spitefully. There will be no next time, she promised herself.

"Why did you feel drugs were necessary, Gyla?"

"It was a mistake."

Psappha recoiled from the tender touch upon her arm.

Psappha

"Don't turn from me because I love you," Gyla said as Psappha started for the door. "Stay close, my love, that I may shelter you with my life."

Contrite, but unable to apologize, Psappha cringed.

Atthis let her kiton slip from her shoulder and Psappha recoiled from her gut response to the sight of creamy breast. Desire and sorrow battled in her mind. Unable to decide between the two, she sheltered her soul with anger.

"Get out of my way, you deceitful whelp of a jungle cur!"

~~ 12 ~~

Psappha went about her daily routine, in spite of her aching head. When she found Gyla's bow and quiver missing, she ordered supper in their quarters, as usual; assuming Gyla had gone hunting and would return at dark.

But, Gongyla did not come. Praxinoa took the untouched plates away sometime after midnight. Sometime later, the lamp in the window flickered and its flame went out. Sunshine slipped between the drapes. Psappha looked up from her tablet, surprised to see that it was no longer dark. Walking stiffly to the window, she saw the usual group of maidens on the practice range and she smiled. When she realized Gongyla was not with them, she ran through the house, searching wildly from room to room. Eventually, she pounded on Atthis' bedroom door, shouting, "Where is she?" Hearing voices inside, she knocked again.

"Hold on, for Ares' sake. I'm coming."

The door opened slightly and a disheveled maiden peered through the crack. Psappha thrust the door wide and pushed through. Atthis lay amid disarrayed covers. Psappha glanced at her, then the maiden and thought she should feel something, but she did not.

"Where is she?" was the only thing on her mind.

"She's gone," Atthis said with obvious pleasure. "Go away and let us sleep."

"Where did she go?"

"To Africa, I suppose. Now, please, Psappha, if you love me, go away. We'll talk tomorrow," Atthis said, and bid the maiden close the door.

Psappha raced through the corridors and out of the house. She scrambled down the path and stumbled past The Lady's park with no thought for the broken pebbles beneath her silken slippers. The narrow streets of New Mytilene were dark and empty. The docks deserted. She saw an Egyptian dragon ship glide into the dawn beyond the harbor and she gasped with pain.

"Oh, Lady, what have I done? She loved me. Why couldn't I let that be enough? Instead, I let Atthis shake my mind like the

124

Psappha

down-rushing wind that falls upon the oaks. Eros, limb loosener, weaver of fictions, bringer of pain, I thought you the most beloved offspring of Earth and Heaven and now your snare has cost me my champion."

Psappha left the docks in a daze of self-pity. She staggered through The Lady's olive grove and limped onto the north beach. Sand crabs scurried to avoid her ruined slippers. Gulls dipped and scolded, arguing over escapees from a sailor's net.

She ignored the young fisherman who stared at her as she shuffled through sand, and tripped over rocks, disregarding the seaweed that entangled her ankles like Ophidia's snakes. The breeze off the water tugged at her braids, pulling strands loose to flutter in her tears.

How futile, how sterile the kiss of the wind, she thought, brushing hair from her eyes. A ragged goat trace led her to the top of the bluff. The edge of the precipice beckoned. She stood there; contemplating Poseidon's frothy pounding on its base, impervious to the spray that soaked her dress.

"Oh, Aphrodite, why have you chastised me so?" she whimpered. "Have I offended some other by my devotion to your golden beauty? Has dark Artemis grown jealous of my faith and chosen to punish me? Will The Lady Cybele desert me now that my unbridled tongue has wronged her servant?

"Aphrodite, you foam-born slut, you blinded my eyes. Gyla was my strength, my life! Why didn't I know that? Now she's left me and it's all my fault!"

Shame and guilt drained her spirit. Aching for oblivion, she stepped closer to the edge.

Strong arms snatched her from Poseidon's siren call.

Gyla, Psappha thought. But no, the scent of fish and hawser grease denied her hope. A sunlight halo obscured her rescuer's face. She felt his heavy muscles ripple as he deposited her in the cool of an overhanging rock.

"Are you all right?"

"I'm fine," she said. To prove it, she rolled onto her side and tried to stand. Her legs refused.

"Here, let me help you."

His voice was rough, as if dried by a lifetime on windy seas. He carried her easily, as Gyla always had, and set her down in a nearby cleft, beside a glowing fire. His smile seemed harmless as he wrapped her in heated fleece.

The firelight accented his old-gold hair. It framed a face as beautiful as any Psappha had ever seen on a man, in spite of the narrow scar that bisected the left side from brow to chin. He had rower's shoulders, like Kerkolos, and the long sinewy legs of a long distance runner.

Behind him, salt-scoured rocks absorbed heat from the rekindled fire and transferred it to Psappha's chilled bones, reminding her of her spray-soaked kiton.

Clutching the lambskin tightly around her, Psappha edged nearer the crackling fire. Her celebrated voice quivered as she asked, "Who are you?"

"Phaeon," he answered simply. The pink line through his brow lent a slight demonic aspect to his face. She wished she could borrow his self-confidence as easily.

The fire seemed suddenly too warm. Psappha scooted back. The lambskin slid beneath her. Phaeon's stare reminded her how sheer her kiton was when wet. The thought made her shiver. She wanted to hide in his masculinity, to let him drive away the shame and wretchedness the women in her life had caused her.

As if sensing her need, he came to her. She watched her hands disappear in his, like ships swallowed by a hungry storm. He urged her to her feet. Standing close, she ran intrepid fingers over his smooth chest and upward to trace the faint laugh-lines beside his mouth, much as she had once examined Alkaios' frown.

Flushed and desperate to bury pain, Psappha let him lower her to the warm sand floor. Phaeon tossed his loincloth aside and her heart fluttered like that of a trapped bird, afraid to stay, yet more afraid to flee. Her kiton whispered as he whisked it away. Her tongue flicked over parched lips. She sucked in his scent as if to absorb his power, but absorption was not enough. Her sagging spirit demanded his submission.

Summoning strength she did not know she had, Psappha shoved Phaeon onto his back. He folded his hands behind his head and grinned up at her. Psappha mounted him disappointed that there would be no protest against her assumption of control. Angry with herself, at him, at Gyla, Atthis and the world, she rode him with the zeal of a battle-hardened mercenary.

For three days, they lived on fish, and wine and the wonder of Eros gone mad. Phaeon's enthusiasm for her put both Alkaios and

Psappha

Kerkolos to shame, but could not rival Iphis in its splendor. The ache remained too deep for tenderness to touch.

Soft rain drew a shimmering curtain over the mouth of the cave. Psappha stretched languidly and rolled toward the fire where Phaeon was busily preparing their breakfast in a flat clay pot that nestled among the flames. Gazing sleepily at his profile, Psappha could not help thinking of Adonis.

Sitting up, she brushed sand from her breasts. "Will it rain all day?" she asked. Her voice seemed to hang in the silence like the smoke rising from the cookery.

"Does it matter?" The scent of savory sauce wafted by her nose as Phaeon stirred the fish.

"Not really, I suppose, but I must see to my home eventually. There are some there who will be worried." She frowned as she envisioned those she thought would not. Her frown deepened when Phaeon turned concerned eyes toward her. "No, no, beloved, do not look at me so. I will not stay long. The school can run quite well without me."

"School?"

"You don't know who I am?"

"You are Selene, The Lady Moon, come down from the sky for a taste of mortal bitchery," he said.

"Ah, yes." She chuckled. "You know who I am. But, I am also Psappha, The Poetess, and, for a little time, I must be about my business."

Phaeon pulled away as if in fear.

"But -- but -- "

"But – but -- " Psappha mimicked, tousling his hair. "Are you a goat that you butt me so?"

"But, The Poetess is not for the likes of me," he reasoned, donning the loincloth that had lain unneeded for several days.

Psappha yanked it off him. "What is this? Nothing is changed. We are as we are. I must go for a time, but I will return." Touched by his sadness, she encircled his thick neck with her arms and twisted her fingers firmly into his hair.

Phaeon loosened her hands with his and tossed her onto the sand, impaling her without warning. Later, she explained why she had gone to the bluff.

"That's no reason to tempt The Fates to take your life," he said.

127

How could she explain that much of value in her was already dead?

~~~~~~

"You haven't slept," Praxinoa accused when Psappha reached to the house. "This must stop. You have neglected the students for days. They deserve better. Come. Sit. I'll prepare a bath for you. When you've finished it and a light repast, you will go and teach your pupils as is your duty."

Psappha felt too drained to argue. The climb up from the beach had turned back the hourglass. Somewhere between The Lady's park and home, she had come to realize that her time with Phaeon had heightened, rather than assuaged her guilt. Shame crippled her tongue.

Wordlessly, she let Praxinoa take charge of her as if she were a babe in swaddling. The steamy, scented water combined with the old nursemaid's skillful hands eased a season's worth of tension from her body but could not reach the tender edges of her soul.

When the bath was finished and Praxinoa went to fetch a bit of supper, Psappha picked up stylus and tablet and cut bitterness into the wax.

"Oh, sweet Melpomymnia, gentle-hearted muse of sorrow, why can't I cry? Where are your tears now, dear muse? I drove her away. What malignant gall remains of the horror I bestowed upon her leaving. My soul retches, but my eyes refuse to spew it forth."

On and on she wrote, pouring heartache into the lyrics, emptying herself until all emotion was gone. Three tablets lay hidden among other secrets by the time Praxinoa returned.

Although the food cook sent was good, Psappha merely pushed it around her plate. Finally, Praxinoa gave up in exasperation. Her scowl was deep as she took her charge's hand and led her to the garden where delighted pupils immediately surrounded her.

The student's happy chatter reminded Psappha of all she tried to throw away. She could no longer permit herself to ignore them. Taking up her lyre, she began to sing -- old songs, written long ago. The new ones were not for publication.

She had safely locked away the baring of her soul.

~~~~~~

The loneliness of the crowded house was near unbearable. Retreating from constant reminders of absent love, and unwilling to use Phaeon as a handy substitute, Psappha took her students to Lesbian Olympus where she whiled away the daylight hours beneath a huge pine

Psappha

with all of Lesbos at her feet. The air stayed clear as crystal most days. If she stayed quiet long enough, the deer came close, reminding her of how much Gyla had loved the mountain.

Psappha's evenings were filled with fragrant flowers and serenading nightingales that only added to her pain.

"Come back to me, Gongyla, here tonight," she sang to the bright full moon. "You, my rose, with your Lydian lyre. Delight hovers forever around you: A beauty desired.

"Even your garment plunders my eyes. I am enchanted: I who once complained to the Cyprus-born goddess, whom I now beseech, never to let this lose my grace, but rather bring you back to me: Amongst all mortal women the one I most desire to see."

Snuggling beneath her comforters, hiding her eyes from The Lady Moon's bright light, Psappha's thoughts harked back to bygone years. She recalled her loneliness while foolishly avoiding the gynakeon and she remembered finding solace in her hands. But, she resented having to use them now.

Instead, she lavished attention on Atthis, drowning pain in artificial passion. Embittered but sated, Psappha sometimes managed to fall into a fitful sleep.

One morning, in their third week on the mountain, someone snatched her covers and she opened her eyes to brilliant sunlight.

"Psappha, I swear I shall stop loving you," Atthis scolded. "Get up for our sake. Unleash your beloved strength from the bed." She teased Psappha's nose with her hair. "Do get up, Psappha, and bathe. I'll have Klies bring your saffron blouse and purple dress. Come, beloved, and stand like a spotless lily beside the pool, sweet with the beauty with which you drive me mad."

Psappha rolled grudgingly out of bed. As she stepped into her bath she heard Atthis call gaily from her door.

"Praxinoa, roast some chestnuts so I can make the girls a proper breakfast. The Gods have granted us a favor. This very day, Psappha, the most marvelous of women, has promised to go back with us to Mytilene, the loveliest of cities."

Psappha did not have the heart to disagree.

They returned to find that another school had opened in their absence, drawing many of their students with its newness.

"Why do you wish to leave us?" Psappha asked when bubbly Timas said she was transferring. "This woman you would follow is a peasant without breeding enough to hide her feet." The instant she spoke, she regretted her tone.

Timas' eyes brimmed with tears. "I do not wish to leave, miladies, but it is the fashion. My father insists. Andromeda has won fame of sorts since Lady Gorgo became her assistant, adding aristocratic sanction.

"Lady Gorgo has a fine family heritage. Not so exalted as yours, milady, but important in my father's business. Please give me your blessings. I do not want to go."

Psappha placed her hands on Timas' young shoulders. "My blessings, Timas. Return to us when you can."

"Oh, I will, milady. My father thinks you old fashioned, but I will change his mind over the winter. Next season I will return to you or I will go no more to school."

Timas was only the first whose parent or guardian blindly followed fashion. There would be many more. Each season brought fewer pupils.

Psappha buried her loneliness in her work. Bits and pieces of her being flowed from her stylus like blood from her wounded pride. As was her habit, she recited verses to herself each evening as she cut memories into the wax.

"When I looked at you, it seemed to me that Hermione was never such as Atthis is. Only Helen could I liken unto you, never an ordinary girl."

The stylus broke in her hand. As she searched for another, she glanced over her shoulder to assure herself that she had bolted the chamber doors, then, picking up a fresh stylus, she whispered as she wrote, "Love, that creature fatal, bittersweet. I should not have dared to touch heaven with my two arms. I should have known the gods could not allow a mortal to share such joy for long."

Each morning, she locked her night's verses into their Cretan box and hid the key. Behind her eyes, she saw a fondly remembered vision of Klies, before she was old enough for braids.

Klies had tried on all her mother's jewels then burst into tears when the bottom of the box popped open. She thought she broke it. Psappha smiled. She remembered comforting the child by letting her pick up the little key and fit it back into its snug compartment.

~~~~~

"I begin to grow tired of Gorgo," Psappha told Atthis one day when they were alone.

Psappha

"Fashions change, Psappha."

"I know they do, Atthis. But so quickly? And to turn so far against us? How can you think Andromeda and Gorgo's kennel, which they call a school, superior to our teaching the virtues of grace and discretion? How can fidelity pass out of style? Perhaps if I chased the young women around the gardens, like the lascivious Gorgo, we could be fashionable again."

"Thou simpleton," Atthis scoffed. "You underestimate yourself. You would have to do little chasing. Now that Iphis has become supreme on Lesbos, our girls make it obvious that they adore you. They would happily compete for your favor, as they compete for mine. But, don't you so much as wink at one of them or your voice of angels will ring from a battered face."

"Should I sit idly by while our best pupils desert us for the promiscuous Andromeda? Wouldn't it be simpler to seduce a few of our prettiest girls to keep them all hoping?"

Psappha ducked from the room just in time to avoid a flying flowerpot.

~~~~~

It was not long before Pittakos ordered Atthis to the new, more stylish establishment. Atthis did not seem to mind.

"I'm a ward of the city," she said. "I must go. Pittakos insists."

"Oh, damn Pittakos! Must he forever be a stone under my foot? You will not go. I won't let you."

"As a ward of the Tyrant, I am subject to his will."

"We don't need his patronage, Atthis. Let me take care of you. Tell Pittakos to release you from your wardship. He can't force you to do his bidding then. We've lost many of our pupils, but not all of them. We have enough and more -- without the city's bounty. I'll accept more writing commissions."

"No, Psappha, you hate confining your muse to other people's ideas."

"I can do it," Psappha insisted. "Tell Pittakos you won't go. Why should you go to Andromeda? She couldn't dance if Eros himself did the piping."

"Psappha," Atthis argued, "I must remain a ward of the city until I marry. To do otherwise would bring disgrace. Iphis may rule fashion, but men rule politics, and marriage is the essence of politics. Why must you be so irrational about this? I'll be in the city. You'll be able to see me. Many of our girls are studying with Gorgo. I'll be able to look after them."

"And what will you teach them, when I am not near to warm your bed?"

"Psappha, I swear it is against my will that I leave you," Atthis said, sounding as sincere as a Phoenician merchant.

"You want to go, you deceitful witch. Have you forgotten what we've had? Will someone else now bedeck your hair, as I did, with wreaths of roses and violets? Will Gorgo drape your lovely neck with garlands of a hundred flowers? Will you lie in Andromeda's arms, and perfume your body with royal perfumes? I gave you all that a fastidious Ionian might desire, and yet you choose to leave me."

Psappha's throat was raw with unshed tears. She had loved the image of Atthis so long it hurt to let go. Each sentence she spoke came out softer than the one before it. "There is no hill, no sacred grove, no stream we haven't visited together. Will you think of me when you go there with her? Never has spring filled any wood with the chorus of nightingales as when we wandered there together. How will you now stand hearing the nightingale's song?"

"Do you want to waste all that we are, Psappha?" Atthis stepped toward her. "I do not want to leave you, but I must," she claimed.

Psappha chose not to believe her. "You want to go," she said.

Atthis sighed. "All right -- All right -- child! I want to go."

"Then go, you bitch! Go to the cow that dares to call herself a woman! Go, and be quick, you faithless sow! You sluttish she-goat! Go! Go, I say, you shameless porna! Go, and return no more to me!"

Psappha regretted her outburst the instant Atthis slammed the door behind her. "Oh, Atthis," she whispered as she watched her cross the garden. "Once, I rendered your beauty the sacrifice of all my thoughts. I worshiped you with all my senses. Now, you've come to hate the thought of Psappha and run off to Andromeda instead."

~~~~~

Psappha got through the remainder of the summer by rote. When the last student left for the winter, she retreated into herself. Tiny bird's feet by her eyes dug trenches with their claws. Her hair faded with her appetite. Poseidon's deep kingdom seemed a bed of rapture compared to the despair of love denied.

Psappha

From a pallet in the orchard, she counted the leaves as they fell from the trees. A squirrel scolded her, and then skittered away. Ants worked at an apple core beside her foot.

The thread of her life grew thin. The clouds seemed to hover over her loneliness like lurking vultures. Her muse deserted her, making her feel like an upended flask of wine, its contents spilled and wasted to the dregs.

I'll go to her, she decided. As soon as I can, I'll go to her. Sacrificing happiness to salvage pride is too high price to pay.

But she had waited too long. Her frail body rebelled against her neglect. She lost strength with each passing day. Autumn chill and false summer heat brought fever. She could not rise from her couch. Eleven Olympiads had come and gone since first she walked on toddling toes through the halls of her father's house. Now, she was too sick to walk, too tired to care. Light faded to one infinitesimal spark of imagined bliss.

Psappha clung to that tenacious thread. Who calls me? Poseidon, my father, I'm too far from the sea. She heard her name through agonies of ice and fire.

Who calls? She fought against the fog. I don't dare cheat Poseidon, she thought. My life is his to take. I cannot lie here like some base-born drudge and die. He would make me wander forever between never and naught. His kingdom is mine by right. I must hang on until he claims me for his own.

She imagined herself plunging into a cold and clammy sea. She shivered, falling deeper into Poseidon's dark domain, then floating upward toward Helios, burning from the nearness of his light.

In her madness, Psappha saw Gyla standing over her, her smile as rewarding as the moon when it appears after a raging storm. She reached for her dark hand and clutched it to her breast. She felt Gyla's free hand on her forehead and she fell, at last, into a deep and dreamless sleep.

The curtain of delirium parted inch by agonizing inch. Psappha heard her name as if through fog. With what strength remained, she willed her eyes to open. The world wore a hazy shroud. She felt a cool damp cloth against her parched skin and looked up brightly, expecting to see Gyla's lovely eyes.

~~ 13 ~~

Praxinoa leaned over her, studying her with worried eyes as soft as the underside of a newly hatched duck. Psappha wished that she had died. But she grew stronger, in spite of herself, as much from Praxinoa's cooking as from any will of her own.

From thin barley gruel to thick rabbit stew, Psappha could have calendarized her recovery by the dishes with which the old nurse tempted her appetite. She was devouring an offering of thick mutton swimming in garlic sauce when Lycos peeked in.

"Well, little sister," he chirped. "You seem to have found a respectable appetite at last." Pulling up a lady's chair, he waited impatiently for her to finish her supper. "Your brother is in Egypt," he said the instant the last bite disappeared.

"What is Charaxos doing in Egypt? And, how do you know where he is when I did not?"

Lycos grinned. "The first ship of the season brought a letter from Alkaios."

"How is he?" she asked, as if she could not tell from the look on his face.

"He's fine. He's helped a score of maidens pay their dues to the Goddess, and he is looking forward to the summer campaign against the Persians. He says the Temple of the Goddess in Naucratis is busier than the one in Athens, so he spent the winter there. That's where he found Charaxos."

"In the Temple of the Goddess?"

"No. Charaxos is a merchant, but it isn't trade that keeps him in Naucratis."

"If not trade or the girls sacrificing their maidenheads in the temple gardens, then what?"

"A rose."

"There are roses in Mytilene."

"Ah, yes," he agreed, his eyes full of mischief. "But no roses to equal the Rose of Naucratis. She shines above them all."

"So," she mused aloud, "a lady entices my wandering brother."

Psappha

"Not a lady, Psappha. A woman."

"Charaxos consorts with pornas?"

"Not a porna, Psappha. The Rose of Naucratis is too renowned a courtesan to be classed as a porna."

"A high class porna then," she sniffed. "My meandering brother will find himself well plucked from the ministrations of such a one. Our father's pride must have bypassed him."

"Oh, he's proud enough," Lycos asserted. "Alkaios wrote that he struts about Naucratis, and well he might. The Rose is desired by kings."

"Don't talk like a cupbearer. Being desired is no claim to station. A porna is a porna no matter reputation or gender." She smiled when he affected a properly chastised demeanor.

"Alkaios did say Charaxos is often short of pocket."

"The cost of trinkets runs high."

"How about your trinket, Adelphi? Has she not cost you dearly enough?"

"She has cost me nothing. I'm alone because of my own foolishness."

"You could still have her," he said.

Psappha shrugged. "It's not the same," she mumbled. "I never loved her. Not the way I love Gongyla, but that no longer matters."

"She'll come back."

"I don't want her!"

"I meant Gongyla," he said with more patience than she felt she deserved.

"You don't know the terrible things I said to her."

"I know what you said to her, and why. She told me. She understood. Anyway, that was long ago. Send for her, or better still, go to her. She loves you."

"If she loves me, where was she when I was so ill?"

"She came. Praxinoa sent her away. You were unconscious," he added quickly when he saw the anger in her eyes. "What good would it have done? You might have been contagious."

Psappha paled from a vision of Gongyla's beautiful face ravaged by disease. Tears that had been hovering at the corners of her eyes slipped free. The taste of regurgitated mutton filled her mouth.

Lycos jumped for a basin and thrust it into her lap. "You are not as well as you pretend," he scolded when the spasms stopped.

"I'm fine," Psappha insisted. "Though I may perish and be damned forever for love of an African queen."

"Send for her."

"No. She will never forgive me."

"She already has. What you need to do is find the courage to forgive yourself."

"My courage shrinks with the years, old friend."

"The years are not so many."

"Dear, sweet Little Fox. Perhaps I should not trust you with my accounts. I'll soon mark the forty-fifth anniversary of my birth."

"Aphrodite must love you dearly, Adelphi. The years have left no mark."

"Not where it shows," she patted his hand. "Not where it shows."

~~~~~

"Psappha! Where is your mind?" Lycos said, when she burst into his office and announced that they were leaving for Africa at once. "We must go over these notes," he said. "You have to approve the expenditures."

"They're approved," she said. "Just tell me if we have enough in the coffers for a trip to Naucratis." She sniffed at his incredulous expression. "Don't you want to see Kios, Little Fox?"

"Of course I want to see Alkaios, but -- "

"Can we afford it?"

"Of course, but what about the students? Much as I'd like to see Alkaios, we can't close the school. The season is just beginning."

"The school will be fine. Klies is here. She can look after things."

"That's another thing," he said. "Don't you want to visit with your daughter?"

"No," Psappha shook her head. "Klies has changed. I don't know her any more. She's become avaricious and seems to have lost her understanding of the language, at least as far as her own mother is concerned. She won't miss me as long as she can play mistress of the gynakeon. I've decided to go to Naucratis. Someone needs to talk to Charaxos and remind him of who he is."

"I'll make the arrangements," Lycos said, looking happier than he had in months.

Psappha

Klies made an excellent teacher. She led the maidens in the intricate patterns she had learned from Atthis, inventing new ones as she danced, enjoying her power and elevated status.

"Ho, Psappha," Lycos called from the gatehouse a few days later. "We have passage on the new moon tide. Will you be ready by then?"

Before she could answer him, Klies appeared at her elbow.

"You're going away?"

"Lycos and I are going to Egypt. You'll be in charge here while I'm gone."

Psappha waved to Lycos, nodded emphatically in response to his querying gestures, and continued toward the orchard, an echo of Klies' pleased smile on her face.

~~~~~

Psappha's trunks were packed. A small pile of items that would not fit into the sea chests lay on her bed. The chest that held her commissioned writings was too large and too full. Behind it was the small, Cretan box in which she had locked her private odes to Atthis and Gongyla.

Going to her dressing table, Psappha picked up her teak jewel box. Turning it over, she flicked the hidden catch with her thumb and lifted the tiny key from its secret place. Just as she reached for the Cretan box, Lycos burst into the room unannounced, waving a scroll, a dozen or so others tucked beneath his elbow.

"This is the best piece you've ever published," he declared. "These, too, are good," he added, tossing a pile of scrolls onto her writing table. "Why weren't they given to me for release like all your others?"

"What are you going on about? You know I authorize no publication except through you." Psappha snatched the scroll and began to read. "Peer of the gods he appears to me -- " The scribe's words swam before her eyes. "Where did you get this?"

"In the marketplace, of course. I bought a copy of every one. I think that one is the best, but you should have trusted them to me."

"I trusted them to no one," Psappha said with anger bubbling in her veins. All thought of Africa vanished from her mind. The verses were hers, her passion and her shame, intended for no eyes save her own. Slowly opening her hand, she stared at the imprint left by the tightly clutched key. Her fingers fumbled as she put it in the lock. The engraved box was empty! The precious private odes were gone. "How could she do this to me?"

"Who?"

Psappha's mind fought the evidence. She wouldn't hurt me intentionally. For mere gold? She couldn't. There must be someone else. Gyla. Gyla knew where I kept the key. "Gongyla sold my soul," she said.

"You must be mistaken," Lycos protested. "Think, Psappha. Who else knew about the key? Gyla would never do anything against your wishes. Certainly nothing that could hurt you. Although these are more likely to enhance your reputation than harm it. These are good. Your best, Adelphi. They will add great esteem to your name."

Psappha had passed disappointment, disillusion and heartbreak and was building rage against the one person she knew would never hurt her. "She was jealous of Atthis."

"Gyla was never jealous of Atthis and you know it."

"She was," Psappha insisted. "That's why she stole the odes and exposed my naked soul before the world."

"Be reasonable, Psappha. If Gongyla was jealous, why did she send you in to Atthis in the first place? Why would she wait until after both she and Atthis were gone to get revenge? Look at this verse, Adelphi. This one says, 'Come back to me, Gongyla.' How could Gongyla steal a verse that was not written until after she left?"

Psappha refused to listen. Doing so would require acceptance of a harsher truth. A truth her mothers' heart could not confront. "It was Gongyla."

"There must be someone else," Lycos persisted. When she refused to look at him, he said, "The copiers know whom they bought them from. I'll go ask them."

"No! Don't ask! I know who it was."

"But --?"

"No."

Lycos dropped his hands.

"Where are you going?"

"Out!"

Out was all she knew. The house no longer felt safe. Tear blinded, she did not see Klies until she bumped into her, nearly knocking her down. Psappha flashed her daughter an automatic smile, then bolted through the portal and raced across the garden to the downhill

Psappha

path beyond with the sparkle of Klies' laughter ringing behind her like a demon's taunt.

~~~~~

"Why are you grinning like a thieving cat?" Psappha snarled at Phaeon, her fury more threatening than the approaching storm. "Haven't I just told you that my soul is exposed to the jests of the mob?"

"But, Psappha," he said. "You've been published before."

"I didn't want these published, you buffoon. They are odes to my own foolishness. Can't you understand how that would shame me?"

"I understand that they are making someone rich. What you need to do is see how many more you can write. And, make sure you're the one to collect next time," he added with a friendly smack on her bottom as if to hurry her on her way. "Who did this to you?"

"I don't want to think about that now," she said. "Right now I . . ." Snatching his loincloth, she took off down the beach, waving it above her head like an elongated banner. She raced along the waterline. Her feet forgot their years as she ran from memories, from emptiness, from truth.

Phaeon caught her by the cleft of the bluff and carried her deep inside. Lightning bolts and pounding surf were as nothing compared to the throbbing frenzy of their mating. But, the storm without could not outlive the storm within. Psappha awoke with her rage intact.

It was late afternoon when she reached the top of the path and hurried home to the sounds of a scuffle. Lycos thrust Klies through the doorway before Psappha reached it.

"What is the meaning of this?" she demanded. "Lycos, you overstep yourself. Take your hands off my daughter."

Instead of releasing her, Lycos grabbed Klies by her shoulders and thrust her toward Psappha. "Tell her!"

Not wanting to hear what she already knew, Psappha took her daughter into her arms and stroked her golden hair.

"Tell her," Lycos grated between clenched teeth.

Klies sobbed against her mother's breast.

Lycos ripped her from Psappha's embrace and said, "Stop your make-believe blubbering, you thankless whelp. Tell your mother what you've done!"

"Let go of her!" Psappha shrieked, pummeling him with her fists. "Stand back, damn you!"

Lycos let go of Klies and positioned himself between Klies and the door. "She sold your scrolls, Adelphi."

Psappha cringed from the look in his eyes when he saw that the information came as no surprise. He made no effort to hide his disgust. Unable to bear his disapproval, Psappha turned belated scrutiny upon her daughter.

"Why, Klies?"

"Why not?" Klies shrugged. "Why should you lose students to Andromeda because people think you old fashioned? Those lyrics prove you are a greater priestess of Iphis than she, or Gorgo could ever be. Lycos is turning away new and returning applicants already. Ask him. You are more famous now than ever. Pittakos will have to let Atthis return.

"And, the gold from the sale of the odes will buy Daphnos a ship of his own. Your daughter will wear purple again. Your coffers will not hold your gold, nor mine."

"What did Daphnos say about your theft?"

"Nothing."

"Nothing? That surprises me. Your husband struck me as a sensible young man."

"He isn't sensible at all," Klies complained. "He won't let me buy him a ship and he insists on living in the new city among a bunch of merchants."

"Might I remind you, young woman, that your father was a merchant."

"But, he was rich. I will not live in dirty little alleys when I can live above it all."

"The verses are mine," Psappha reiterated. "You had no right to profit from them, nor will you. From this day forth not a dram of gold will pass from my hand to yours."

Klies looked at her askance then shoved Lycos out of her way and darted from the room.

Psappha made no move to follow. She returned to Phaeon as a last resort. With him, she was not required to think or feel. With him, she could simply be, reinventing herself from hour to hour.

Winter had not yet locked the island in its grip the morning Psappha awoke and knew she could hide on the beach no longer. Last night's fire slept under warm ashes, giving off little or no heat, making her grateful for the thick, down coverlet she had given him long months before.

She opened one eye at a time, then grabbed a rabbit-skin cape and scrambled to her feet. Klies pushed past her, azure eyes widening

Psappha

as she got a full view of Phaeon, nude and uncovered on the tousled bed. Psappha yanked the displaced coverlet over him then glared at her daughter.

"I had to come," Klies whined. "My friends snicker behind their hands when your name is mentioned. The way you are carrying on with that uncouth barbarian has all of Lesbos laughing."

The uncouth barbarian was awake and grinning, leaning on one elbow, watching.

"Psappha, my love. Hand me my clothes so I can build a proper fire."

Psappha smiled ruefully to the clutter of garments left from their enthusiasm for each other the night before. Since he seemed about to rise without them, she quickly gathered Phaeon's and tossed them at him.

Seeing Klies' obvious interest in the activity beneath the down, Psappha took her arm and turned her away. "You dare to come here to hurt me by saying I am a reproach to you?"

"What else could I do but come here and insist that you be more discrete? Your fame is great. No one of your stature can flaunt unfashionable conduct without censure."

The admiration in Klies' eyes as she watched Phaeon putting logs on the fire told Psappha that her impertinent daughter would not mind being censured for such as he.

The cave grew suddenly too warm. Psappha threw off the stifling skins, too angry to care that she was nude without them. The shock on Klies' face was more than welcome.

"If you insist on the society of the notorious, you may do so to your heart's content," she said. "Have your fill of it. On my part, Klies, I am not inclined to disregard the bad temper of youth.

"I haven't forgotten the extent of your treachery. I know what to expect from you, so you had best mend your ways, and be careful, Klies. I am easy going but I have power enough, still, to chastise you severely."

Until she said it, Psappha had never stopped to realize that she had power and wealth to spare. Her select group had grown to such proportions that now there were as many instructors as there had once been students. Her expanded home consisted of three houses and a huddle of guesthouses, workrooms and outbuildings.

141

But, no matter how many servants she hired, it was still Psappha who welcomed guests, even those as unexpected as her elder brother, who arrived a few days later, unannounced.

~~~~~

Psappha greeted him in her private parlor. "Charaxos, do sit down. You look like you're about to have apoplexy."

Psappha's senses recoiled from her brother's dissipated appearance. His eyes looked peeled. Tiny capillaries traced jagged lines across the sallow yellow of his eyeballs as if to draw attention to the grotesque, dilated pupils. His paunch lopped over his girdle like that of an overage eunuch. He strode back and forth before her like a one-man army without orders.

"You must stop seeing the fisherman," he sputtered.

"By whose dictates, Charaxos? Surely not yours."

"Yes, by Zeus, by my order, Psappha. By my authority as senior male member of our family, I forbid you to go to him again."

"Your authority, Charaxos? I think you know what you can do with your pompous authority. If you ever had any authority over me, which you did not, you forfeited it long ago."

His bulbous face reddened. "It is beneath the dignity of the House of Scamandronomos for my sister's name to be linked to that of a common fisherman," he persisted. "A fisherman whom you flaunt like a prize sheepdog, according to Klies."

"Leave Klies out of this, Charaxos. How dare you come here after a lifetime of neglect and presume to dictate to me? Where were you when our mother died? Chasing pornas, I've no doubt. The whole of Aegean society is laughing at your antics, yet you dare to question my decorum. So -- Phaeon is a fisherman. He is, at least, a respectable one. How much better that than your notorious Rose?"

Charaxos purpled as if he wore a noose. "I won't have you use that tone with me, Psappha. You must not see him again or I will cease to support your disobedience."

"You won't have me use that tone," she chuckled. "You won't have me use that tone?" Her laughter rose like leaves caught in a whirlwind. When it subsided, she asked, "What tone would you have me use, you fool? The God of Ridicule cannot devise enough barbs to hurl at your folly.

"You will not support, brother mine? You prove your stupidity. I support this household. What familial monies your debauchery has left you are but a mustard seed, compared to the harvest of wealth I've earned without your patronage.

"This house belongs to Alkaios. The others are mine, bought and paid for. You have no claim to them. Attempt to displace me and you will only add to the stench you've already brought to the name you dare say I besmirch." Psappha turned away in disgust.

Charaxos stepped in front of her, his opium-ravaged eyes pleading. "You can't intend to sanctify this outrageous relationship," he sputtered. "Even our rash ancestor, Ariadne, chose a king upon whom to bestow her favors. You can't mean to impose a base-born man on our great tradition."

"Great tradition?" Psappha loosed a sardonic chuckle. "Which great tradition, Charaxos? The stupid princess who got puffed up and abandoned or the foolish king murdered by his adulterous wife? Our entire aristocracy is descended from an army of idiots who fought a ten year war to preserve the honor of a woman who had happily sacrificed it to a beautiful young man rather than waste her own youth and beauty on an impotent ass. Take your great tradition, your orders, and your over-indulged appetites back to your porna and try to convince her of your illustrious heritage after your money runs out. The only tradition she understands is the sacrifice in the temple garden.

"Go, Charaxos! Go, and trouble me no more. What I do with my life is no concern of yours. I'll marry, or not marry, whom and when I choose. Go," she said more gently, "and stop by the gatehouse. I've instructed Lycos to give you a small purse. You'll need it for your pipes and your porna."

~~~~~

Not even her brother's misplaced arrogance could lessen Psappha's love for her orchard. Its early blossoms scented the air long before she reached them. The pale green beneath her favorite tree seemed a welcoming carpet. When she sat upon it, the sweet fragrance of thyme rose around her.

Lycos flopped to the ground beside her, chewing on a blade of mint until her questing eyes insisted that he say what he came to say.

"You should release him, Adelphi."

"Not you, too, Lycos. I thought you would understand and want me happy."

"I do understand. Better than you do, perhaps. Forgive me, sweet sister, but have you thought of the future?"

"What of the future? Isn't today enough? I'm not alone, Lycos. You know what that means to me. I never need be alone again. Phaeon will see to that."

"Will you marry him?"

"I might."

"You don't love him." His level gaze left her no chance to deny it.

"I love him -- as much as I can."

"Is that enough, Adelphi?"

"Phaeon thinks so."

"For now," he allowed. "But what of the future? He's young, Psappha, shouldn't he raise sons of his loins to bring comfort to his later years? You're no longer a girl, Adelphi. Your days of bearing are past. True, you are as beautiful as you ever were. More beautiful, I think, but the years will not always be so kind."

"Don't speak foolishness, Lycos. You talk as if I was halfway to my bier, when I am at the height of my powers as a woman. Were I any younger, I could not begin to match Phaeon's vigor."

"That may also be true, Adelphi, but he is in the full flush of youth. My years are as yours and it has been a while since I stopped counting the silver in my hair. What of Phaeon's love when the years make their tardy mark on you?"

"I'll blow out the candles," she said, hoping to divert him.

"You must free him."

"I know, Lycos. I know --"

"Now, Psappha. Don't put it off. The longer you postpone it the harder it will be on him. I believe he truly loves you."

Psappha

~~ 14 ~~

Psappha's funereal white kiton flared behind her, billowing with warm salt air. Sand oozed between her toes. She loosened her braids as she walked, letting her hair fall in fawn-red, undimmed waves. From the bluff, she saw Phaeon's boat bobbing on the water. It looked like a child's toy in the sheltered cove. Once more, my love, and then goodbye, she promised herself as he stepped ashore to greet her.

The night combined all that was rich and vibrant in their relationship. Youth mated Pleasure beyond a poet's wildest dreams.

In the morning, Psappha's eyes brimmed with tears as she told him of her decision.

"You will marry me," he said, refusing to allow her sacrifice.

"No, no, my love. It will not do." Struggling for the right words, she resorted to familiar lyric form. "If my breasts were still capable of giving suck, and my womb were able to bear children," she said. "I would not hesitate, but would come running to be your bride. But age is already writing on my face and Hera hastens not to fly to me with Her gift of pain. You must find a lovely daughter of Illustrious Aphrodite and take her swiftly for your own. I will go again among the maidens and you will come and sing to us of her of the violet-scented breast and golden tresses."

"You're talking rot, Psappha. Your body is rich in treasures. I love you and will have no other for my bride."

"If you love me, Phaeon, choose a more youthful companion for your bed. I couldn't endure being married to a young man," she lied. "I am too old."

He crushed her to him. She pulled away.

"Psappha," he pleaded, dropping to his knees on the hard, dirt floor.

The pain in his eyes almost changed her mind. She stared beyond him, storing new memories with which to bury the old.

There was the bed on which he taught forgetfulness, the hearth where blazing logs had failed to compete with the raging fires created between them, the goatskin that welcomed their animal pairing.

Psappha shook her head, composing lyrics in her mind as she ran her fingers through his tousled hair. "Stand up, fair youth, and look me in the face as friend to friend. Unveil the beauty that is in your eyes," she said, maintaining form to dull the pain. "Our time has been a beautiful time, Phaeon. But I, you must know, love delicate living. For me, richness and beauty belong to the desire for the sun."

She could see he did not believe her, but she continued, unheeding. "I could not forsake luxury for the life you lead and you, my darling, are too proud to accept my bounty. It is best that we part. To go on any longer would tarnish that glory which has been ours." He made no move to stop her as she opened the door.

"Goodbye, my brave and beautiful dolphin," she whispered in parting. "May you ever sleep in the bosom of a tender companion," she said as she stumbled. Then, she squared her shoulders and went on, not looking back.

~~~~~

Psappha did not ask if Atthis came to stay, she did not care. With Phaeon out of the picture and her love lyrics making the rounds, the tide of fashion waxed firmly in her favor. Atthis' arrival was no surprise. Nor did skilled Atthis lack for willing pupils.

Out of guilt, as well as half-forgotten habit, Psappha showered her with presents. When Lycos complained of the cost, she wrote for publication. "Why not?" Klies had said. Why not, indeed? Psappha asked herself. What does it matter? The world puts value on my simple words. Why shouldn't I? No amount of anger will change Klies; Gyla has taken herself beyond my reach, and Atthis?

She shrugged as she chose a fresh wax tablet.

"Why does the daughter of Pandion, the heavenly swallow, weary me?" Psappha mumbled, thinking of Atthis as she puzzled over the words. Writing deliberately for the public without a commission was different. The poem refused to behave.

Laying her stylus aside, she studied her reflection in the mirror. Once there was beauty there and I thought you ugly, she told the womanly face that stared back at her. How blind I was. I am grown old without my notice, and, Atthis? She tried to picture Atthis as she had seen her earlier that day. She could not. Her mind showed her only remembered visions. I love the child, she realized, but the child no longer exists. Did she ever truly exist? Except within my stubborn mind? She looked again at the first lines of the poem. It's true, she

Psappha

decided. I have grown tired of Atthis. I loved the child and refused to see the woman.

~~~~~

Summer faded into autumn. One by one, the maidens called farewell from the decks of homebound ships. Psappha wandered aimlessly, remembering when the house rumbled with people. Against her will, she recalled another time when she had felt this dismal. The house had been full then, but she had refused to hear.

She remembered Praxinoa wrapping her in her mother's deepest-purple cloak, as she took her place in the funeral procession; eyes down, concentrating on the dust kicked up by the pallbearers who walked immediately before her, with the bier on four stalwart shoulders.

In the back of the orchard, just beyond the laurel hedge, the bearers set their burden on the pyre and stepped away. Someone had handed Psappha a knife. She remembered that her fingers trembled when she pulled the pins from her hair, releasing her braids.

The crowd moaned as she lifted each braid and slashed it, placing shorn tresses tenderly upon her mother's still breast. The false piety of the wailing professional mourners' insulted her senses. Their keening death chant cut her ears. She screamed. She saw them nod approvingly and she laughed -- and laughed -- and laughed.

Psappha touched her cheek as she recalled the sting of Alkaios' palm. She had stared at him in disbelief, then gratitude, as tears, long withheld, rushed from her eyes, unchecked.

Alone in the quiet house, Psappha remembered throwing herself to the ground beside her mother's open grave. On that day, long before she threw away her official maidenhood, she cried the last of her childhood onto the breast of Earth, the only mother that remained.

Psappha shoved the memory from her mind, along with the pile of tablets on her worktable. There would be time, and more, to transfer their contents to papyrus later. She felt as if she had nothing but time. Although she had refused all invitations to share a student's bed, she would miss them. She enjoyed their bubbling presence. She did not look forward to spending the winter closed in with Atthis.

Trying to dredge words from the oozing swamp of her laggard brain, Psappha clenched her stylus. It broke. She reached for another, broke it, threw it aside and picked up a third. Thinking of Atthis not as she was now, a sated practitioner of a courtesan's arts, but as she had seemed when first she saw her, so young, so innocent, so very long ago. The words began to flow.

147

Peggy Ullman Bell

"Gentle Atthis, you will remember forever our life together in the glory of our youth, for all the many things both pure and beautiful we did together. A sadness wrings my heart, remembering.

"I was not the one who changed," Psappha mumbled as her stylus cut the words into the wax.

"Remember, Atthis, when I first saw you. You ran in beauty, strong and young, your golden hair a glory in the sun. Truly, I drank that beauty with my soul. The man with me thought me a poor walking-companion, so lost was I in the magic of your spell.

"Those times I walked with my friends, in the city, I passed your dwelling. Sometimes, I scarcely heard them. My spirit was yours alone. I thought, then, I would come and speak to you, but you were fleet of foot and soon gone. A fair sight it was to see you. I was so young then, so in love with love and life and beauty.

"I remember, Atthis, how we came upon you in The Lady's park. Such an awkward, graceful child you were, gamboling among the trees like a spring fawn, so beautiful in your gangly elegance. Even then, you reflected the kiss of Terpsichore as you flitted upon the grass. I remember well your startled, flashing eyes as you peered at us from behind a bay tree.

"I felt so mature and grandly remote from you, but my vagrant heart was already forfeit to that soul-eyed girl. We walked away from you, but my thoughts stayed behind. I carried the vision of your darling face with me, completely unable to dispel the memory."

Having been committed to wax, the memory was gone. At last, she knew Atthis as a dream of her own invention. And, Alkaios? He, too, was a fantasy lover, a convenient tool of her self-education. And, Kerkolos? No dream he, and yet, no true reality, a symbol, perhaps, of what society deemed right and respectable, a husband, and an unexpectedly proficient lover. And, Gyla? Gyla is gone more surely than Kerkolos, she thought. Enough! Enough and more! I cannot bear it!

Hours later, a soft tap on her door told her it was time to join the household at dinner. Busy with her stylus, she ignored her hunger until Praxinoa entered with a lamp.

The light wavered. Psappha turned in time to see Praxinoa sway.

"You're ill," she said, jumping to her feet. "You should have sent someone else with the lamp," she said as she took Praxinoa's elbow.

"I am not too ill to serve thee," the old nursemaid countered through a cough.

Psappha

"You must go at once and rest," Psappha insisted.

"After I help you dress for dinner."

"No," Psappha said. "I'll have something brought here. I don't need help for that. Now, get you gone and don't leave your bed until you are fit."

She shivered from the damp chill that seeped in as Praxinoa left. How long before this weather draws off all her strength? Psappha wondered as she returned to her writing table.

The humid cold reminded her of caves. She wrote of Selene, The Lady Moon. She wrote of how Selene peeked into the cave on Mount Latmos, becoming enthralled by the beautiful youth sleeping there. From deep in her tortured soul, she summoned a tale of how the Lady Moon kept Endymion asleep, eternally young, to enjoy his slumbering love. That alone, was capable of warming Her ethereal heart, as She aroused his dreaming passions with pearly kisses.

Psappha threw the tablet into the fire where it hissed and spat as the wax melted. Psappha thought the sound appropriate. Each time she had carved the word young into her tablet, she became more dissatisfied, more confused, her mind a cauldron of emotion. The ache of frustrated passion stole all other appetites, but she would not see Phaeon again. For his sake, if not her own.

~~~~~

Unable to tolerate the loneliness of her chambers a moment longer, Psappha wandered into the garden. The creaking of the cog-wheel over the well, the slosh of the water as it tumbled from the pots, the murmuring of the well-man coaxing the ox around its hoof-cut path eased her from thoughts of verdant jungles into cool, bright moonlight.

The sound of muffled weeping attracted her attention. Following it, she found Anaktoria, the fleet-footed maiden of Lydia, hunched behind a rock.

"What is it, child, that brings tears to your lovely eyes?"

"Oh, my lady, I must leave thee."

"But, sweet nymph that is no cause for weeping. Of course you must go, as you always do, at the end of the season, before winter bolts the harbor doors with ice, to return on the first breath of spring."

"No, my lady. I must leave now. I cannot stay the season. My father has ordered that I sail at once."

Psappha brushed a strand of straight, black hair from the maiden's tear streaked face.

"It will be all right, Anaktoria. I won't be here in any case. Lycos and I are sailing to Egypt with the new moon. Perhaps we can come visit you on our way home. Would you like that?"

Instead of smiling as expected, the girl began to sob. Psappha grasped her shoulders and gave her a firm shake. "Stop this, Anaktoria. Stop crying and tell me what is wrong."

Anaktoria tossed her head as if to shake away her tears. Her lovely hair fell behind her shoulders like a soft dark cape. " I go to the Temple, milady. You cannot visit me."

"No!" Psappha protested. "You cannot! Surely the knife would break before it could stop the flow of your beautiful children."

"I do not go to the priesthood, milady, although I would prefer it. I must go, within the month, to the sacred garden of Ishtar to await the purchaser of my maidenhead."

Psappha tasted gall. A man joking about the Temple gardens is one thing, she thought. Having one of my lovelies trapped by barbaric custom is quite another. Rage brought tears to her eyes.

Seeing them, Anaktoria began to cry anew. Composing her face, Psappha took both of the maiden's hands in hers. "I swear to you, Anaktoria, that although I, like you, had but one maidenhead, I did not fear the breaching of Aphrodite's threshold."

"But you knew to whom you would cast it away," the maiden sniffed.

Psappha smiled, remembering. "Yes. I knew, and so shall you. I've heard that lovers can arrange to meet in the Temple garden on the night of the sacrifice to keep strangers from tasting beloved fruit. It will be so with you."

"My lover can never be my husband."

"So much sweeter will be the sacrifice," Psappha soothed. "Could you give a more precious gift to one who will see you wed another?"

"My lover has no need of a maidenhead, milady. She has not yet lost her own."

I have failed this tender creature, Psappha thought. I should have prepared her for the outer world of marriage and men. My students must learn to thrive in whatever environment The Fates may thrust them. This cannot, will not, happen again. I will somehow teach them all that they need to know.

Psappha

But, resolutions for the future did nothing for the immediate problem. Psappha searched her mind and found no ready answers. There is not enough time. Or, is there?

"Could you give yourself to a man you know?" she asked.

"If I must give myself to a man at all, it would be better if I knew him. But, I know no men, milady."

"I shall send a message to your father at once," Psappha said. "If he will permit you to travel with us, I will take you to a man in Naucratis who is the gentlest of lovers. He was my first," she confided with a smile.

Anaktoria apparently found no comfort in Psappha's revelation. "How will I suffer the touch of any man after I have lain in my lover's arms and known the joy's of Eros' true mating?" she asked.

"The man I would have you meet in the gardens is a true and tender friend, Anaktoria. He will teach you that Eros has another face which can smile as kindly as the side which you've already seen."

"But, even if what you say is true, milady, and I do not doubt you, the wedding will follow. How will I suffer the touch of the unknown man my parents have chosen as my husband?"

"I did not go to my marriage bed in purity, little one, and yet I swear to you that night was sweet enough to me and neither have you anything to fear."

"Can the night be sweet without love, milady?"

"It may not be without love, dark flower. Aphrodite, like Eros, has many faces. You will be astonished. Silver-throated Hera is not miserly with her gifts."

Gazing beyond the grounds, Psappha saw the twin harbors of Mytilene. A lone trader rocked at anchor near the estuary. Recognizing the bright profile of an Egyptian dragon ship, she knew that, like Anaktoria, only one could fill the void within her soul.

Spinning away from the view, she tossed the maiden an encouraging smile and hurried away. This time she would not be distracted from her goal. She almost forgot to wave 'Good morning' to the gardener in her rush. Her whole body tingled as she hammered on the gatehouse door.

"Lycos!" she shouted, bursting in without waiting for an answer. "You're sleeping my life away, Little Fox. Unleash yourself from that bed. We're going to Africa."

Lycos stumbled from his alcove, rumpled and bleary-eyed.

"Come, you sluggard, start packing!"

She left as abruptly as she had come, giving him no time for protests.

Back at the main house, she dispatched a messenger with passage money, gave Praxinoa's substitute enough instructions to keep her busy past nightfall, and then she hurried to the quarters behind the kitchen.

She found the old nurse shivering in swelter. "We're going to Egypt," she announced. "On the way we'll visit your home."

"I have no home," Praxinoa murmured. "My people are no more. They've been carried out of their land to serve pagan masters." She covered a racking cough with her hand. "I'm sorry," she said when it stilled. "I forgot you're not of my faith."

Psappha seated herself on the edge of the narrow cot, pleased with the compliment. For the first time, in a long time, she looked closely at the woman who had warmed the fringes of her life for so many years. The years had not been kind. Praxinoa's once olive skin was sallow; her raven hair had more silver than gray. How could I have been so unobservant? Taking an emaciated hand into hers she said, "Perhaps your God is also mine. Aren't He and Zeus, when he's on his best behavior, much the same?"

A pained, expression of disapproval filled Praxinoa's eyes. Psappha tried a different approach in search of a smile. "Do you remember Gongyla's story of a rash young man. Did she ever tell you what happened to him?"

Praxinoa's disease-ravaged face brightened as she recited the tale of the traveler's homecoming.

"When the young man returned from his journey, he found his father had died and left all he owned to a slave. He left his son the choice of a single item from the estate, nothing more. The young man thought and grieved. He prayed long and loud to the One God for guidance. 'Which one thing should I choose,' he asked, but the Lord God left the choice to him."

Psappha smiled, noticing Praxinoa's adaptation of Gongyla's story.

"He chose the slave, of course," Praxinoa whispered hoarsely. "The young man's father was very wise. If he had left the inheritance to his son, who was absent, the slave would have squandered it. Thinking it his own, he guarded it well."

"Very clever," Psappha said, trying to smile.

Psappha

"It has been said cleverness is the childhood of wisdom," Praxinoa said. "You have always been quite clever. Are you also wise?"

Psappha lowered her eyes, ashamed before the sad wisdom in Praxinoa's eyes. "The young man in the story was not wise," she said, avoiding the question. "Cleverness is also the childhood of avarice. I heard that the older the young man got, the more selfish he became," she said, trying not to think of Klies.

"One day he went to a prophet who told him all he had would one day belong to his neighbor."

"How could that be?" Again, speaking caused Praxinoa to cough.

"The prophet did not say," Psappha continued when the hacking stopped. "Anyway, the young man, now old, made up his mind to thwart the prophecy. He took all he owned to the market and sold it. With the gold he received, he bought a huge diamond, which he had sewn onto his turban. 'Now,' he thought. 'The poor man cannot steal my wealth.'"

"But, the prophet said his neighbor would one day own it," Praxinoa prompted in a hoarse whisper.

"And, so he did," Psappha said. "One day the rich old man went down by the sea. A strong wind came and blew his turban far out into the water. 'Well,' he thought. 'The prophet was wrong. The poor man did not get it after all.'

"A few days later, as the poor man's wife cleaned a large fish he had netted, she found the diamond inside."

Praxinoa smiled. "His just due, I'm sure." Her chuckle died amid racking coughs. Psappha knelt and gathered the old nurse in her arms.

When the spasm subsided, Praxinoa pulled her coverings tighter although the heat in the tiny room beside the kitchen was oppressive. "You have been foolish, like the young man, Psappha. You've squandered your love on the unworthy and let your child squander what is yours. But, at least you need not worry about the penalties of avarice."

"Perhaps I do," Psappha said. "There is a thing I covet, yet dare not hope to own."

"How can that be, my child? You have wealth beyond a Sybarites dream. Your fame is greater than any woman dares to hope."

"That is the problem, old one. 'Greater than any woman dares hope.' No matter how great my school becomes, or how widely read my lyrics, I remain a woman and I want more. I enjoy the gold my work has brought me, but I desire a greater compensation. I want recognition from The League of Poets. I burn for--"

She saw the ache her paltry complaining added to the pain in Praxinoa's eyes, and she cursed the Fate who ordered the destruction of so beautiful a spirit. "Sweet Praxinoa, I am going to Egypt and you must come with me."

Praxinoa rewarded her with a cautious smile. "Why, Psappha? Why do you want to leave your home? Why now, when winter is almost here and your time will be your own for months?"

"Because of winter, I suppose, because Lesbian winters are cold. Because I am alone, and that has never pleased me. You'll feel much better in the dryness of Valley of the Nile."

"I'll feel better in my grave, Psappha. I'll not see another spring."

"Hush. Don't speak of it. We're going to Egypt where you'll drink sunshine and nectar. The life-giving juices of Apollo's fruit will soon have you up and bossing me around again."

"Don't delude yourself, Psappha. No amount of sunshine, or fruit can change my fate. I will go with you, if it makes you happy, but before I do, I would have your promise."

"Anything, Praxinoa. Anything."

"You must swear to me that when my numbered days are gone you will not burn my body."

"Hush. Don't speak of it. Your days are far from over." Even as she spoke, she knew she hoped in vain. The light was growing dim in Praxinoa's eyes.

"Promise me," she repeated. "You must have my body prepared in the manner of the Egyptians and taken to Bethlehem to be lain in the sepulcher of my father. Swear by whatever power most binds you."

Psappha nodded. But, what power binds me? She wondered. The Lady? No, she abhors oaths. Aphrodite? No. She's too fickle. Apollo? No. His gift of words and music come only on his whim. Zeus? No. He belongs to foolish warmongers. Poseidon? No. He will claim me when it suits him, but he helps me only if he chooses. Hera? No. She has no further need of me. My days of blood and babes are behind me.

Is there no god who has proved faithful, no goddess who has not abandoned me in my hour of my need? She smiled into Praxinoa's

Psappha

tired eyes. "By Artemis, I swear it. By Artemis, dark shadow of Musicos, who, if she has not done me service, has, at least, done me no ill."

Praxinoa let her lashes fall.

Psappha kissed her drawn forehead and determined to hasten their journey to warmer climes.

~~~~~

The ship lay becalmed off the coast of Phoenicia. The once great seafaring confederation sprawled like the reluctant slave it had become. High on a seaside promontory, the Temple of Ishtar reminded Psappha of the many maidens who had sacrificed their pride to the man-made goddess of Babylon.

Looking at Tyre, her double-glory tarnished but undaunted, Psappha thought, instead, of Carthage. It had been years since that city had crossed her mind. Or, has it always been hiding there, she wondered as soft words echoed in her mind. 'A green land, beyond a white land, beyond the land of the Carthaginians.' Ah, but, Gyla, my sweet, sweet love, I cannot see so far.

Taking a deep, sustaining breath of salty air, Psappha left the rail and returned to the cabin below. The one next to the one Atthis occupied, which Psappha pointedly ignored.

Praxinoa's cabin was dank and silent, except for the old nursemaid's wheezing breath. At least for now, no blood-spotted cough disturbed her sleep. "Will she wake, Lycos?"

"She'll come around," he assured her sadly. "She may not wish to, but she will, for a while."

"What do you mean, not want to? Praxinoa loves life as Poseidon loves the shore."

"I've seen this sickness before, Adelphi. It is not a pleasant way to die."

Praxinoa moaned fretfully. Lycos filled a spoon with the elixir he had extorted from the Asklepians before they sailed. He dropped as much of it as he could into the old nursemaid's half-opened mouth.

When most of the elixir trickled toward Praxinoa's chin, Psappha pushed Lycos aside. Taking some of the elixir into her mouth, she placed her lips on Praxinoa's and let the potion flow, from her tongue, into the old one's constricted throat. She laid her cheek against the almost imperceptible pulse in Praxinoa's limp wrist and felt a scream rise from her gut.

"Where is this nameless, useless One God of yours, Beloved? Why does he let The Fates treat you so cruelly? Oh, Lycos, why must she die? Why not me? I wasted the love the Fates gave me all because of a love long dead. Why can't I be the one to die? Why didn't Phaeon let me fall from that cliff? All I brought him was pain. All I bring anyone is pain, even myself."

Great, wracking sobs tore at her. She cried inconsolably until the sleep of exhaustion claimed her.

Lycos did not wake her when Praxinoa's breathing faltered and went still.

Psappha

15

Psappha stood with white knuckled fists clutching the starboard railing. This was the doorway to Praxinoa's ancestral homeland and Psappha felt as excluded from it as the old nurse had believed herself to be. She was glad the Port of Joppa had no facilities for docking larger ships. The lighter bobbed against the hull, but she had no wish to go ashore.

Praxinoa had told her charge enough about her family, and her father, for Psappha to know that her presence at the burial would only make things awkward. The lighter would carry Praxinoa's body on the first leg of its journey to Bethlehem. Hired mourners, faithful to the One God, would accompany the sarcophagus to its final resting-place.

Standing here, watching the oars pull the lighter closer to the shore, Psappha recalled all that she could of Praxinoa. Hearing the clatter of the rising anchor-chain, she sighed heavily, letting memory fill yet another void in her life.

The sky beyond the mountains changed to an excitement of color. The long oars dipped, and the ship pulled slowly away from shore. "May your next life bring you greater joy," Psappha whispered in farewell. "May your One God be enough to grant you the happiness you so boundlessly deserve."

~~~~~~

"Doricha is here," Lycos whispered in Psappha's ear before she entered her brother's house. "Atthis is with her."

"Why did she not wait for me?"

Before he could answer, Atthis opened the door and welcomed Psappha as if she and not Doricha was mistress of the household. Psappha frowned as Atthis bowed in greeting and bade her enter.

Atthis led them to the great hall where Doricha lounged on an ornate couch, her ginger hair splayed on the cushions. Charaxos lolled on the opposite couch like an indulgent potentate. The look that passed between Atthis and Doricha left no doubt that they knew each other more than well.

157

Psappha whirled away in disgust, bumping into Lycos who then followed her outside. "We will sail at once," she said when he had closed the door behind them. "I will not stay in the same house with pornas."

"There is no ship," Atthis said from the reopened doorway. "We will have to winter here."

"You may have to winter here, not I. The harbor overflows with ships."

"None will sail this late in the season except those who hug the coast plying their trade with the Ionians."

"One of those will do. Lycos, send word to the harbor that The Poetess desires passage on the next vessel leaving port."

"I will not sail on any tadpole trader," Atthis said.

"I did not invite you," Psappha replied. "Stay, if you wish. The porna should make you perfect company."

"You wrong her, Psappha. Doricha was never a porna by choice. Iadmon sold her against her will. She has done no entertaining of that sort since Charaxos purchased her and set her free."

"She hasn't needed to," Psappha countered. "Her retirement has been purchased at great expense to my brother, I'm sure."

"Psappha!" Charaxos posed in the doorway like a threatening storm. "I'll not have you ranting on my doorstep."

"Better your doorstep than within your brothel, Brother."

"Silence," he commanded, casting an embarrassed glance toward the gathering crowd.

Lycos tugged at her arm. She shook him off. "I'll not have you making decisions for me either," she told him. He backed away looking so crestfallen some of her anger dissipated. "All right, Little Fox. We'll go now."

"No," Charaxos sputtered. "You shall not! You will not shame me by refusing my hospitality."

"I can add no shame to your tarnished reputation, Charaxos, only to my own. I will not share a roof with your harlot and her paramour." She turned to go.

"No," he stopped her with a whisper. His face had turned a mottled scarlet.

"Charaxos," she said softly. "I cannot stay here. When, if ever, you learn where true values lie, come to me."

"I will stay here," Atthis said. "Doricha is expecting a guest and has asked my assistance."

158

Psappha

"Of course," Psappha sniffed. "You are leaving, Charaxos?" she asked expectantly. He cringed from her sneer.

"You're wrong, Psappha," Atthis defended. "The guest Doricha hopes for is not that sort. It is rumored that Solon may stop here on his current tour."

Psappha snickered. "You've kissed the God of Darkness if you think the world's greatest statesman will visit the Rose of Naucratis. It almost makes me pity you. For all her airs," she said without apology, "your precious Rose is a porna. She would be walking the streets, leaving 'follow me' imprints in the dust, if she had not bewitched my brother."

Charaxos' face turned crimson.

"She loves him," Atthis said.

"She loves his gold. As you will learn to your sorrow, Charaxos, when your money runs out."

"She is good to him," Atthis persisted.

"You are under her spell yourself," Psappha accused in spite of Lycos' attempts to silence her. "Was your taste so completely shaken by your affair with Andromeda that you can no longer judge food from garbage? Or, have you always preferred gutter twat?" Atthis' blow grazed her cheek. She lunged in return, then stopped mid-stride, threw back her head and laughed. "Stay with your porna, Atthis. 'Tis more than you deserve."

Psappha pushed through the gathered onlookers, frowning at Lycos when he caught up with her. "I thought I sent you to find us a ship."

"We don't need a ship, Adelphi. We can winter with Alkaios."

With Alkaios' good humor to brace her flagging spirits, Psappha filled tablets faster than Lycos could get the finished lyrics copied and aboard the coastal vessels for distribution.

"Dark Cybelean warrior, in some distant land . . . " he read from the latest one. " . . . remembering the magic of the night." He mumbled under his breath for a few lines, then exclaimed, "This is wonderful, Adelphi. The best of the lot."

"It's a poem, nothing more," she demurred, not wishing to discuss it.

"Is it?" Alkaios doubted.

"Don't you have something to do?"

"Not a thing," he drawled, stretching his long frame and lazily clasping his hands behind his head. "Don't you?"

"Not a thing," she mimicked his teasing tone. She dismissed Lycos with a wave of her hand, and, "Get on with your work," for good measure. After he had gathered up the finished scrolls and carried them away, she turned to Alkaios and said, "Now, I have to get busy."

"You work too hard."

"You're the one who works too hard," she objected.   "Not working at all has to be extremely strenuous."

"No," he grinned, "but watching you work is. I think what you need is a long slow trip. In fact, I have just the thing for you in mind."

"Oh, you do, do you?" She mocked his impish grin. "Are you trying to get rid of me?"

"Never." He sat up and studied her face intently. When she caught him at it, he veiled his eyes and said, "You are a bright light in a dark and drunken tunnel, Spha. My poor poems sparkle with reflected genius when you're around."

"You overdo your flattery, Kios.   I think you have some mysterious motive for your sudden suggestion."

"I do," he admitted. "Come. Help me empty another flagon. You've written enough sad epics for today."

"Have I become a burden to you, with my brooding? Is that why you want me to leave?"

"As burdensome as an empty vat at a Dionysia," he responded drolly, handing her a brimming goblet.

"Empty?"

"Aye, Spha. Your cup is empty. The poems you produce so prolifically are but dregs of a once rich brew. Clear your fire-shooting eyes, velvet-voiced one. Your talent turns lowly dregs into ambrosia, but you are capable of challenging the Muses."

He refilled her goblet, while letting her know by his expression that he had not strayed from his analogy. "I want you to take the island route to Mytilene."

When she would have protested, he stayed her with an upheld palm and a shake of his head. "Visit the temples and gardens, Spha. Refill your spirit with beauty and light. By the time you reach Lesbos, things will be better for you. I promise."

"What makes you an authority on my fate?"

"The gods whisper to me," he teased, refusing to be serious another moment. Instead, he became playfully argumentative and continued in that vein long after Lycos returned from the copy shop. Together, the three of them reviewed old arguments, instigated new

Psappha

ones and drank their way through several more flagons.   They exhausted subjects and themselves, waxing profound and prophetic into the morning hours.

Lycos had long since curled into a sleeping ball on the hearth when Psappha took exception to Alkaios' opinion of the Trojan War. "You are a greater fool than I thought, you insufferable sot. Do you actually believe that men fought for ten years over a silly king's faithless wife, and nothing more? Look at the story! What do you have? As men tell it, you have supposedly intelligent men, of all cities, dying to defend the honor of one minor king who was not man enough to keep his wife at home, while quarreling among themselves for the privilege of despoiling women other men thought they owned.

"I tell you, Helen was a woman in love, nothing more. Menelaus and his greedy brother wanted control of the Hellesport and used her as an excuse, as if men ever need an excuse for their bloodthirsty games of grab and grovel."

"Surely you aren't saying that Helen had no part in it," Alkaios slurred.

"Of course she had a part," Psappha admitted, accenting with a wave of her arm that sent wine slopping onto the hearth without her notice. "Of course she had a part, but who are we to say what that part was? Who are we to judge her?   Who are we to pretend to know what those who knew her thought of her? History is a plague if you take it without question.

"Homer was a man, or men, no one is sure. What can a man know of a woman's mind? Can you claim to comprehend the many facets of mine? No. Of course, you can't. Nor I yours. But, I ask you, Kios, how might the story read if written by a woman's hand. How would the years of battle sound if told by Helen or Klytemnestra? What might Penelope have had to say about Odysseus' adventures? In her version, might not her troubles exceed his in import? History is written, and oft revised, by men, Alkaios, and men, when it comes to their precious honor, are unmitigated fools."

"Ah, Spha, you make me glad I'm dishonorable." Alkaios laughed. Four empty flagons flanked the one with which he had originated the discussion. Now, he brought it full circle. "You need to sail away from this den of fools, Spha. Lycos! Wake up! Find Spha a berth on an island hopper."

"There is only one fool here, Kios. If we go, you will be all alone, with only your cellar for company."

"Lycos will stay with me. Won't you, Little Fox? I have work for him to do."

"No, Kios, I won't leave without him."

"I will come in the spring," Lycos said, rubbing his eyes. "You could do with some time alone."

"I despise being alone!"

"Aye," Alkaios said. "But, you work better that way and I need Lycos here."

Psappha knew she had lost and still she argued. "You said I worked too hard."

"Aye," Alkaios toasted her with yet another flagon, "you do. But I have other work for Lycos."

"What are you plotting . . .?" she asked hazily. She received a brimming goblet in reply.

~~~~~

Dionysian gongs throbbed in Psappha's temples as she boarded the squat Samosan trader. Later, in her cabin, she unrolled the bundle Lycos thrust upon her at the last minute and smiled to find two flagons of Chianti. When her stomach stopped trying to trade places with her brain, she realized that Alkaios had gotten her onto the boat without revealing his reason for doing so. She had no idea what chicanery he was up to and her head hurt too much to care.

The little red ship rolled and rocked from port to port. When they reached the Ionian Dodecapolis, Psappha indulged herself with brief shopping sprees in several ports while the Captain exchanged cargoes.

The diversion soon grew tedious. By the time they reached Samos, Psappha was more than happy to accept his invitation to linger a while at his home. At that point, she would have accepted any excuse to keep her feet on solid ground for more than an afternoon.

The little, red ship bobbed impudently close to wintering Carthaginian triremes. Smaller craft scurried over the placid harbor like servants preparing a banquet. Behind the Samosan Acropolis, the island rose in tiers, an amphitheater designed for the Immortals.

Psappha was in no hurry to reach Mytilene. She spent as much time as possible wandering the countryside. The captain's wife was something of a shrew. It took Psappha several weeks to realize the woman was jealous of her freedom. The captain's wife would have liked to roam the island as she did. But, they both knew she would die in the arms of her grandchildren with the desire unfulfilled.

Psappha

The woman's fate, like that of too many of her former students saddened Psappha and made her hunger for Mytilene, and free-spirited Lesbian maidens who had not yet felt the restrictions of a true gynakeon. She thought of all the countries she had visited and those that her students had described. Soon freedom will be only a memory, she thought mournfully. I pray the memory does not completely fade.

There came a time when Psappha knew she had to leave the sanctuary of the captain's home or be stuck there with both him and his discontented wife throughout the long winter ahead. Memory haunted her as she made one last tour of the rocky island. Her kiton caught on some brambles beside the well-worn path to Hera's Temple. Psappha heard it rip as she yanked it loose, but she continued up-hill unperturbed. At a gurgling spring, she paused to perch on a path-side rock and removed her sandals. A few paces farther on, she tied her kiton up like a goose girl.

The famous Samosan Temple of Hera stood on the crest. White columns pointed to the red-tiled roof like virgin fingers reaching for the blood of womanhood. The huge statue of The Lady, Hera, wore a high, basket-like headdress over a marriage veil. In Her extended hands, She held ancient betrothal scarves. Someone had piled roses around Her alabaster feet.

"Oh, Queenly Hera," Psappha prayed. "Take present shape beside me, down from my dreams in that beautiful form which once appeared at the summons of kings, the sons of Atreus, who, when they had brought to an end the destruction of Troy set out from the river Scamander.

"Now, I, Psappha, daughter of Scamandronomos, beseech Thee, Lady, that, as in the past, so again may I do things pure and beautiful among the maids of Mytilene whom so often I have taught to sing and dance at your festivals. And, even as the sons of Atreus, by grace of you and your fellow gods, set out from Troy, so in prayer I, daughter of the Illian heir Scamandronomos, entreat Thee, Hera, protect me on this my returning journey to the pure and beautiful island you found for him."

Psappha was reluctant to leave the temple grounds. All the flowers she loved were there, their beauty unexcelled by the flamboyance of Hera's birds. The bold peacocks screeched their dominion over beds of heavy-scented herbs and roses; sounding like laboring women in the throes of Hera's appointed rounds.

163

Peggy Ullman Bell

Psappha watched their courting rituals until Helios rode low over the sea. The path she chose for her descent took her along the top of the island. The sandals by the spring stayed for someone else to find. Pausing on a rough outcrop, she imagined that, if she looked long enough and hard enough, she would see Lesbos -- thirty miles distant, beyond Chios.

She strolled slowly toward her lodgings deep in thought, unaware of her surroundings for a time. She heard voices and she stopped. A gathering of women, out of doors, on Samos and most of the places she had visited was rare enough to make her hide, lest her unexpected presence frighten them.

They danced around a boulder, which had been worn smooth by a thousand women's caresses. Their paeans to The Mother sent shivers to her soul. A stubborn lump stuck in her throat as she watched a pageant unfold. The priestess separated herself from the worshipers and strode to lands edge, the jewels on her long cape shimmered as she walked. Her crown looked like pink-gold in the sunset. Two of the women left the shrine and followed her. Together, they removed the crown and placed it ceremonially upon the lush ground.

The myriad of tightly woven braids upon the woman's head reminded Psappha of Medusa's legend. Of course, she thought, wondering why she had never thought of it before. Medusa must have been a jungle queen in braids. Her power alone would be enough to set the men struggling for supernatural explanations.

The women reached as one to lift away the priestess's velvet cape. When they stepped back, Psappha gasped. Lyrics sprang into her mind. Beautiful, beloved - strong and free - I see my perfected self in thee.

The cinnamon-skinned priestess bent to speak to her attendants. Psappha composed the next line of her lyric in her mind.

Tall, true Amazonian willow bending in the wind. Unbroken, unflinching -- the willow leans to kiss sweet Earth from which she springs, roots tied to bosom, reaching for clouds - resilient, firm. Exultant is my song, Oh, willow. Exultant is my song.

The priestess straightened, her arms stretched overhead.

Life blows thunder yet you, my beloved, reach enveloping branches -- sanctuary -- willow tall and softly whispers acceptance, love -- the siren's call. Are we not sisters after all?

The priestess dove into the cerulean foam.

Psappha stopped a sob with her fist.

164

Psappha

Lycos arrived in Mytilene before her. He greeted her with a letter from Alkaios.

"Whatever Providence bestows upon you," she read, "receive it with a thankful heart. Do not defer the joys of life while you build yourself a monument more lasting than bronze. A word once sent abroad, flies irrevocably. I, Alkaios, will one day fade from memory but what is best of Psappha shall live beyond the pyre." She read it again to herself, and then she shrugged. "What, pray tell, does he mean by all of that?"

"You'll see," Lycos said, hiding his mouth with his hand.

Psappha could see mischief in his eyes. Experience told her she would get no enlightenment from him, so she let it pass. There was much else to occupy her thoughts. Requests and petitions had mounted in her absence.

Psappha left such things to Lycos, while she divided her time between her school and her work. Alkaios, he told her, was in Syracuse. Each day brought more messages from travelers hoping to find welcome in the house of The Poetess. Lycos unrolled them all with an air of expectation.

Psappha read only those queries he insisted she must and she resented every interruption.

It was not as easy to ignore her guests. Rules of hospitality older than time demanded that she appear in the great hall every evening. It was there that she permitted Lycos to press correspondence upon her. The pretense of reading allowed her to be mentally absent. It had all become a bore. Sometimes, to avoid unwanted conversation, she sat for long moments tapping her palm with a scroll as if deep in thought.

She posed thus now, but she had read the scroll -- twice. A broad smile teased the corners of her mouth. Charaxos is coming home! Alone! She gloried in the thought, happy for the first time on months. Golden Nereids, she prayed, her elation subdued by caution. Grant my brother's safe return, I beseech thee, that his desire may be fulfilled, and that, undoing in every way his former mistakes, he may become a joy to his friends and a sorrow to his enemies, so that we may be shamed before no one.

May he desire to hold his sister in due honor, Golden Ones, and may he find a desirable wife among decent young women.

Having finished her protections, Psappha laid the scroll on the table and stabbed the contents of her platter. While conveying the filled blade to her lips, she mumbled, "As for you, Doricha, you obscene and evil bitch with your nose set to the ground, may you go off and do your hunting elsewhere!"

She signaled for her tablet and stylus so she could note the beginnings of a poem before it deserted her. Feeling better, now that her Muse was with her, she turned belated attention to her guests.

An animated discussion centered upon a dignified, silver-haired gentleman with a clear, cultured voice. He criticized a new play by Streichoris concerning a maiden so virtuous she chose Death rather than loose her maidenhead unmarried. Psappha set her half-empty goblet on the serving table and commented, "An interesting premise, milord. Interesting, but unlikely."

"You do not find the theme believable, milady?"

"Not in the least, milord." Psappha noted that his eyes sparked with humor at the prospect of debate, she imagined hers were the same. "Maidenhood is a commodity of value to proprietary males," she argued. "A healthy young female might consider an intact hymen more burden than virtue."

"Did you find it so, milady?" The stranger's magnetic eyes twinkled.

Psappha smiled, meeting his challenge. "I am a daughter of Aphrodite, milord. The disposal of my maidenhead was, rightly, a choice I reserved for myself."

"A most remarkable accomplishment for a gynakeoni," he said.

"Perhaps, milord, since men consider gynakeoni little better than animals, caged for their exclusive enjoyment and profit. But, there are no gynakia on Lesbos, milord. Lesbian men are wise enough to know that a caged beast eats many trainers before it is subdued."

Solon glanced at the stunned expressions on some nearby faces and he chuckled, a warm, musical ripple. Raising his goblet, he said, "I salute thee, milady, you have made my argument. Gentlemen? A toast to . . .?"

"Your hostess, milord. I am pleased to welcome to my home a man who recognizes gynakia for the absurdities they are."

"Greetings, Illustrious Psappha. I should have recognized you by your irrefutable logic. Accept, dear lady, a toast to your brilliant mind. Alkaios did not exaggerate. Solon of Athens hails thee, oh Poetess."

Psappha

Psappha's hand rose as far as her waist before she gulped her surprise and willed her fist to lay quiet at her side rather than stuff itself into a gaping mouth, which she barely managed to clamp.

"Forgive me, Master Solon, I should have welcomed you at my gate." She cast an angry gaze around the crowded hall in search of Lycos. She spotted him near a Theban courtier and beckoned him to her side. "How is it that I was not told of so illustrious a guest?"

Rather than appearing chastised, Lycos stole furtive glances toward the entrance. To Psappha, he looked more like a fox than ever; a wily fox with his ear cocked for the bay of the hounds.

"Lycos, I asked you a question."

"He did not tell you because I did not tell him," Solon said.

Psappha scrutinized the statesman's face. Of course, she mused, he would not wish to be the center of attention. "Please allow me to welcome you properly now, Master Solon. I am grateful for the opportunity to entertain you."

"And I, Lady Psappha, am grateful for the opportunity to converse with you. Your fame is more far-reaching than you know."

"Not far-reaching enough, I'm afraid."

"What more do you want, Illustrious Psappha?"

"Nothing that can be obtained in a world being taken over by gynakia, milord. You mentioned Alkaios. The honor I desire is one he can attain. Are you familiar with his poetry, milord?"

Before he could respond, the ringing of a sistrum halted all conversation. Lycos looked suspiciously unsurprised. He lifted his hand and the musicians struck up a flourish. A flick of his wrist brought servants hastening to draw the couches from the center of the hall.

"Would you care to share my couch during the entertainment?" Solon asked.

Psappha was about to say, "Of course," when a troop of nude temple dancers twirled into the room, filling the center of the hall. She stood entranced while the Cybelean dancers whirled and stamped to the rhythm of brass castanets. Their breasts swayed, their stomachs undulated, the coins on their collars and belts jingled in time with the music as they gyrated. A gong reverberated beyond the door and the dancers wilted to the floor, their noses pressed to the cool tiles.

Thinking the spectacle an extravaganza for Solon's benefit, Psappha rewarded Lycos with a broad smile of forgiveness. Only he could arrange such wonder on short notice. When he grinned back at her like a boastful child, she knew the surprises were not over.

His next one came as a cloud of smoke in the doorway that quickly changed to amber. Psappha heard him chuckle as a High Priestess of Cybele stepped from its midst.

The High Priestess was a magnificence of opulence. Delicate gold chains crowned her multitude of braids, hanging in delicate swags on her high dark forehead, their ends forming shimmering ribbons reaching to the shoulders of her jewel-encrusted, purple and scarlet cape. Folded away from her shoulders, the cape revealed a pearl-dressed, saffron kiton draped after the fashion of the Egyptians. A heavy collar of gold coins lay upon high cinnamon breasts, accenting the swan-like curve of her neck.

Psappha blinked, then stared, then blinked again. Her heart thumped red behind her eyes. Her throat locked and she could not speak. She felt as if the floor had fallen from beneath her. Yet, she stood on solid marble, afraid to breathe for fear that what she saw was an apparition that would vanish with the smoke.

Every hair, every capillary, every inch of Psappha's skin ached for Gyla's touch. A pulsating tremor began deep in her gut, flowing lava-hot to Aphrodite's temple where it vibrated like a purring leopard as Gyla undulated through the throng.

Aphrodite, you marvelous, you wondrous purveyor of a thousand dreams, she comes! Hold back my tongue, you Harpies. Let not my words destroy me again.

Gyla studied her with a serene, tender smile. Then, she snapped her many-ringed fingers and the dancing resumed. Under cover of inattention, she left the hall through the family exit.

Psappha followed, too dazed to grasp the papyrus scroll the great Solon of Athens extended toward her as she passed.

Psappha

16

Light from tall candles danced like fireflies on Gyla's ceremonial finery. The door to the adjacent chamber stood ajar, the room busy with servants as if Lycos had anticipated Gyla's return. Psappha waved them away. She ached to serve her love with her own hands.

Psappha reached and pushed the magnificence of brocade from Gyla's shoulders, letting the cape fall in a heap.

Gyla reached to take Psappha in her arms but Psappha shook her head, holding her off, touching a finger to Gyla's full lips to stop her protest.

"It is your turn to be Ianthe," she whispered, afraid to trust her voice.

Perfect emerald scarabs held Gyla's sheer garment in place. Psappha worked at them with impatient fingers until, at last, one after the other, they came free and she tossed them aside. The diaphanous under-gown drifted floor-ward, covering the temple robe like summer sunshine on a bed of many-colored flowers.

Stepping back, Psappha forgot to breathe. Fragile, gold chains lay upon dark braids like garlands of infinitesimal flowers. She reached. The proud head bent. She twined her fingers in the golden links and lifted them away like a monarch's crown. The wide collar of gold adorned cinnamon-warm flesh as if its row upon row of shimmering coins were part of Gyla's supple body.

Psappha's fingers fumbled the catch. Gyla unhooked the collar and cast it weightlessly aside. Psappha's breath escaped in a rush. She stood, uncertain as to how to proceed. Always before, she had but to follow another's lead. Reversing that confused her, stopped her. She could not help staring rudely as Gyla strode to the bed and stretched upon it like a long, lithe cat, beckoning with sultry eyes and seductive smile.

Psappha's garments flew from her like leaves caught up in an autumn breeze. They fluttered to the floor behind her as she crossed the room to perch on the edge of the mattress with her chilled feet tucked beneath the hot moistness of Aphrodite's altar. Her hands trembled as she reached, with feather touch, to trace Gyla's ageless brow. Her fingertips followed the tiny crease of eyelid, brushed over glistening lashes, which framed misty, almond eyes. They drifted from high cheekbone to firm jaw, roaming beyond the cup of ear to caress pierced lobes and remove the diamonds that dangled from them. A tingle traveled up her arms as her fingers drifted, petal soft, down gentle curve of throat like twin brushes painting invisible swirls on pulsating breasts.

She flicked up-tilted nipples turned black with passion, molding lush contours between damp palms. Her hands flowed over sloping hips to taut thighs, trailing across Aphrodite's fragrant altar and pausing there like pilgrims at Delphi awaiting the divination of the Oracle.

Her too-long-lonely eyes followed the journey of her hands. The map they drew became the guiding line for starved lips. Avid hunger unleashed, found nourishment at last.

The consummate divinity of Iphis became reality. Devotion became instruction as Psappha's silent tongue spoke the love she had so long denied.

Teacher and student divorced roles. Barriers ripped and vanished. They merged. The joining, begun so long ago, was, at last, complete. They became a coalescence of image and reflection, shadow and substance, blended, melded -- one.

~~~~~

Psappha awoke to a world abundant with birdsong that seemed as nothing compared with the singing in her blood. Years had fallen from her spirit. She snuggled into Gyla's arms, her smile answered by a welcoming curve of luxuriant lips temptingly close to her own. Testing their texture, she found them full and warm as never before. The pride she had so long accepted, as her due, was at last a gift that she had won. Her spirit cried for all the wasted years, but only for an instant.

This is no time for recriminations, even self-deserved, she thought as she used the tips of her braids as painter's brushes to map each curve and contour of Gyla's precious body.

Gooseflesh covered Gyla's arms as Psappha drew the auburn strands over them. Her hair had never looked as lovely to her as now. With feather-light touch, she traced ebony areola, lingering upon cinnamon breasts, reluctant to move on, yet hungry for the trail.

Slowly, Psappha painted an invisible spiral on Gyla's taut stomach, flicking ever so gently over the crimped pelt that guarded the

Psappha

altar of Aphrodite. With her braid tips, she wrote her name on Gyla's thighs, smiling when her efforts evoked a shiver.

"Oh, no," Gyla chuckled when Psappha would have painted the soles of her feet. "Enough is enough, my lady. You have made your point."

When she would have rolled Psappha onto her back, she met resistance. "Not this time," Psappha said. "This time, you are Iphis and I intend to worship you fully."

Bending down, she placed a kiss on Gyla's lashes, then, with her lips, she followed every tracing made by hand and hair, but still she would not yield. Her tongue stretched to savor every flavor available on cinnamon flesh, from the salty tang beneath full breasts to the sweet oceanic wonder of the altar. Lessons learned by instinct led her questing tongue as it delved fragrant depths, craving more, then more.

Finally, her need to worship quieted, she allowed Gyla to resume the lead, only to snatch it from her moments later. A quiet chorus of whimpers and purrs escaped their lips as they spent the long night competing for dominance while both indulged in total surrender to one another, and to Eros.

~~~~~

Lycos' cubicle smelled of nutmeg oil and bee's wax. Psappha fidgeted, her cheek resting against Gyla's hand. "If Lycos wished to see us, he could at least be prompt," she complained. Gyla gently tweaked her ear. Psappha wiggled into a more comfortable position and sighed, resigning herself to wait.

It wasn't long. Lycos burst into his cramped office like a winter storm, scurried to his worktable, tossed scrolls and tablets in every direction, found the one he searched for and handed it to her. She scanned it, rolled it up, blinked, unrolled it and read it again.

"Conference of Poets . . . Syracuse . . . The Illustrious Psappha . . . invitation . . . member . . ." She mumbled the words as the scroll blurred before her eyes.

"It's true, Adelphi." Lycos beamed. "Solon of Athens left it for you."

Gyla took the message from Psappha's trembling hands and read it aloud.

"The servants of the Muses have, this second year of the fifty-third Olympiad, chosen to admit to their Conference of Poets, held each year in Syracuse, The Illustrious Psappha of Lesbos, known to many as The Poetess. We, therefore, send forth this invitation, by the

171

poet Solon, that she join us there and become, if she chooses, a member of our League." Re-rolling the scroll, Gyla tapped it in her palm, her eyes wet with pride. "You will go," she said, making Psappha's decision for her.

"I will go nowhere without you," Psappha insisted.

"We will all go," Lycos chirped. "I wouldn't miss this for anything. They have never invited a woman before. Don't you realize what an honor this is, Adelphi?"

Psappha smiled. "Of course, I realize it, you goose. What do you think I've been aiming toward these long years past?"

"Me, I thought," Gongyla offered.

~~~~~

Awakened by the cacophony reminiscent of a wharf, Psappha wondered if the ship could have reached the Isthmus of Corinth so soon. The voyage passed so swiftly, she thought as she tickled Gyla awake.

Psappha was dressed and on deck before her champion got her eyes open. Word of the honor bestowed upon her had preceded them. She clung to the railing with one hand while waving to the welcoming throng with the other, swelling with pride as they sang chorus after chorus of her own verses.

The merry crowd bore her straight into the city. Psappha sighed with wonder at the beauty of Apollo's temple, high above the Agora on a sacred pinnacle, reached by seemingly endless stairs. Stepping from her chair, she found the marble warm beneath her feet. The crowd came in whispers behind her as she climbed.

Treading upon the garden of the Gods, she paused, breathless before the magnificence of the Acrocorinth, across and above the Agora to the south. She looked forward to the night when, Gyla said, the lights in the sacred citadel would look like the windows of heaven.

Standing before Apollo's temple, surveying the myriad scenes below, Psappha felt as if she stood atop Olympus with the world of men at her feet, which is where, in her deepest heart, she had always wished to be.

"Oh blessed Poseidon, Earth-Shaker, Father of Ocean, look upon your daughter now, on the doorstep of your brilliant nephew, on the threshold of all I most desire. For this, you saved me long ago.

"Many times, I've cursed the selfishness with which you stole my beautiful ones. For that, Mighty Poseidon, forgive your errant daughter. I did not know, nor understand, where lay the perfect blending of my

Psappha

being. Carry me yet a little farther, Great Ocean, for I go to claim a lesser, though hard-won, glory.

"I have received true happiness from the golden Muses. My words will live after me. The poets of Hellas number Psappha of Lesbos among them.

"Hither to me now, tender Graces and lovely-haired Muses. Sweet, rose-armed, pure Graces, hither to Psappha. Come hither, daughters of Zeus, that I may once more, on the morrow, create again a lyric worthy of your love.

"Once before you honored me by giving me your own song for my own. Hither again, lovely ones. Arise, once more, my lute divine, and make yourself my voice."

Walking from the temple, Psappha's eyes rested on the series of cavernous reservoirs, each with a marble facade and portico, that held the sacred water of the spring, Pirene, on the shrine's west slope. As she watched the old men at their games, she tried to remember how the spring had gotten its name. She could not. She left them to their silent gambling and continued down to the Agora where Gyla waited.

A hushed crowd followed them until they reached the white road to Lecharon, from which they were to sail for Syracuse. There, people lined the shoulders of the paving to sing them along with their cheers.

Near Lecharon, the bleating of a flock of goats being driven into Zeus' temple turned Psappha's stomach. She could not help distrusting priests and gods who, unable to bleed painlessly themselves, murdered The Lady's sacred creatures to appease their jealousy.

A grubby merchant in desert robes insinuated a small, jewel-encrusted mirror in front of her frown.

"Ah, sir," he proclaimed, addressing Lycos, who had come up behind her. "It is for such beauty as this that my master makes his magic glass."

Psappha laughed and placed her hand in the crook of Gyla's arm. Together, the three of them made their way through the crowds, passing booths bright with fabrics from unknown lands, brought to Corinth by Phoenician traders; stalls overflowing with figurines and presided over by stiff-bearded Egyptians.

They dawdled near stalls of rare oils; tables strewn with exotic herbs; brocade-bedecked bins of rare spices.

"Here, milady, I have fine cloth of byssus brought with great difficulty from Assyria," a merchant chanted. "Here is gossamer silk fit for a princess. It was, in fact, purchased at great cost from a prince of Persia who had it woven for a bride."

Psappha paused to finger some jewelry.

"Ah ha," exclaimed the merchant. "I see you have excellent taste. That is fine Egyptian enamel. See how delicately they have painted the figures upon it. This necklace is the work of a master in a craft that has few masters. Only the perfection of this chain of cut-glass beads from my own country can surpass its beauty."

He draped the glass chain around her throat and held a looking glass for her.

"See, gentle lady, how the facets of the glass pick up the tone of your lovely skin and dress it in the colors of your apparel?" When Gyla offered to buy it for her, Psappha shook her head and they moved on.

Sacred prostitutes watched their approach from the entrance to The Temple of Aphrodite. In the haze of her happiness, Psappha allowed herself to appreciate their collective beauty. At their behest, she and Gyla entered the temple, leaving Lycos to contemplate the virtue of a quad of nearby bearers.

Psappha prostrated herself before the statue of the Goddess, her gratitude extending to her much-maligned patron. The adulation in her eyes did not change when she turned them from Aphrodite to Gyla. "Let's not go directly to Syracuse," she bubbled as they left the temple. "Let's go first to Delphi. It isn't far."

"I have no wish to consult the oracle of Apollo," Gyla grumbled.

Psappha patted her hand and said, "The oracle does not get her wisdom from Apollo. Nor from Dionysus," she added in an aside to Lycos. "I've heard it said that the prophecies come from The Mother. The Lady's Crones claim She lived there for aeons before the men's gods came. Wouldn't you like to have Her word on our future?"

"Isn't it better to let the Fates weave their webs in secret?" Lycos asked.

"Like you and Alkaios?" Psappha said. "I've wandered blind too long. This time I want forewarning. You may go on ahead if you have no wish to know your future."

~~~~~

The fertile valley of the Pleistos was below and behind them. Gongyla paused on the overlook above the inlet, looking as if she would rather dive into its depths than enter Pythia's dark abode. Psappha pulled her from the edge and led her to Castalia's fountain.

174

Psappha

"You need not drink from this," Gyla insisted. "The gift of poetry you have is more than the water could bestow."

Psappha laughed. "Perhaps to your prejudiced ear," she said. "But it pays to accept each gift the gods may offer."

The mouth of the ancient cave of the oracle leered at her. The sacred smoke insulted her nostrils. It filled the cave with a gray cloud reminiscent of hemp fields being readied for planting. She stared in dismay as the priestess swayed before her. She wanted to run and would have if Gyla had not held her fast with her stalwart stance and forbidding expression.

Gyla's tall form and planted feet seemed to say, 'we are here and we will stay. I did not wish to come.' So, Psappha held her ground as her spirit rushed away from her intuitive sense of The Mother's presence to cower in the far corners of her mind.

When, at last, the oracle came, Psappha strained her ears to hear, but could not. When the priestess had gone, an assistant came to her and said, "Your answer is this. You shall lie soon and long in the arms of your strongest and most constant love." Psappha thanked her and hurried away.

The sun was high in the sky when they left the cave. The way to the docks led them past open corrals filled with bellowing cattle. They hurried past a refinery where naked slaves stirred great vats of boiling fleece; slaughter pens swarming with green flies; swine pens oozing slime.

"Well?" Gyla asked, having remained silent longer than Psappha expected.

"The priestess said I shall lie long in your arms," Psappha told her.

Gyla frowned. "Are you sure you heard it correctly? Oracles often talk in riddles. Could it have had a different meaning?"

"She said I would lie soon and long in the arms of my strongest and most constant love. What else could it mean?"

Gyla eyed Psappha, her expression thoughtful, perplexed. She dragged her feet as they approached the ship in spite of Psappha's sudden impatience. "There was nothing else?"

"There was nothing else," Psappha insisted. "But, she did say it would be soon, and it shall be, if you will stop dawdling and hasten with me to our cabin."

~~~~~

Peggy Ullman Bell

Psappha lounged in a deck chair, glad that Lycos had chosen to sail without them. She felt the usual thrill of longing and terror as Gyla climbed to the lookout atop the mast. Moments later, she descended like a swooping eagle to lash the water near a dolphin playing in the wake. It no longer frightened Psappha to see her lover float downward from her lofty perch. As on the ship where they first met, it was an everyday routine. Now, having finally claimed what had long been hers, she took pride in the oarsmen's admiring gasps.

Nude, except for a pretense of loincloth, Gyla was more spectacular in her simplicity than Hera's peacocks in full array. She returned to the deck with water droplets on her oiled flesh. Psappha leaned away, brushing her arm.

"Stand back, you gorgeous fool, you're drenching me with your drippings."

Gyla laughed. Psappha's pulse fluttered as high, cone-shaped breasts quivered mere inches from her nose. A flash of ivory, in startling contrast to full, sensuous lips, brought scorching juices to the temple between her thighs. Twinkling black eyes evoked wild, mindless yearning. Her flesh screamed it's craving while her spirit wept from an excess of tenderness. Her muse hid from a love too great for mere songs to describe.

~~~~~

No matter how hard Psappha tried, the words would not come.

"It is impossible," she growled, hurling her stylus across the cabin. The tablet followed.

For days, she had tried to compose a proper ode for the Conference, when she would much rather have been on deck watching Gyla swim, instead of storming around the rocking cubical, each false start angering her. She had closed her porthole earlier so she could not hear the goings on outside. Every gasp from admiring crewmen only served to frustrate her further.

The close air in the cabin grew warmer by the hour. Each time she thought her muse had deserted her forever she stiffened her shoulders, retrieved her tablet, found a fresh stylus and attacked her task again, renewing concentration with each chewed stylus. Every line came in bits and pieces, like a festering tooth from the mouth of a doddering fool.

A momentary break in the rhythm of the oars distracted her. In her mind's eye, she could see Gyla plummet from her rookery into the foaming wake. "Be still my heart," she chided, scratching the letters into the tablet almost as fast as she could think. "For me you cannot throw out, in rapid, hymn-spurting inspiration, an Adonis song which in beauty of style shall please the Goddesses. Dishonoring Desire and heart-conquering Aphrodite have made you speechless. Brain-destroying Peitho, from her flagon of gold has poured her sweet nectar upon your wits."

She laid the tablet with her private collection and took up another. Her reluctant talent tried once more to answer her direction. One by one the words appeared, as if of themselves, upon the wax. She sounded them, savoring their effect. "You dishonor the good gifts of the muses, my friends, when you say, 'We will crown you, dear Psappha, the best player of the clear sweet lyre.' Know you not that my skin is all wrinkled with age, and my hair has turned from dark to white? As sure as Starry Night follows Rose-armed Dawn and brings darkness to the ends of the earth, so Death tracks every living thing, and catches it in the end."

~~~~~

Dawn had not yet penetrated the cabin when they heard a clatter followed by a clunk. Psappha and Gyla faced one another across a lamp-lit table, listening to the sounds the seamen made as they rolled empty casks from the stern to cargo nets amidships. The captain had explained last night that the sailors lowered the casks into lighters and rowed them ashore. He said they often stopped here for fresh water.

Sometime later, the full lighters bumped against the hull while being hoisted and offloaded. "I've heard it said the water here is sweeter than that of Corfu," Psappha commented. "Though it seems a waste to make an extra stop."

Gyla glanced up from the apple she was peeling. "The stop at Leucas is not extra, my love. We will not dock at Corfu. The ship will lie offshore here, awaiting others before crossing the narrows. It will give me a lovely time to swim. Besides, we are yet a long way from Syracuse and the crew wanted to sacrifice to Apollo to assure safe passage."

"There is a temple here?"

"No, Little One. A shrine only, but it will do. Finish your breakfast and we will go on deck to see."

"I've already finished." Psappha pushed her chair back and went around the table. "I have no desire to see anything other than your beauty. Can't we stay inside a little longer?"

Shaking her head, Gyla got up and opened the door. "Come. We'll have years in which to hide in the warmth of our light. We'll never be parted again."

Psappha's face clouded.

"No," Gyla assured her, "not even then. The Mother would not be so cruel. We will be together through eternity, as we were meant to be."

"Don't speak of it. You'll tempt the Gods."

"Life does not end when Death comes to carry us from Earth, Little One. Even the men's multitudinous deities would not be so frivolous."

"The gods think Death is a misfortune," Psappha countered. "Else they would have died."

At Gyla's urging she stepped across the threshold then stopped, backing into the cabin, the scroll sticky in her hand.

"I don't want to go out there. The walls of Poseidon's kingdom crouch above like vultures."

"It's just a sea-chewed island," Gyla said, taking firm hold of Psappha's arm and propelling her onto the deck. Centuries of storms had eaten the shoreline into a monstrous apple-core with a jagged promontory above and a diminishing inlet below.

Psappha shuddered, caught by a deepening sense of foreboding. She burrowed into Gyla's protective embrace and watched, with one eye, as the cumbersome water-boats shuttled from ship to shore and back.

The ship snuggled into the under-cut like a duckling beneath its mother's wing. A contingent of scrubbed oarsmen scrambled over the side and into a small painted skiff. Curiosity overruling apprehension, Psappha approached the rail.

"Where are they going?"

"To the shrine. See -- there." Gyla pointed to where a bit of roof jutted above the sharp edge of the projecting cliff.

Psappha ran across the deck to the swinging, rope ladder.

"What is this?" Gyla teased as she caught up. "A moment ago you were a trembling dove. Now, of a sudden, you're an eagle seeking to fly to the top of the world."

"No eagle I, Beloved." Psappha chuckled at the mischief in Gyla's dark eyes. "I would give thanks to Apollo for lending me his gift of song. I forgot to do it at Corinth. Come with me."

"Not I, Little Love. The water invites me."

"Please, I don't want to go alone."

Psappha

"You aren't alone. You will never be alone again, my lady. Wherever you are, I will be near. Wherever you go, I will go, if only in spirit. We are one, Psappha. I will always watch over you. My heart is ever with you and I will not be far. Go, nightingale, bestow your bountiful gifts upon your God, then hasten to me and we will honor The Mother together."

~~~~~

The freshet-carved path up from the indented waterline was slippery with moss. Psappha wound her way around rocks, carrying the copy of her acceptance speech as a gift for Apollo. She stumbled often in the dim light of the water-cut, but she refused all offers of assistance. Ascending a sharp curve, she blinked from sudden sunlight. The shrine gleamed upon flat, flowered lawns. The grasses waved in the gentle, salt breeze.

She slumped onto a marble bench to catch her breath, fanning herself with the scroll, admiring the gulls as they skimmed among tumbling clouds. Moments later, the shrine stood empty and she continued toward it. Her step quickened as she approached the altar. Time seemed nonexistent.

"Golden Apollo," she recited, her knees on the grooved, penitent-worn stone. "Great has been your gift to me. Truly, you have sent your sister, Artemis, to be my companion. I dared expect no grander gift. Yet, in your benevolence you have deigned to grant another.

"Long have your lyrics filled my mind and flowed through me to your sacred lyre, yet I dared not hope to be considered equal to those of your servants most highly praised. Yet, this also, Oh Bountiful Musicos, you have seen fit to bestow upon me. I offer thanks, Oh Wondrous Apollo, that in this world of men, Psappha shall wear honor. Many praises shall I sing to thee, Phoebes Apollo. Psappha of Lesbos bears, for thee, a grateful heart."

She left the poem on the altar stone with a silent thank you to Alkaios, beloved meddler.

Someone had planted mint and thyme on the path to the edge of the promontory. Fragrance rose with each step she took. At land's end, she opened her arms to encompass the bay and called out, "Blessed art thou, Father of Ocean. Again, you carry your hereditary daughter in your gentle arms. I go to claim an honor of which I dared

179

not voice my dreams. My heart is full, Earth-shaker. The Lady has granted all my prayers, both great and small. No mortal could imagine more than that which is now mine. There is no glory left for me to acquire, save immortality.

"With your blessing, and that of your divine nephew, my songs have earned me a small portion even of that. Psappha sings your praises, Mighty Poseidon. The Poetess hails your holy name."

Shading her eyes, Psappha surveyed her surroundings. The cerulean sea mirrored the iridescent sky. Gulls invented script on the face of lamb's wool clouds. Poseidon whispered his love to the inverted cliff. A rising breeze kissed her hair, sensuously unfurling her braids. She walked away from the little temple, feeling as if she could touch the Queen of Heaven by the mere extension of her hand.

At the edge of the cliff, she leaned forward and looked down. The ship rocked in the shadow of the overhang. From where she stood, it looked like a toy in a tub. She could barely make out Gyla's lovely form halfway up the mast.

Gyla looked up and waved. Psappha felt the ground shift beneath her feet. Gyla dove into the tranquil water. A tremor threw Psappha to the ground.

"No, Father of Ocean. Not now," she shouted as she jumped up and ran for the sanctuary of Apollo's shrine.

"I'm not ready," she cried when the temple shook.

"Earthshaker! Stop," she commanded as the precipice fell away in a deafening crash of falling rock.

"Gyla!" Psappha screamed. The pathway was gone. The little temple stood with its marble toes exposed to open air. The cove below was empty of all but waves.

Psappha stared, uncomprehending.

"Damn you, Poseidon! You can't have her! She's mine!" she wailed, and then, with a shriek that would have made an eagle weep, she followed her love into the sea.

Velvet-voiced Psappha would sing no more among the maids of Mytilene.

~~~~~~~~~~~~~~~~~~~~~~~~

Psappha